# 2½ Minutes

A novel by

## Don Miller

Also by Don Miller

*INVITATION*

*Commonguy.com*

Published by Don Miller

ISBN # 978-0-9839612-6-0

Cover design by Leah Henderson

# DEDICATION

*This novel is dedicated to Mom and Rick*

# ACKNOWLEDGEMENTS

My special thanks to:

Dr. Dennis Hensley for his exceptional editing services.

Leah Henderson for the perfect cover design.

# 2½ Minutes

## Prologue

Eve hadn't planned on driving. She didn't know how many beers she'd had. She didn't care. It'd be poetic justice, anyway, if Doug's hot-rod, fire-engine-red '70 Ford pickup truck got busted up.

It was a balmy, moonlit Friday night in May of 1974, but the serenity of this midnight was the farthest thing from Eve's mind. Windows down, feeling the wind gush as it whipped her straight, shoulder-length black hair, she drove back to Richmond, Indiana – alone. She wasn't driving home. She was driving to Doug's apartment, which he'd told her to clear out of a half-hour ago. Home no longer existed.

Her head buzzed. At twenty, life was supposed to be bursting with exuberance and anticipation. But, not so for Eve Kessler. Her life was a disaster. She couldn't make a go of *anything*. She'd moved in with Doug four years ago and had *never* found a way to keep him happy. This wasn't the first time he'd kicked her out. It was, however, the first time he'd told her to move out because the bouncy blonde sitting on the other side of him at the bar was moving in.

*God, what a mess.* She couldn't move in with her mother, Etta, again. The same guy who'd been Etta's source of booze money the last time Eve had been there still bunked with her. He'd been there for more than a year and, considering it was with Etta, that amounted to a long-term relationship. Woody – or whatever his name was – had made no secret of his fantasy that Eve would stay the night and share her bed with him. Her mother had been furious, but not with the jerk. No. She'd told

Eve to get out, as if it were Eve's fault that Etta specialized in luring a never-ending line of lechers to her revolving boudoir.

Eve flicked her cigarette butt out the window. She was *not* going to ask Val and Vicki about crashing at their place. Her friendship with Val had never been the same after she'd taken up housekeeping with Doug. They were still friends, but not the trusted confidants they'd been in school. And, considering the rumors that had been wafting around about Valerie DeBolt and Vicki Buholtz – the Volt Twins as they were dubbed – she wasn't anxious to spend a night at their pad.

*Nobody* was going to offer any help. She'd never done anything to deserve this piece-of-crap life. She'd never hurt anyone. It wasn't her fault she'd been born of a self-destructive, scheming, good-for-nothing user. It wasn't her fault she didn't have a dad to lean on, that her father was "anonymous," as Etta had haughtily asserted, claiming he could've been any one of a dozen guys, some name unknown, who she'd joined for a two-day free-for-all.

Eve's head reeled as she drove and wallowed in self-pity. She'd decided to drive back roads to traverse the twenty-five miles to Richmond from the Triangle dance bar in Greenville, Ohio. The last thing she needed was a three-day stint in jail for drunken driving. She didn't know why Doug always wanted to go to the Triangle. It was legal to drink beer in Ohio at eighteen, but her being underage in Indiana had never stopped Doug from handing her whatever he wanted her to drink. He seemed drawn to the place. "Let's go to the Triangle." Maybe he still went there for the younger girls. He was twenty-five, but who knew – she'd never been able figure out what he wanted. Maybe *Babe* from the bar was still a teenybopper.

Eve was agitated. *No place to live. No job. Nobody gives a crap; just get out of the way, Eve. No life. I'm following in my pathetic mother's footsteps. What's the point? There is no point.*

Five miles from Richmond, near the village of Middleboro, the souped-up pickup approached a gravel quarry that had a sheer-rock drop-off that pitched more than one hundred feet straight down. Eve knew the cliff was there, just ten car-lengths from the road. She rounded a curve and eyed the narrow, grassy slope leading up to the abyss.

*Screw it. I'm done.* She mashed the accelerator to the floor, turned the wheel slightly to the right, and felt the two passenger-side tires bump down off the edge of the pavement. The gravel and grass berm pulled the pickup harder to the right. The left-side wheels dropped off the pavement. The truck climbed the gentle incline at eighty miles per hour, angling away from the road… closer and closer to the precipice. Three seconds, and it would plunge over.

*No! Don't abandon Brent!*

Eve jerked the steering wheel to the left. The truck skidded sideways on the bumpy ground. Both right wheels caught in a gulley, and the pickup launched into a spinning roll. On its second roll, the petite body of Eve Kessler flew out the driver's side window, hurtling twenty feet into the air and then plummeting back down. Over and over the pickup careened, closing to within a foot of the cliff. Eve tumbled and somersaulted behind the mangled mass of metal as if she were tethered to it. Her world was black.

# Chapter 1

I wonder who that girl is. She's a goner. Her face is so pale... snow-white around the blue-black lumps. Can't get a good look at her.

The sterile room has cabinets along two walls and medical equipment everywhere else. All the paraphernalia and the four people hovering over the gurney make it hard to see the poor girl laid out in the middle of the room.

The middle-aged nurse taking the girl's pulse says, "She been unresponsive all the way in?" The nurse must be in charge. She looks tense.

"Yeah," one of the two guys in blue uniform says. "We couldn't get any blood pressure at the scene, so we really scrambled. Pulse was one-sixty. Respirations been running anywhere from twenty to forty."

Boss Nurse glances sideways at a younger nurse – she looks younger than me – and commands, "Steph, get that heart monitor on her, and help me get an IV set up!" Then Boss feels the motionless girl's neck. "Ted, tell 'em to get Dr. Kenner in here! Stat!" One of the blue uniform guys – the one who'd been talking – Ted, I guess – jumps like he's hit by lightning. "Hand me the sixteen-gauge," Boss orders Steph. "Pulse is thready and weak, hardly there at all. She's losin' a lotta blood somewhere."

The other blue uniform guy looks worried, like he's scared Boss is going to make *him* do something. Ted ducks back in. "Kenner and the trauma team are on the way!"

Steph runs past the scared guy, grabs some wires off a monitor stand, and whizzes her hands around, sticking suction-cups to the girl's body. The monitor starts beeping, and the screen shows a bump with each beep. The beeps are slowing down.

"Tell 'em to make sure Respiratory's coming."

"Got it." Ted hurries back out.

"And get Lab, too," Boss demands as she pushes a needle in the girl's arm. "She smells like a brewery, and they're gonna wanna know how bad.

"We're gonna lose her before they get here!" Boss yells. She starts CPR, like they do on *Marcus Welby*.

In rushes a guy who looks as tense as Boss, maybe a tad less frantic. Must be Dr. Kenner. Three people surge in behind him. Ted and the other blue uniform guy squeeze out. Lab Girl stands at the door with her goody tray, looking panic-puzzled, like she can't figure out how to get from where she is to where she's supposed to be.

No more beeps on the heart monitor. Dr. Kenner starts barking. "Get a CBC, lytes, cross, and type for two units of blood – no, make it three." He looks around. "Where's Lab?"

"I'm tryin' to get up there," Lab Girl squeaks, wedging her way through the group.

Doc looks at another girl holding an armload of equipment. She's ready to leap at his command. "Get her tubed." Then he pushes Boss over with his body and takes over the chest compressions. "She just flatlined when we walked in the door, right?"

"Yeah," Boss says. "She was barely alive when she got here. Belly's boggy. She's losin' blood in there."

"What happened to her?" Doc asks the air.

Ted has crept back to the door to watch. "Rolled a pickup truck out by Middleboro Stone Quarry. Came about an inch from goin' over the edge. Neighbor was lookin' out the kitchen window and saw headlights bouncin' all over the place and knew there was a wreck. My guess is the call came in before the truck was done flippin' over. We got her here fast. Everything happened right this time... well, except the crash, I guess."

Boss gives Ted an "idiot" glance. For a split second, Steph and Ted's eyes meet, and they actually smile at each other.

*That's* out of character for this scene. I bet they've got a thing going.

"Close that door!" Doc commands, cutting Ted out of the picture. "And give me one milligram epi." Boss already has a shot prepared and hands it to him. Doc pushes the needle into the girl's chest, eases the fluid into her, and watches her for a minute. Nothing happens. "Get ready to shock her."

Steph almost falls over herself getting the shocker ready. Doc grabs the paddles from her.

"Clear!"

He thrusts the paddles down onto the girl's chest. Her torso jumps, and her arms and legs jerk.

He resumes the chest compressions.

The girl's eyes roll open, but I don't see any life in them. That can't be good. The heart monitor is quiet as can be.

Now there's distress in Doc's voice. "Shock her again. Gimme the paddles! Clear!"

The girl jumps and jerks some more, but then she's still again. It looks like a losing battle to me. For a moment, the action stops, and they all look at each other.

"Again," Doc says.

All this is fascinating, but I'm ready to quit this dream. Whatever possessed me to have such a real-feeling, stupid dream about watching some girl die? I don't like that haunting look in her eyes. I should be freaking out, but it's like I just want to watch and see what happens... except for those dead eyes. I need to wake up. *Close her eyes! I've had enough of this. Wake up! Come on! Enough. Wake up!*

## Chapter 2

What's happening? The dream won't stop. Feels like I'm floating, but that can't be... hovering in this corner, watching them trying to save that ghost-eyed girl. How do I get down? She's gonna die. Her heart line is flat. No bumps, no beeps. She's already dead.

Wait! What the heck? She looks like me, just all bruised and deathly white. But, I'm right here. Can't be down there at the same time. Wherever here is. Up here? Just floating? That can't be, either. I think I wrecked Doug's truck, but I don't even hurt. I feel great! Is she dead? Could that be me? No. No way. Can't be! Dead? Am I *dead*? No. No. Oh, no! She *is* me! What now? I just stay up in this corner? Forever? How do I move? I can't even see myself up here, just down there. Dead. I should be scared. I should be really, *really* scared!

Who's here? Where are you? I know somebody else is up here! I can feel you. Talk to me. Who are you? Let me see you!

Uh-oh. We're moving. Where are you taking me? Hey! We just went through the ceiling. Oh, wow, I feel good! Who are you? Are you making me feel like this? So much joy and warmth. So much! Is it coming from you? How do you do that?

Do you see that tunnel up there? *Do* you? Are we going in it? I don't think we should. Can we stop? Please? Closer and closer. Will you stay with me? Why can't I see you? I know you're here. I *feel* you. *Wow!* Look at that bright light! Do you see that light? At the end of the tunnel?

*Oh, man!* Feels *sooooo* good! Better and better and better! Every second. Are you doing this to me? I can't talk anymore. It's too much. Just feel. Keeps getting more. More and more and more. This has *got* to be heaven! How could *I* be in heaven? *Ohhhhhhh!*

Into the tunnel. Rocketing! Faster and faster and faster. The tunnel whooshes by. There are two with me. I can't see them, but they're there. They know me. I should know them; they feel like home. They're guiding me. Now, they're talking to me – without words – reassuring me. I know what they're saying: everything will be okay. They know what I'm thinking. It's like we're living inside each other. Faster still. My ecstasy grows ever more intense. Bursting! Peace and love and joy! Coming from the light? We're getting closer and closer to the light. So bright! So pure! Impossibly light. Now there are more with me. Millions! I'm in them, and they're in me. Nothing but peace and love and joy and oneness – complete belonging. I'm part of everyone and everything: the universe, every molecule, God. All things are one. All in me. Infinite ecstasy! There is nothing else.

Something's happening. *Knowledge* is gushing into me. All at once, blossoming in me at the speed of light! I know everything – everything that ever was and everything that ever will be. I understand the forces of life. It all fits perfectly. I have no more questions. Existence is love. Boundless love. Love everyone! Love more than humanly possible. Way more. Nothing else matters.

We're almost there, almost to the light. Please, take me faster. Please! Now! I want to be there now!

Wait! There's my life! My whole life – everything I ever did from the time I was born. I see every act. I feel every emotion. All at once. I see every detail and every person in each scene. I feel all of the emotions, mine and *theirs*. Everything is brilliant, much more crystalline than when it happened. The colors, the sounds, the smells – even the emotions – all *so* vivid. And I understand. Life happens. It's all chaos, and it just happens. People do what something inside them leads them to. Nobody was evil. Nobody *is* evil. Nothing was done wrong. It just was. I didn't do it wrong. Everybody would have felt better if there had been more love. There should have been more love.

I see myself at birth. I feel my small, intense emotions, mostly anger, as I kick and scream, but my own feelings are not foremost. My consciousness is drawn to my mother's emotions. My anger is miniscule compared to hers. She doesn't hate me, but she hates the pain I've given her and the prospect that she might have to take care of me. She feels no sense of bonding or motherhood. She's exhausted from eleven hours of labor and nine months of sustaining an ever-expanding creature within.

The doctor asks if she has a name for her daughter. She feels a moment of malicious pleasure and victory as she replies, "Eve." My name is a dig at her adoptive parents and their pressure to bring her into the fold of their faith and their church: Eve, the temptress who doomed mankind to the consequences of original sin.

A nurse asks if she wants to hold her new baby girl. She feels revulsion. "Too tired. Take her away."

As I absorb the scene and emotions, I feel a twinge of regret for bringing such hardship upon my mother. But, I understand. No one is at fault. I didn't do anything wrong by being born. Yet, I caused her pain.

My mother couldn't help how she felt. Her life had been fated to be filled with emotional torture from the time she'd been conceived. When she'd been ten months old, she'd been abandoned by her own irresponsible mother, left lying on a blanket in a damp corner of a bus depot in the middle of a freezing January night, filthy and malnourished.

She'd been named Loretta by an Indianapolis children's home. She'd lived there until she was five, and from the beginning she had been a disciplinary nightmare. The home's approach to behavior adjustment had had little to do with nurturing and much to do with inflicting pain and instilling fear. She'd been apportioned an abundance of both. My mother can't be faulted for her misdirected life choices. She is not evil.

I see everything at once, yet in sequence. Some scenes – those that mark milestones in my life – stand out. There is evaluation of my every act. Although I'm not alone – a supreme presence, or all, joins me in reviewing my life – I am the judge. Feeling the emotions my actions spawned in others, I wish I'd done better. However, my judgment isn't harsh. If I could do it over, I'd try to instill more love. As I evaluate my life, the one with me makes me feel comforted and safe and, above all, loved.

I see myself at eighteen months, toddling around my mother's small, dirty two-bedroom house wearing only my overnight soaked and soiled diaper. My mother lies on the couch, hung over, eyes slits, silent, avoiding motion. I amplify her pain. I bump into things, stumble around, plop down, and make noise. She pretends I'm not there. I don't feel hate in her, just a longing for me to go away.

Lying on the coffee table is a fork and the remainder of the TV dinner she ate two bites of late last night before she passed out. I grasp the fork and teeter into the kitchenette area of the combined living-dining-kitchen space, displaying my prize with tines pointed up. I trip on the leg of a chair and fall. The fork pierces my right cheek. With blood running down my cheek, out of my mouth, and off my chin, I scream.

My mother doesn't move for a half-minute. I feel anger well up in her. She staggers out the front door and slams it furiously. She returns a minute later with the woman who lives next door, Gloria. My mother is cursing me, ranting about how unbearable I am. She still doesn't hate me, but she's consumed with anger.

As I watch this moment, I wish I could have engulfed her in love.

Gloria picks me up, pulls the fork out of my cheek, and takes me to the hospital. My mother does not go with her.

I see myself, sobbing, cheek bandaged, being carried from the hospital by a medium-built, soft-skinned, middle-aged woman with short, stylish white hair: my grandma, Sarah Kessler. She holds me tight as a balding, thin man her height holds the door for us: my grandpa, Everett. I'm clean, dressed in a new sleeper, and wrapped in a blanket.

Gran is filled with both love and anguish. She aches for Etta and feels responsible for my being neglected and wounded. A craving to bequeath me a happy, comfortable, productive life overwhelms her.

Absorbing the scene, I understand the hopes she'd had to create those circumstances for Etta, as my mother always

insisted I call her. When they adopted her at five, Gran and
Grandpa could not have imagined the extent of the unhappy
child's torment. Gran, a third-grade teacher, had been unable to
conceive. She and Grandpa loved children and decided to adopt
one whose life they would have an opportunity to turn from
hopeless to heartwarming. Gran and Grandpa devoted
themselves to Etta, but were not able to undo the damage that
had already been scorched into her. Etta was bent on self-
destruction, becoming more defiant and wayward at every turn.

The more Gran and Grandpa tried to bring Etta into a loving
relationship, the more she did to break their hearts. Counseling
had no impact. Her grades were deplorable because she wanted
them to be. At twelve, she began intermittently staying out all
night, hanging out with high-school kids, and drinking. At
thirteen, she became sexually active.

At fifteen, my mother became pregnant with me. Gran and
Grandpa did everything they could for her while she carried me
and after I was born. When I was six months old, Etta told them
they were suffocating her and she was going to California with a
thirty-year-old man; she'd give me away there. To try to save
both Etta and me, Grandpa offered to buy her a little house a few
blocks from their two-story, colonial-style brick home adjacent
to Earlham College. They told Etta they wouldn't intrude on her
life, but she'd be welcome to come home anytime, and they'd
babysit me anytime she wanted. They put her house in her name
with no strings attached. Etta accepted the house, but after she
moved out, to spite them, she didn't visit or make contact.

As Gran carries me out of the hospital, she's rent with
emotions. She feels utter failure for bringing no happiness to
Etta and for driving her further from any relationship with God
and their church. Bringing these things into Etta's life were the
reasons they'd adopted her in the first place, and they'd agonized
for years attempting to achieve those goals. Gran is besieged
with guilt for having allowed me to be subjected to the neglect
that came with being in Etta's custody. Clutching me to her, she
feels devotion more strongly than she's ever felt for anyone,
including Grandpa.

Grandpa is also besieged by a mix of emotions. Though a
kindhearted, generous man, he's infuriated about the hole Etta
has gouged into their lives. He's disgusted with himself for his

commitment and persistence thirteen years ago toward adopting an "Etta" to save. He is filled with resolve to ensure that I flourish. He loves me unconditionally and without bounds.

I see myself at my second birthday, the perfect picture of a happy, healthy, well-loved child. There are gifts: dolls, a tricycle, clothes. I blow out two candles on a cake with help from Grandpa while they sing "Happy Birthday." Grandpa and Gran are delighted. I adore them. As I see the beginning of this scene I'm pleased. There is much love.

We hear a knock at the front door. Grandpa opens it. Etta pushes in past him, shrieking. "I see how much you worship my daughter, *not* your granddaughter. Well, I've got news. I'd have borne a grandson for you to get all gooshy over, too, but I got rid of it last week. Yeah, and they did a number on me. I won't be pumpin' out any more kids. But, seein' all the fuss you're makin' over her, I'm thinkin' I'm gonna take her back now. Not that I *want* her. But I don't want *you* to have her."

"Etta, get out," Grandpa tells her, his voice rising. "We're Eve's legal grandparents, and Child Care Services has determined you're not fit to raise her. We've started the process of obtaining custody. You leave us alone."

My mother sneers at Grandpa. "I could just grab her and take her right now, but I think I'll wait. Let you get more attached. Maybe for a few more months. Or maybe weeks. Maybe days or hours. I'll snatch her when you're not looking. Maybe when she's out playin' in the yard, or maybe at the grocery store. Maybe I'll sneak in at night, maybe midnight, maybe around three, shove a gag in her mouth, and just walk out of your house with her. Better keep her with you *all* the time. Keep 'er inside. Lock your doors. Like *that* could keep me out. Maybe you should take turns sleeping – somebody always be awake with her. Maybe, just to be sure, you'd better both stay awake all the time. Never sleep again."

"I'll get a restraining order if I have to!" Grandpa yells. "Now, get out!"

Etta spews venom. "Don't like my company anymore? Don't like *me* anymore? *You* raised me! You won't do any better with *her*. Just watch: she'll turn out worse than me. You'll just fail again."

"Get out of here right now! Sarah, call the police! *Now!* Etta, don't you *ever* set foot in this house again. You come *near* her, and I'll see you in jail or Hell!

Gran's fingers quiver as they dial.

"*Fuck you!*" She whirls and storms out, screaming, "I'll be back! *Bet* on that!"

I experience all their emotions. Gran, on her knees, pulls me to her. She's shaking, tears streaming down her cheeks. Grandpa is livid. He clutches his chest, as if his heart is being crushed. My mother feels nothing for me, only her own rage and twisted satisfaction at the pain she's creating in. At two years, old I watch my mother and feel something akin to love. It isn't the all-consuming adulation radiating from within me for Gran and Grandpa, yet a bond tugs at me.

As I take in the scene, I feel regret, not guilt, that such pain was generated because of me. I wish I had infused more love.

I see the special days of my childhood: my third, fourth, and fifth birthdays; the Christmases those years; outings and vacations with Gran and Grandpa. My days are filled with joy and love. Life is wonderful. Etta is absent during these years, but I know she's my mother, and sometimes I think of her and wish she'd visit me. I see myself in church Sunday after Sunday, sitting between Gran and Grandpa. I see them teach and guide me: counting, the alphabet, the golden rule, confidence in my abilities, trust in myself, faith in God. I bring joy to them. They are *everything* to me.

I absorb these scenes, and I'm pleased.

I see my sixth birthday. It's Saturday, and Grandpa and Gran take me to Grand Lake near Celina in Ohio. Gran's older sister and her only living sibling, Auntie Ruth, lives there, and she and Uncle Theo have a pontoon boat. Uncle Theo moves slowly and uses a cane but loves to be on the water on calm days. What he lacks in health and mobility he makes up for with the joy he takes in life. His wit, sparkling eyes, and ready laugh make being with him delightful.

Today is a beautiful, sunny day, and we spend the afternoon on the lake. There's a table on the boat, and Grandpa, Uncle Theo, and I are playing Crazy Eights. Auntie Ruth steers the crawling boat at the back, and Gran sits beside her chatting. I'm wearing a pink and white checked dress, and my long, black hair is pulled into a ponytail. In one corner of the boat rest a covered cake pan and a half dozen wrapped packages. Grandpa has set 2:00, an hour from now, as the time for the birthday celebration to begin, and I'm tingling with anticipation.

"Are you ready for your big day Monday?" Auntie Ruth asks me.

"I can't wait! Molly, my best friend from Sunday School, will be in my class. We both have the same dress, and we're going to wear them the first day."

"Well, I bet Molly won't be as pretty in hers as you'll be in yours," Uncle Theo says with a twinkle.

Grandpa beams. "Nobody there will be as pretty as Eve. God broke the mold after he made her."

"Aw, Every grandpa thinks that about his granddaughter," I say.

"I know. It just amazes me how silly all those other grandpas are. Anybody can see I'm the one who's right."

"I hope they have something left for you to learn in kindergarten," Auntie Ruth says. "Gran has already taught you the alphabet and counting. How's your reading and adding and subtracting going?"

"They've got it all figured out," Grandpa says. "They're going to make Eve the teacher."

"Quit, Grandpa. I don't know how to be a teacher."

At precisely 2:00 on Grandpa's watch, the cake is set on the table and the lid is removed. Six candles are lit, and I bounce on my toes while "Happy Birthday" is rendered. I blow out the candles to the secret wish that every birthday will be as wonderful as today. I sit back in my chair as Gran, eyes gleaming, hands me my first gift. The world is perfect.

I see us driving home at dusk. It's a long way. I sit in the back seat behind Gran. She says, "Eve, look at the big gravel pit over there." Then all becomes chaos.

Grandpa grabs his chest and slumps over the steering wheel. The car veers off the road toward the pit. Gran grabs the steering wheel and jerks it. The car skids back onto the pavement, sliding sideways across the road. I see a tree race at us. I scream just before the tree explodes into Gran's car door.

## Chapter 3

I see myself at the cemetery. Two caskets are prepared for lowering side by side. It's drizzling rain, and I stand under a tent, my mother close behind but not touching me. She's skinny but attractive: makeup done well, black dress fitted perfectly, hair up, perfumed. Standing close with an arm around her lower back is Brad, a man I've never seen before.

Our church pastor looks at me as he concludes the service. He's spent hours with me, reassuring me Grandpa and Grandma are in heaven, a glorious place where they wait for me with open arms. I'll reunite with them when I die. All I have to do is live my life in the way they've taught me.

He's also tried to explain to me, in the most tender words he can garner, what a massive stroke does to a person. And that Auntie Ruth and Uncle Theo are not here with me now because when she heard about Gran and Grandpa, that's what happened to Auntie Ruth.

I stand silently in front of my mother as Gran and Grandpa are lowered into the ground. I have no more tears to cry. I try to pray. I'm crushed.

As I take in this scene, I feel Etta's excitement, her anticipation, as if she's stuck gold. She's gratified that they're dead. She has no thoughts or feelings regarding me. She doesn't hate me, which places me above almost everyone else she knows. I feel my young soul pull toward her.

Brad feels smug. Standing at the gravesite, he can hardly keep from grinning. I have no emotions regarding him, and he has none for me.

I see a scene from that night in my mother's house. The door on the awning-covered stoop that's surrounded by weedy grass opens into an L-shaped kitchenette. The sink and short counter are covered with stacked dirty dishes. Etta and Brad sit at the two-person table smoking, talking, and drinking beer. They exude an aura of exhilaration. He makes a phone call. I sit on a grungy chair in the living area of the linoleum-floored room, watching them.

Brad hangs up the phone and smirks. "Stedman says we need to get the will read right away. He's settin' it up for day after tomorrow. He says his dad will never recover from the infection he got from the kidney surgery he had last month, and his days at the law firm are done. But, we have to get it read fast anyway, just in case the old man comes out of his coma."

"Did he say how much?"

"Stedman says the $250,000 insurance policy that goes into Eve's trust fund is all we'll see. He says there ain't much more than that. They dumped most of their savings into keeping you going and their co-pay for medical expenses for the old man's ticker. He says his fee to rearrange the trust distribution will be whatever he can recover from the estate."

"How much is he rakin' in?"

"He wouldn't say. Just acted like it wasn't enough and he was doin' us a big favor."

"When do we get the two-fifty?"

"It was set up to hand out ten grand a year to her guardians for upkeep and save the rest 'til she's eighteen to give her over the next four years. He says he's sure he can get the upkeep raised to twenty grand a year, which would get almost all the money to us before she's eighteen."

"He's positive he can get her to us?"

"He says he already filed the paperwork, and it's a done deal. You're her mother and her only natural relative. It don't matter who the will named as guardians. He can break that part of it."

"So, when do we get the first twenty?"

"Soon as the judge okays the changes. He says he's lined up the right judge, and it shouldn't take a month. We just need to get to his office and sign papers tomorrow."

Brad and my mother knew each other from haunting the same bars. He was living with another woman when he heard about Gran and Grandpa's accident. He called my mother the next day and moved into her house the night before the funeral, forcing her previous man-of-the-month out.

Brad works at the Kemper Cabinets factory and has a friend there whose lawyer is Mark Stedman. The family law firm was created by Stedman's father, who is well-respected and was a friend of Grandpa. The day after the accident, Brad's friend told him he'd bumped into Mark Stedman, who'd told him the Stedman firm was in charge of administering the estate. Stedman had suggested that the settlement could be massaged in my mother's favor, insinuating that the legal fee arrangement would also require massaging. Brad then contacted my mother, and the day before the funeral they met together with Stedman.

I hadn't known any of this at the time but had gradually patched parts of the puzzle together. Now, as my life unfolds before me, I understand how it all happened. I don't judge Brad or my mother. They had little choice in how they'd become the people who'd made these decisions. Their actions were neither good nor bad. It was just the way it happened. The only judgment I render as I see the scene is that I should've made my presence felt – added a measure of love.

I see myself a few weeks later, standing by the door to the cubicle I sleep in, watching Etta and Brad fight. I'm underfed and disheveled, wearing the birthday dress Gran and Grandpa intended for my first day of kindergarten. Though Etta has not taken me to kindergarten, I've worn the dress every day. It's dirty, crumpled, and has a torn sleeve where Etta, in a fit one afternoon, grabbed me and slung me aside, trying to make me be anywhere other than in her sight.

It's evening, and Etta is sprawled at the table, drunk. Brad looms over her, screeching. "You're comin' with me, right now! The branch bank is open for a half-hour yet, and you're gonna sign a cashier's check for twenty grand. I got you the whole two-fifty, and my share's gonna be the first twenty. Then I'm outta here, and you can deal with your life however you want."

Etta is bawling. "C'mon, Brad, I *gotta* have some cash. Stick around, and we'll share it *all*."

He pulls her to her feet and backhands her across the face. She gasps and crumples to the floor. My eyes are glued to them, but I make no sound.

"Brad! Please!" Her nose and mouth are bleeding.

He grabs her by the arm and drags her to the bathroom. "Clean up. And I mean fast! We're goin' to the bank."

Ten minutes later and no longer bleeding, she's as presentable as she can make herself. He pulls her out the front door. I shuffle to my bed and lie down on top of the covers, leaving the bedroom door open.

Hours later, Etta stumbles back into the house, followed by a man I've never seen. She leans into him and rubs her hands on him. He doesn't see me. She knows I can see them but makes no attempt to screen their cavorting. Lying in bed watching and listening, I want to help her but don't know what to do.

## Chapter 4

I see myself at school. I'm in the first grade, at recess on a sunny early autumn day. My routine is entrenched. I sit on a playground bench and watch the other children. My long black hair, which used to be silky from Grandma's frequent brushing, is ratty. My dress is dingy and torn. I smell bad.

I feel the emotions of my classmates.

Five boys are playing tag. One squeals in delight as he ducks left and avoids being tagged by an inch. The one who missed shouts out, "Aw, man," and sweeps to his right, seeking a new runner. This time the chaser turns left in anticipation before his target does, and they collide and tumble in a wild, laughing, gangly roll.

Four others play keep-away with a dodgeball. The three around the perimeter are laughing and shouting.

"Throw it here!"

"Watch out, here he comes!"

"I'm open, I'm open!"

I feel the frustration building in the boy in the center as each charge fails to secure the ball, until finally he continues a charge after the ball has been dished off, plowing the passer down.

"Hey, get off me!"

"I tripped."

As the other two boys run to join in the action, the tackler jumps up and grabs the ball from the boy carrying it. They start over, with the boy who lost the ball now in the middle.

Two girls and a boy sit on the merry-go-round and pull snacks packed by their mothers out of their snack sacks.

"I got a chocolate chip cookie," says one of the boys.

"I've got a Twinkie," the girl replies.

The other boy says, "Here's a cheese cracker."

They eye each other's prizes and begin negotiating. In 15 seconds they reach agreements, make trades, and open wrappers with satisfaction.

Molly is playing hopscotch with three other girls. They all giggle as they skip through their turns and run back to get in line to do it again. They revel in a spirit of camaraderie. Molly and I haven't spoken since the accident.

My frolicking classmates don't notice me on the bench. My teacher, Mrs. Kerr, stands nearby. She watches over the playground, also seemingly unaware of me.

As I absorb this scene, I feel her concern. She doesn't look at me, but I'm foremost in her mind. She knows about me, my grandparents, my mother's history, and a little of my home life. She aches for me and wants to help but doesn't believe she has a right to step in. Seeing her now, I wish I had done something to show her I would be okay, something to make her feel better.

I see myself that winter during lunch sitting at a table with the seats on both sides of me vacant. With help from Mrs. Kerr, I've learned to give more attention to hygiene. I now wash myself each morning. I scrub my clothes in the bathroom sink each night before wearing them the next day. I comb my hair and brush my teeth using utensils she's given me. However, there are things about me that keep my classmates distant; things I can't change.

I never laugh or smile. I miss Gran and Grandpa terribly. I worry about Etta and how I can avoid making her angry. The man she brought home the night Brad had dragged her to the bank lives with us. Wilson. He isn't nice. Etta seems to try everything to make him stay. I wish he'd go away. There is nothing pleasant about my life. I'm somber and drab. My demeanor isn't inviting to other kids. I melt into the background.

Sitting alone this day, I see a boy I don't recognize carry a tray from the food line. He's shorter than me, skinny, and has light hair with a pineapple-do sticking up at his forehead. His dancing, bright blue eyes scan the room for an empty seat and land on me. He makes his way to the seat on my right and sits.

He smiles at me. "Hi. I'm Tom. It's my first day at Westview. My dad retired from the Air Force, and we just moved here. I have cousins in Richmond. What's your name?"

"Eve."

That is the extent of our conversation. The next day, again he sits by me – and the next and the next and the next, mostly in silence. The first day of the following week, he doesn't play ball at recess but instead comes straight out of the schoolhouse to my bench and sits.

"Hi, Eve. Why do you always sit on this bench?"

"I dunno."

"Do you wanna play?"

I shrug.

"Well, if we don't go play, can I sit here, too?"

"If you want."

"Can I be your friend?"

"If you want."

"Do you have any other friends?"

"I don't think so."

"Everybody should have a friend. I'll be yours."

"Okay."

Absorbing this scene, I feel Tom's emotions. He's happy. Tom is a nice boy. Even though he's only seven, he knows he's helping me, and it makes him feel good. My feelings are confused, a misunderstood mix of yearning to reach out to him and fear of again being thrust aside.

I see myself in the third grade. Tom escorts me home from school on a warm spring afternoon. We're best friends.

He's better at arithmetic than I am. "You wanna work on homework problems together?" he asks.

"Sure." I smile at him. "We can sit outside on the step."

He'd been inside our house before, but I'm nervous about it. I've learned to clean, dust, and sweep, and I try to keep up on it, in case he has occasion to come in. However, I can't control what Etta and her boyfriends do to the place when I'm at school. She's usually drunk and embarrassing by afternoon. I might find anything from spilled beer to dirty underwear lying about. Two weeks ago, I walked in to the sight of her and the current boyfriend, Grant, sitting naked on the floor.

Today, we hear commotion when we're a half-block away. As we get close, something crashes and breaks inside. Grant – he's huge – is yelling at Etta, accusing her of stealing his money. She's screaming back at him, saying he can't live there for free. Her ranting stops abruptly in mid-sentence. As we stand in front of our stoop, not knowing what to do, Grant charges out the door, sending the screen door crashing off its hinges. The door misses Tom by inches as the brute bounds out of the house. He shoves us out of his way, knocking us both to the ground before jumping into his dilapidated car and peeling away.

Tom jumps up, pulls me to my feet, and runs into the house with me at his heels. The place looks tornado-ravaged. In the midst of overturned furniture, broken lamps, and plaster fragments, Etta lies on the floor, unconscious, blood oozing from the side of her head.

Tom races to the neighbor's house and pounds on the door. Gloria, the same woman who took me to the hospital when I was eighteen months old, runs behind him to our house. She rouses Etta and bandages her head. Etta refuses to go to the hospital. Gloria eases Etta into bed and helps Tom and me clean the place up.

As I relive it, I feel everyone's emotions. Gloria, though she has a plethora of her own problems, wishes she could take me away from Etta and into her care. Her heart breaks for me. Tom is worried about my mother and me. The nine-year-old boy wants to protect us both... especially me. Grant felt nothing but fury. Etta's head is spinning from too much alcohol and the beating. She's in pain and beyond anger. She wants to die. I'm ashamed. I long for Tom to think I'm a normal kid with a normal life. He knows it isn't so. My circumstances draw him closer to me.

I see Tom and me in the sixth grade, on the last day of class. School has just let out, and we stroll along the sidewalk. It's an exciting day. High-school kids drive past us celebrating freedom day. Radios blare: The Animals' "House of the Rising Sun," The Beatles' "Can't Buy Me Love."

Tom is more than a year older than me. He's a gangly fourteen-year-old. His voice is in the midst of changing. He's self-conscious. At twelve, I'm well-advanced into puberty. I'm five-feet-two, and my body compares favorably to most of the freshman girls. My early development inhibits him even more.

Carloads of exuberant boys ogle the short-skirted sixth-grade girls as they drive by, filling the air with catcalls.

"Hey, you sweet little thing, ditch him and come with us!"

"Look at that choice young one!"

"Come with me, honey!"

"Hey, whatcha doin' later?"

"What's a fine piece like you doin' with a geek like that?"

Tom turns beet-red. I'm embarrassed for us both.

"They're idiots, Tom. I hate them. You're the nicest boy I ever met."

He doesn't reply – can't talk over the lump in his throat.

"Tom, I love you." We'd never uttered those words. "I always will. You're the most important thing in my life. The only thing, really."

He flicks away a vagrant tear. "You're so much cooler than me. You don't have to walk with me."

"Stop it, Tom!" I drop my books to the ground, turn to him, put my arms around his neck, and kiss him on the cheek. I *have* to make him feel better. He turns yet redder.

As I watch the scene replay, I feel his panic. He'd felt my breasts brush his chest, triggering his mind to shout that I was no longer a kid like him. *She's way out of your league, you idiot!* He wanted to dissolve into the sidewalk.

My emotion was desire to lift him, to make him see how good he was – make him see through the charade to the truth. I couldn't.

Again, my judgment of my actions results in regret. Not guilt. There was much love, both Tom's and mine, and that was good. Regardless, I made him feel inept instead of noble. I should have done better.

I see a scene of Tom and me in early August, two weeks before we enter seventh grade. This is one of many similar scenes from that summer. Tom's parents kept close tabs on him, but they knew some of my story, and they trusted him. They allowed him to spend a lot of time with me. They could see that I desperately needed a friend, and they were trying to do their part to help someone in need.

Today, we're walking along the tree-covered, gorge-like west bank of the Whitewater River, our favorite place. We walk and sit here several days each week. I'm wearing a pair of too-small, old, brown shorts that I've patched, a sloppy green tee shirt I washed this morning after Etta took it off last night, and dirty sneakers worn through on the sides. I'm walking behind him through an underbrush patch.

"I'm gonna miss it down here when it's too cold this winter," I say.

"Maybe we'll come anyway. It'd be better than walkin' around school or the mall." His voice cracks up an octave on "mall."

I know what he's getting at. "C'mon, Tom. You *know* I couldn't care less what anybody thinks about us. I can't help it if I look older than I am. I wish I didn't."

"No, you look great. Everybody thinks so. Half the guys in high school want to date you. I mean, you look like you belong in high school, and I belong in grade school. Just listen to me. Even my voice proclaims, 'Almost ready for puberty,' and you – I mean, *look* at you. It was bad enough the last day of school, but you get more... more, well... every day."

We come to a clearing overlooking the river and sit in the grass.

"Nobody thinks I'm a high schooler. I'm barely five feet."

"Height don't matter, believe me. I'm five-nine, and anybody who takes one look at me would say, 'That fifth grader sure is tall. It isn't the height. It's the rest of the package."

"I can't help it, Tom. I wish I could. I'll wear clothes that hide it. I never want to be with anybody but you. I wish we could go away from here, just you and me. Forever."

"Someday I'll take you away. I promise you that. As soon as we're out of school, I'll get you away from this place. If you still want me to."

"I'll go anywhere you want to take me. I'd go now if we could. One thing will be kinda cool about school starting, though: we'll see each other every day. I can't believe we didn't get in the same home room or any of the same classes, but I want to spend every second we can together. I think I like you better all gangly and with your voice squeaky sometimes. If that fools the other girls into thinking you're too young, that just gives me that much longer to get my claws hooked in you deeper. I wanna make sure everybody knows from day one that you're my guy, and anybody that tries to steal you is gonna have to deal with me."

"You must be blind, Eve. I don't have a clue what you see in me."

"You saved me, Tom. You're my knight in shining armor. My life would be awful without you. I love you. I know we're too young for that, but I do. I always will."

"I love you, too, Eve," he squeaks. "C'mon, let's go on down and wade."

He stands and offers his hand to help me up. We snake our way down to the river hand in hand, take our shoes off, and silently he leads me through the cold, shallow water.

On the return trip, I finally mention the topic we've promised to avoid bringing up but that's been foremost in both of our minds.

"I wish you weren't going on vacation tomorrow," I say. "Two weeks is too long."

"I have to go. I tried to get them to let me stay here, but they won't. 'Your father's brother and your cousins live in Wisconsin, and the family has to stay in touch. You're going, and don't ask again.' That's all I get out of them."

"I know. I mean, we should feel good that you have family to visit. I sure wish I did. But still, I don't know how I'll get by without seeing you for two whole weeks."

"It's tearing me apart too, Eve. I mean, I bawled like a baby last night in bed 'cause I couldn't stop thinkin' about how much I'm gonna miss you."

"Well, that makes me feel a little bit better," I say and smile at him. "At least knowing I'm not the only one. God, I miss you already. I can't wait till you get back."

We both know we're too young for the feelings kindling in us. Nonetheless, our emotions can't be denied. There have been no kisses other than that peck on the cheek on the last day of school, but we know we're in love. We're enthralled when we're together.

Tom's family arrives back home just before midnight on the day before school opens; it's too late for us to talk. I see myself on the morning of the first day of school, anxious and excited, wearing my prettiest worn-out dress. I've laid out a dingy, loose button-down sweater to throw on before I go. It makes my chest look less prominent. I'm washing breakfast dishes. Etta is sleeping off last night's booze. Gil is the guy who has provided for Etta's needs for the last six months.

Gil is a big, burly man with dark skin; thick, wavy, dark hair; beady, near-black eyes. He has a history of police work and was on the force in Indianapolis, and before that in Chicago. He moved to Richmond last year and opened a private investigator business, renting a third-floor one-room office in one of the downtown Main Street buildings. During the time he's lived with us, I've gained some vague knowledge about him. His childhood in Houston, Texas, amounted to street gang life. His private investigation practice is sleazy. Gil is hot-tempered and shady. He leers at women. He's mean when he's drunk, which is often. I cook his food and wash his clothes, but I don't like or trust him.

This morning, he sits behind me at the table as I lean over the sink. I feel uncomfortable, but I don't look around.

"So, you start seventh grade today."

"Uh-huh."

"It's time, you know."

Apprehension rises within me – something in his tone. I don't reply. I hear his chair slide back from the table.

"Listen to me. Don't make a sound. If you do, I'm gonna hit you in back of your head and knock you senseless. By seventh grade, a girl needs to know what makes this world tick. If you don't, you're gonna get blindsided. I'm gonna help you understand."

My apprehension is now terror. I freeze.

"That's it. Keep still. Not a sound."

His hands grasp my hips. I'm crawling out of my skin, horrified. My head is screaming. My body is rigid.

He slides me sideways from the sink so I'm leaning over the counter. He reaches up under my dress and pulls my underwear down and off. He grips my waist, lifts me up, and pushes my torso forward so I'm supported by the counter, my feet off the ground.

"This is probably gonna hurt some. You gotta learn what it's like. Don't you make a peep."

I see the scene unfold. The act is neither good nor evil. It happened. Gil is not the devil. His decisions and actions result from the life circumstances that have been thrust upon him. He's never had any love in his life. As I watch, I relive my pain, both physical and emotional. Gil feels power, everything around him at his command. He's gratified. When he releases me, I slither off the counter into a heap on the floor and silently weep. He has no pity or empathy for me. He feels bolstered as he zips his pants and swaggers to the front door – a great start to his day.

"That's what life's about, Eve," he says. "Someday, you'll thank me for this."

## Chapter 5

I lie on the floor shaking and heaving for ten minutes after Gil is gone before deciding I can't stay here all day. I can't be here when Etta wakes. I have to pull myself together and go to school. If I'm ready in fifteen minutes, I can make it.

I arrive at Dennis Middle School without having spoken to anyone. The last time Tom and I were together, we lamented the fact that we didn't have any classes together. Now, I thank God for that. I can't face him.

There he is, in the hall at the first class change. He sees me. I turn around so our eyes don't meet, hurry away from him, and duck into the nearest restroom. I wait until the bell rings before venturing into the hall and then shuffle into General Science two minutes after class has begun.

"I'll overlook being late on the first day," Mr. Jackson admonishes. "Next time, Miss Kessler, you go to the office." I don't look at him or acknowledge his words. All of the seats away from the teacher's desk are taken, so I take a front-row seat and look at my feet.

By lunchtime, I still haven't spoken to anyone. The thought of eating makes me want to vomit. I stand in the hall, having determined to avoid the cafeteria but not knowing where to go. I falter, stare at nothing, and then abruptly perceive Tom wave, smile, and rush toward me. Again, I turn and dart into the nearest restroom, lock myself in a stall, and stay there through the lunch period. I try not to think.

At the end of day bell, I lurch out of my seat and bolt for the door. When I reach the street sidewalk, I glance back at the entrance doors and see Tom standing there staring at me. Our eyes lock for a second, and then I turn and hurry away.

As I see these scenes unfold, my inability to cope is incidental to me. Tom's emotions are overwhelming. He's devastated. All he thought of for the past two weeks was reuniting with me. His fourteen-year-old passion is intense. His world revolves around me, and I've wrenched it out from under him in one day. I ran from him, sliced out his heart. He assumes that, during his two-week absence, I've been swept off my feet by an older, more mature guy. His world crashes.

I judge myself more harshly for this act. I should have risen above my own difficulties. My actions have shattered Tom. He was pure love. In return, I've given him agony. I could not have been more cruel.

After deserting Tom, I walk for a long time. It's almost dark when I slink in our front door. Gil and Etta are smoking and drinking at the table and watching *Bonanza*. There's an empty pizza box between them.

Etta doesn't acknowledge my entrance, but Gil does. "You're out late. We wondered if you were comin' home at all. Had to order pizza. How was your day?"

"Okay," I mumble as I walk into my bedroom and close the door.

I come back out after midnight, after they're asleep. I pick up a half-empty pack of cigarettes and a lighter from the table and walk out onto the stoop. I sit on the concrete, lean back against the wall, and puff at my first cigarette. After two hours, the pack is empty, and I go back to bed. I don't sleep.

I see scenes of sameness over the next six months of my life. My days at school resemble those of the early first grade. I keep to myself; most days, I speak to no one. From time to time, I see Tom looking at me with the anguished expression that has become permanent on his face. He never approaches me.

Etta and Gil keep their cigarettes locked in her dresser to prevent them from disappearing. Taking care to avoid hitting the same store twice, I steal a carton a month.

I don't sleep much. A couple nights a week, after Etta has passed out, Gil enters my room. He's always clad in just a tee shirt. He pulls my covers down and strips me of whatever I'm wearing. He's quiet and usually shows me a balled fist on his way in. He wouldn't have to threaten. I don't care.

After a few weeks, Etta figures out what's going on and treats me even more icily. The last thing she wants from me is competition.

Most nights, regardless of how cold it is, after they're asleep I go out, sit on the stoop, stare at the sky, and smoke a half-pack.

I see myself in April, smoking on the porch after midnight. Valerie DeBolt, a girl who lives three houses down and across the street, calls to me. "Hey, aren't you a little young to smoke?"

I ignore her. She's a sophomore party girl – long, straight, silky white-blonde hair; wide brown eyes that don't go with the hair color; perfect, sparkling teeth; high, rosy cheeks; and her smile, legs, and breasts just won't quit. As far as I know, she's the sexiest package in Richmond High School and, to make sure nobody misses that fact, she wears the tightest, skimpiest clothes the stores dare to sell. I've seen her smoking on her own porch many nights, usually with three or four other partiers. She's never given me the time of day. Tonight, she's smoking alone.

She descends her porch steps and walks to our house carrying her pocket transistor radio. She's bouncing her hips and swinging her elbows to Mick Jagger screeching "Satisfaction." I want to go inside, but I'm not going to waste the rest of my cigarette just to avoid her.

"Do you drink, too?"

I don't respond.

"You're Eve Kessler. I've seen you around. What happened to that boy you always hung out with?"

"Mind your own business."

"So, you do speak."

"What do you want?"

"Just thought I'd come over for some girl talk. We might as well smoke together. Do you mind?"

"Do whatever you want."

"C'mon, don't be so tough. I know you could use a friend."

"Friends are useless."

She sits and smokes until I've emptied my pack.

"I'm goin' in."

"Hey, if you ever want to talk, I'll listen."

I turn and walk into the house.

As I observe my rudeness in this scene, I feel Valerie's emotions. She's not offended. She's curious. She's toying with me to see how I react. She's seen me around the neighborhood since I was a little girl, and she's intrigued by the change in me. All I feel is desire to be left alone.

I see several similar scenes. Valerie makes a night trek to our house about once a week when I'm out smoking. By late May, I've lightened up. Although I fight it, I crave someone to talk to. She sways over at 1:00 on a pitch-black morning near the end of the school year.

"How ya doin', Eve?"

"Hi, Val."

"Out late t'night."

"Yeah."

"You're 'bout thirteen, right?"

"I will be in June."

"I been tryin' to figure you out. You smoke all the time. Your mom's a shameless drunk, but I've never seen you drink."

"Don't wanna end up like her."

"You've never, ever had a drink?"

"Nope."

"You want one?"

"Nope."

"How 'bout sex?" She lifts her eyebrows. "I gave it up when I was fourteen. You still a virgin?"

I take a long puff and stare at the street. I take another and blow it out. "Nope."

"You gotta be kiddin' me! Who was it? That boy you always used to hang with? Is that what split you up?"

I smoke the rest of my cigarette while she looks at me, waiting for an answer.

"You ever been raped?"

Her mouth gapes. "No way. Not you. Who?"

I jerk my thumb over my shoulder.

"Your mom's boyfriend? No way! When?"

"Most recently, 'bout forty-five minutes ago."

"You're makin' it up. That didn't happen."

"You think I care whether you believe it or not?"

"Naw, you're way to cool about it. No way.... Has it happened before?"

"About twice a week for the last eight months."

She's quiet, shakes her head, and tries to decide whether I'm lying. "You'd have barely been twelve. Does he use rubbers?"

"Yeah. Lubricated. Makes him think he's doin' me a favor."

"How can you live with it?"

"You call this livin'?"

## Chapter 6

I see another late night in mid-June, smoking on the porch with Val.

"Again tonight?" she says. "You gotta get outta this."

My stock has risen in Val's mind since my divulgence three weeks ago. Now, instead of considering me an underling, she sort of looks up to me.

"You got any great ideas?"

"Maybe," she says. "You know Vicki Buholtz?"

"Yeah, I know who she is. I've seen her hangin' on your porch, drinkin' and workin' up boys. You two are thick. They call you the Volt Twins, right?" I smirk. "Val De*Bolt* and Vic Bu*holtz*?"

As I sit smoking, I mull over my impression of Vicki. She doesn't play by the rules. The only authority she recognizes is her own whim. There is no set of consequences severe enough to divert her, once she's decided to do some bizarre thing or other. It's not that she's dumb – she's as smart as anybody in her class – she just doesn't care a whit what anybody thinks. She's tall and solidly built – not heavy, but no featherweight. Her insignia is her thick, dark-blonde, kinky mane pushing out away from her head as it finds its way down to her shoulders. It usually shows reddish roots that go with her green eyes. She wears tight jeans and black boots most of the time and has been expelled more than once for wearing them to school. Most kids are in awe; they think she's fearless. To me, Vicki Buholtz seems foolish and reckless.

"Vic ain't all that bad," Val says, as if she's reading my mind. "She just wants to live life – try everything, ya know."

"Seems wild and crazy to me."

"Well, yeah, she *is* wild and crazy. But not because she doesn't know any better. I mean, she's thought through how she wants to be, and the stuff she does, she does 'cause she decided it's the right move for her. None of it just happens. She's *never* caught in a situation she didn't want."

"Well, *good* for her. My whole life's nothin' *but* bein' caught in situations I don't want."

"That's what I'm talkin' about. Get out of it! Vicki could help."

"What the heck could she do for me? Why would she care?"

"I'm tellin' you, she ain't so bad. She don't wanna see *anybody* get taken advantage of. Somebody who can't protect themself gettin' busted around by some brainless beast really sets her off. And she'll stand up to anybody. I've seen her kick the shit out of boys a lot bigger than she is."

"Does she even know who I am?"

"Yeah, I told her all about you."

"Great. I'm sure *that's* gonna make my life better."

"No. She *wants* to get involved. She lives with her mom, on the other side of Main. Her mom's pretty cool. Most parents with a kid like Vic would change 'em or die tryin', but her mom supports her. It's like she kind of admires Vic's spirit or balls or something."

"So, what's she wanna do? She think she's gonna come over here and kick the crap outta big, bad Gilberto Bartolo? He carries a gun, ya know. And I *know* he's used it – on people."

Val's eyes widen. "You gotta let her get you outta here! She says you could live at her house. She already talked to her mom about what's goin' on with you. It was actually her mom's idea. And Vic's all for it. She wanted me to tell you."

I smoke two cigarettes before I say anything. Vicki Buholtz is the last person on earth I'd have thought I'd ever befriend. Move into her home? I grunt a laugh. I don't really know much about her firsthand – don't know where she lives or have a clue what her mom might be like – but then, how could *anything* be worse than getting raped by Gil Bartolo twice a week?

"When?"

"You could move in anytime you want.  We'll both help you move."

I smoke another cigarette in silence and stare at nothing.  I flick the butt into the grass and say, "Okay."

As I absorb this scene, I feel Val's emotions.  She's excited.  She's awestruck by the knowledge that she lives three houses from a den where child rapes have been occurring for almost a year – by a guy who has shot people.  She wants to save me from the devil.  She thinks that even though I'm only twelve, in some ways I'm beyond being a teenager.  She wants my unique perspective to come into her circle of friends.

I sense almost no emotion in myself.  I think I'll be better off out of Etta's house.  I feel a twinge of guilt about abandoning her.  I judge my interaction with Val and my decision to move out as passable, but I wish I'd done something to help Etta.

Several scenes from the next three months whiz by me.

Two days after I decide to move out, Val, after seeing Gil leave at 7:30 in the morning, calls Vicki and her mother, Joyce Ann, and the three of them arrive before 8:00.  Etta won't come to until at least 10:00.  It doesn't take five minutes to put my belongings in the boxes Val brought and toss them in the trunk of Joyce Ann's sea green Chevy Bel Air.  I scribble a note to Etta: *Moved out.*

Joyce Ann's house isn't big.  It has a combined kitchen/dining/living room, a main bedroom with a half-bath, Vic's bedroom, a bathroom, and third tiny bedroom with no closet, where I sleep on a blanket on the floor.  Val's boxes are my dresser.  The move-in is quicker than the move-out was.  We take the boxes from the trunk to my bedroom floor, and we're done.

"Okay," Joyce Ann says, "let's get to know each other.  C'mon out to the table.  You want something to drink?  I'm having coffee, but we've got lemonade if you'd like."

"Or beer," Vic adds.

"Water is fine," I say.

Vic pulls two beers out of the refrigerator, pops the tops, hands one to Val, takes a swig from the other, and sits.  Joyce Ann runs me a glass of water and turns on the stove burner under a tea kettle.

"I just can't believe what the girls tell me you've had to live through," Joyce Ann says. "I've heard a few things about your mom, and I knew about the crash with your grandparents, but I would've never guessed how tough your life has been. We're happy to have you here. It's not much, but life here should be a lot better than what it sounds like you've been having."

"Thanks, Joyce Ann. I was gettin' by, but there was nothing fun about livin' with Etta. I really do appreciate you lettin' me move in. I'll help out. I can do all the housework, and I'll do the wash and cook if you let me."

"Helping out is fine, but we won't pressure you to. Do whatever you feel comfortable with. Your schoolwork should come first. And God knows you probably need some time to sort things out. Has he really been doing that to you since you were twelve?"

"Yeah. Always used rubbers, though, so I don't have to worry. I'm just glad I won't have to put up with it anymore."

"He should be put in jail."

"I'd castrate the sumbitch," Vic adds. "In fact, I'm real tempted to sneak in your old bed tonight and just wait for his ass with my knife. I know I could do it. You can't believe how much advantage you get with the element of surprise. He'd be a girl 'fore he had any clue I wasn't you."

"Remind me to never make you mad at *me*," Val says.

"I don't care about him," I say. "Don't care if he goes to jail or not. Don't care if he lives or dies. Long as I never have to lay eyes on him again. It's really nice, what you're doin' for me, though. There's really no way I can pay you for it. But, like I say, I'll do my share of the work around the house. More, if you want me to."

"We're going to get along just fine," Joyce Ann says. "You just do what you feel like doing. If that turns out to be nothing, I'll understand, and it'll be just fine. You've had to do way too much for a girl your age already. You hungry? Vic and I sort of catch as catch can around here. There's usually somethin' in the fridge and cupboard, but we don't very often actually sit down to a meal. You're pretty skinny. You must be hungry."

"I'm good. I don't need much – won't eat you out of house and home."

"Honey, you worry too much about being an inconvenience. Don't. I'm just glad we could help. And if there's anything you need, just let me or Vic know. You won't have a hard life here."

Vic and her mother are nice to me. I do most of the cooking and cleaning, although Joyce Ann continues to protest that I do too much. Settling in with them, I feel cautious relief.

Two weeks after moving out, I can no longer ignore the voice telling me I should check on Etta. I walk to her house in the early afternoon, when she should be up and Gil should be at work. I approach the house cautiously from the side and linger near the windows to listen. The TV is on, and there is no conversation. I step up to the screen door and peer in. Etta sits at the table in a housecoat with her back to me, watching a soap opera with a cigarette in one hand and a beer in the other. I tap on the door. No response. I rap louder.

"Who's there?" she asks without turning to look.

"It's me, Eve."

Now she turns. She squints at me and takes a long drag on the cigarette. She blows out a lungful of smoke and says, "You back?"

"No. I'm not moving back in. I just wanted to see you. Let you know I'm okay. Can I come in?"

"I don't care. Suit yourself."

I open the screen door and walk in. The house is a wreck: clothes strewn on the floor, dirty dishes piled in the sink. Nothing has been cleaned since I left. "Have you been okay since I moved out?"

"Why wouldn't I be? Gil's been a little rowdier. I'd say that's a good thing."

"Is he treating you all right?"

"Sure. Why wouldn't he?"

"I could help straighten up a little, if you'd like."

"Be my guest. A little sprucin' couldn't hurt."

She turns back to the television. I pick up clothes and put a load in the washer. Then I do the dishes, sweep the floor, put the laundry load in the dryer, and another load in the washer. It's almost 4:00. Gil will be home soon. Etta has laid her head on the table and gone to sleep. I touch her shoulder, and she cracks her eyelids.

"I'd better be going," I say.

"Time is it?"

"Almost four."

"He'll be coming. Don't need you here when he walks in."

"All right. Maybe I'll stop by again in a couple weeks."

"Whatever."

"Okay. Bye, Etta."

I walk back to Joyce Ann's, worrying about Etta.

Most evenings, the Volt Twins hang out with their gang – juniors and seniors, a mix of girls and boys. They go out of their way to bring me into the club. I don't fit. I'm young, introverted, and self-conscious. However, it's a bawdy group, and they've made it their challenge to pull me out of my shell. After a couple of weeks, my participation expands from single-word responses, except to the boys. Occasionally, I laugh. After a month, I've succumbed to their persistence that I share their beer. After two months, my shyness is gone, and I'm the pride of the pack.

I see a scene from autumn of my eighth-grade year. At 8:30, the Volt Twins and I pile into the backseat of Dan Bloomfield's car. Marilyn, a longtime member of Val and Vic's group, is practically lying on him in the front, her left hand around his neck, and I can guess where her right hand is. He drives us two miles north of town, past the Highland Golf Course, to a ranch house back a gravel lane. Our destination is Vic's date-for-the-night, Gerald's, home. We hear rock and roll music booming from the house as we turn onto the drive.

Gerald is a senior, as is Val's boyfriend, Denny, who meets us. He's already blitzed. He sweeps Val into his arms, and she throws her arms around his neck as they lock mouths. His hands move down to slip under her loose mini-skirt, pulling her tight against him. There are a dozen kids here and no adults. I'm the only one not paired off.

The party is unconstrained and already in full swing. Ten seconds after we're inside, Vic returns from the refrigerator with two uncapped beers in hand and extends one to me. She disappears out the back door with Gerald. My beer is empty in five minutes, and I get myself another. Two couples, including

Denny and Val, are dancing – if you can call mashing groins and groping dancing – in the unlighted living room. Two other drunk couples have slid the kitchen table and chairs against one wall and are on the floor, having a hilarious time playing a concocted, make-up-rules-as-you-go combination of Twister and Spin-the-Bottle. I lean against the side of the archway between the living room and kitchen, grinning and watching the clumsy hysterics as I tip my third bottle straight up and drain it.

Everybody knows I'm here, but they all go about their own antics, from time to time giving me a "watch this" look and a chuckle. By 10:00, I've finished nine beers, and I'm babbling to anyone who'll listen. Val and Vic have disappeared with their boyfriends. The kitchen game has degenerated to the boys leaning against one wall, pitching coins at the girls sitting against the wall across the room. The rule is that their beer bottle has to be tilted up to their mouth with one hand while they pitch with the other. The short-skirted, loose topped girls sit leaning forward with their legs spread. A hit to the crotch is one point, and a coin down the top, being a more difficult shot, is two points. As they giggle and guffaw, I keep score and gab on about anything and nothing.

The game degenerates, and I stumble to the fridge, keeping my right hand on the wall to steady myself. No longer able to keep score, I'm coherent enough to know the need for scorekeeping has evaporated anyway. I clamp the neck of my sloshing bottle with my left hand and weave through the living room toward the open front door and the porch as The Troggs' "Wild Thing" blasts from the stereo. One drunk couple is rooting on the living room on the couch, half-naked and oblivious to my presence.

Somehow I make it to the front door and the porch railing. I double over the railing and wretch into the flower bed below. My bottle slips out of my hand. Lurching for it, my right toe catches on my left calf, and I topple head-first onto the wooden deck. I groan, roll over onto my back, and pass out.

There are lots of scenes during the winter with Val, her girlfriends, and me. Partying and boys are the predominant topics. They especially get a kick out of talking about sex. How long this guy's is. How this one moves. The positions they've tried, mastered.  The number of times they've done it in one night.  The number of guys they've done in one night.

I try to act like it's all cool, try to fit in.  I don't understand their excitement.  I've done it fifty-seven times – I'd kept track of exactly how many times Gil raped me – and there isn't a single aspect about any one of those experiences I have any interest in sharing with these girls or anyone else.

Val keeps after me about it.  I'd gotten really messed up by Gil, she tells me.

"Sex can be the best thing ever.  Sooner or later, you gotta loosen up, or your life'll never turn out.  You gotta start havin' *fun* with boys.  Soon as you're ready, I'll set you up.  I'll pick you out a nice guy – gentle, maybe even sensitive."

Vic is more brazen.  "You gotta let 'em ride ya.  Ride them! You gotta *live*, girl.  Get your share outta life!"

Through all their prodding, I remain unconvinced.  I've been there and have no desire to experience it again.  On the other hand, they do have one point.  I don't have much of a life. I see nothing in my future – not that I have a desire for any particular future.

I finally tell Val I'll give it a shot.  If the guy seems okay, I might do it.

I see myself at another bash in late March.  Boones Farm is the beverage of the night, and I've downed half of a bottle.  Val introduces me to a junior boy, Manny Willison.  He's her height and has a dark complexion, brown eyes, and black hair cut short, counter to the fashion.  He might have some Puerto Rican blood in him.  There are about twenty people here, and the house has plenty of private spots.  "I'll leave you two alone to talk," Val says, abandoning me.

"Eve.  That's a pretty name," he says.  "It fits you."

The thought that flits through my mind is how I came to have that name.  "What about Manny?  I've never met anybody named Manny."

He smiles at me.  "It's actually Manuel, but please, please, don't tell anybody."  He notices that my cup is empty.  "Let me refill that.  You wanna go out and sit on the porch?  It's a little cool, but other than that, it's nice."

"Sure.  It's hot in here anyway."

We sit on a porch swing for half an hour and talk a little but mostly stare at the stars. He sits a couple of inches from me, not touching. He's nice and doesn't seem to mind the sparse conversation. He's brought a full bottle out to the porch, and we kill it while we sit.

He rises to get another bottle and looks down at me. "You know what I'm hoping?" I look up at him. "I'm hoping you've never been kissed. I'd really like to be the first."

I don't tell him he would be. I'd kissed Tom on the cheek, but that was as close as I'd ever gotten to being kissed. I think, *Kissing was never part of Gil's routine*, and wish I'd squelched the thought before it entered my head.

He reaches for my hands and gently lifts. I stand. He places his hands lightly on my temples and leans in. He kisses me, and after a few seconds I kiss back. *He's okay. This is as good a night as any.* I take his hand and lead him back into the house. We wind our way through the crowd and find an open bedroom door. We go in, and I close it.

Val is waiting on me at Vic's house the next day when I get home from school. "Did you do it? How was he? So what did you think? Are you gonna get with him again?" She's bubbling over.

"It was okay. You picked a nice guy. I like Manny. I think he liked me – at least, he acted like it. He didn't pressure me. Never even suggested anything, really. It was me. I led him to the bedroom, but I'm not gonna compare notes with you, Val. You'll just have to guess at the details. Yeah, if he wants to, I'd probably do it again."

I'm reserved. Val is flush with excitement.

I see lots of scenes of Manny and me from that spring. We're a couple. We have six dates in April. Each time, we wind up either in bed or in the backseat of his big white Ford Galaxy. During May, we're together two or three times a week. We enjoy each other's company. We go to movies, to restaurants, for moonlight walks. I feel like my life is beginning, that maybe my future could bear happiness.

We have a lot of sex. I never feel giddy about it like Val and her friends. I let on like it's good, as if each time is some kind of meaningful experience, but it never is. It's okay, better than getting raped by Gil, but it'd be no sacrifice to live without it. I instigate most of the intimacy, mainly because I think I'm supposed to. Manny doesn't pressure me but is never hesitant.

On a warm, sunny Saturday afternoon in May, Manny takes me to Whitewater State Park on Brookville Lake for a picnic. We tote our oversized blanket and picnic basket into the woods and find a grassy spot surrounded by trees and brush. We have a beautiful view of the deep blue lake and the vivid colors of spring extending to and along its shoreline, lush greens accented with zones of yellow and lavender flower fields. It smells like spring.

The content of the basket is Manny's composition. It's a variety of cheeses, crackers, and meats supplemented with potato chips and two cherry pie packs. We have paper plates, plastic utensils, and paper cups to be filled with his special complement, a bottle of red wine. As he uncorks the bottle and pours us each a cup, he says, "And I've got another bottle in the car. Just in case we spill this one or something. I didn't put it in the basket. You know, I didn't want you to get the idea that I was just bringing you here to get you drunk."

"And then have your way with me?" I finish his thought.

"You know I would never try to coerce you into... um... compromising your... um... gentility."

"Oh, big words for a country boy. But how could you possibly coerce me? I'm too willing."

He grins. "Just one of the many traits I adore about you."

"Well, Manny, here's what I think about your being prepared for a possible spilling of the wine. I think you are not well-prepared. If we spill it, the mood of the moment will suffer while you go scampering back to the car to fetch that other bottle. So, while I lay out our feast, why don't you trot right back to the car and bring it now? You know, on this lumpy grass, it's a sure bet the bottle's gonna topple over."

"Be right back." He jumps up and jogs off toward the car.

We nibble on lunch, sitting side by side on the blanket, leaning on each other. After enjoying lunch, nature, talking, and teasing for an hour, I finish the last sip from the first bottle. He turns my chin toward him, and we share a long, intimate kiss. Out of breath, he whispers in my ear, "I love you, Eve Kessler."

I pull his mouth hard on mine and impart a sense of urgency. I lie back and pull him down on me. Half an hour later, we snuggle together under the blanket, relishing the feel of our skin against each other.

"This is going to be a great summer," he says. "I'll be working in my uncle's landscaping business, so I'll have some cash. We can spend every weekend together. I'll take you to movies and out to eat every Friday and Saturday. And the rest of the time, when I'm not working, we can just hang out."

"What? You're not bringing me back here again? You don't like this?"

"God, I *love* this! I'd bring you here every day!"

"Oh, now I think you're *too* eager. Like maybe this really *is* what you had in mind. You know, take me where nobody will see, so people won't talk about you hanging out with a little eighth-grader."

"C'mon, Eve. You'll be a freshman. And let me tell you, there aint *nothin'* 'little girl' about you. You put every other girl I ever dated to shame. I don't know how you do it, but you're way past a freshman, or even a sophomore."

"So, you really don't mind bein' seen hangin' out with little Eve Kessler? And you won't be tryin' to avoid me in the halls at school next year?"

"I mean it, Eve. Quit that. Man, I'm the luckiest guy in the whole school. I'll be right beside you every second, protecting what's mine from all the vultures in the halls."

"You think you're luckier than Denny, or whoever Vic might try out on any given night?"

"Well, Denny's graduatin', so technically he don't count. I mean, I know Val's your friend, and I don't wanna say she's not good."

"Because you know damn well she's the best. You'd probably trade me for her in a minute if you could."

"No way, Eve. Never."

"Okay, I won't make you choose between me and Val. But, what about a night with Vic? Surely, that'd make your heart skip a beat."

"Are you kidding? It'd make my heart stop. She scares the crap outta me. I'd be limp as a slug."

"That'd be a first. In fact, I'd pay to see it. From what I can tell, that slug don't know the meaning of limp."

I see myself at the end of my eighth-grade year. It's graduation night, early June. Val invited me to Denny's graduation party, but I've had a headache all day and begged off.

Tonight, I feel bad about abandoning Manny. By 9:30, the headache is gone, and I walk fifteen blocks to the party to share the rest of the night with him. I cut through a neighbor's yard to save walking around the block and approach the party house through the back yard. A dozen cars are parked back here. I see Manny's Ford and go out of my way to walk past my favorite ride. As I get close, I hear music from inside: The Turtles' "Happy Together"... our song. My initial reaction is to smile. I notice the car jostle. I peek in the window.

I don't know the girl rocking on him, but there's enough light for me to see Manny's shocked face peering around her at me.

## Chapter 7

Scenes from the half-year after my last look into Manny Willison's eyes flash by. I grow progressively wilder. My appearance becomes more like Val's, the embodiment of sex. I consume alcohol more and more heavily. Before Manny, in spite of everything, my grades had stayed decent. Now, I'm barely passing. I've lost count of my sexual partners. Sex does nothing for me, but I binge on it anyway.

I see myself on a Saturday night in November of my freshman year, again at a party with Val and Vic. They're seniors now, and Vic is getting further from my comfort zone. The boys she attracts are no longer boys. Twenty is too young for her. She experiments with drugs. Anything goes with her.

This is Vic's kind of party. The crowd is rough, and there are no rules. We're at a farmhouse far from town. The place is owned by a thirty-something, fat, bearded biker. Most of the party animals are toughs cut from the same mold. I'm worried that the place is a drug den. Vic fits in. She's high on something, God knows what. Val isn't far behind her, out in the backyard, tantalizing two of the brutes.

I see a guy who looks as out of place as I feel. He's just under six feet tall, and thin with wavy, dark blond hair. He sees me notice him, and we walk toward each other. "You don't look like the other guys here," I say loudly, trying to overpower The Doors blaring "Light My Fire."

He gives me a nervous grin. "My cousin wanted to come," he shouts back. His cousin – other side of his family, no blood relation, he says – told him to come to this thing if he wanted to "get his eyes opened."

"*She* talked me into coming," I say, pointing to Vic standing and swaying on a Harley in the middle of the high-ceilinged living room. She's tipping a whiskey bottle straight up from her lips, draining the contents while three of the hells angels grasp strategic body parts to keep her from falling. "I live at her mother's house. Don't ask. It's a long story."

"I'm Larry. You look like you don't belong here any more than me."

"I'm Eve. You got a car?"

"Yep. I brought my cousin so, I better see if he wants out, too. Either way, let's go."

We skirt past his cousin in the kitchen. Cousin looks even younger and more innocent than Larry, but when Larry says "I'm leaving. You coming?" Cousin shakes his head. He's in the midst of being massaged by two wild-haired, long-legged sirens who look as if they've lived their entire lives in strip joints. He can't bring himself to leave.

Larry grabs my hand. "Let's go."

It's 10:00 when Larry and I get in his navy blue Mustang. We're unsettled by the lawlessness of the renegades ruling over this party. He looks at me as we speed down the long gravel drive. "You wanna go somewhere? Get a burger or something?"

"Yeah."

We stop at McDonalds and talk for an hour, first about the party and then about who we are. He's a wrestler, a senior. His family is middle-class, he says, but to me the picture he paints describes rich.

I'm careful what I tell him. My mom's an alcoholic. I moved out when I was an eighth-grader – couldn't take it anymore. The motorcycle dancer wasn't quite as crazy back then, and she and her mom offered me a spare bedroom. I accepted the offer, and I cook and clean for them. Over the past six months, I've let myself get a bit out of control, but after tonight, I'm toning it down.

He asks me if I'd like to go see *Bonnie and Clyde* with him tomorrow afternoon.

"Sure."

I see scenes of Larry and me during the next two weeks. It is the first two-week period since I stumbled onto Manny and my substitute at last year's graduation that I haven't had sex with someone. Larry and I go out three times and become friends. Our third outing, on a Saturday night, is to dinner at Nickerson Farms, fifteen miles west of town. It's a nice family restaurant. It doesn't serve alcohol.

Larry insists on buying me a steak dinner, and it's more than I can eat. He has an appetite that makes up for mine and finishes it for me. Most of the talk during the drive and dinner, in response to my questioning, is about him and his family – their holiday plans, his dad's plastering business, his summer experiences working there, his wrestling team and bouts, and school. Larry is open and genuine. I feel as though I know everything about him.

"Okay, somehow you've extracted every facet of my life from me. Now, it's your turn to let loose some of your mysterious secrets."

"Oh, you already know all the main stuff. And there's nothing very mysterious or secret about the rest. Mostly drudgery."

"Not convinced. I know you're not proud of your mother, and it was bad enough that you moved out, but I don't know the details. I know she was adopted and you lived with your grandparents until you lost them in an accident. I know you lived with Vicki Buholtz, of all people, and have been tight with Val DeBolt, the sex goddess of Richmond High. I know you went with Manny Willison for a while and broke it off when he cheated on you. And I know you're not proud of the life you've lived. That's pretty much it. I can't believe you know every tiny detail about me, and all I know about you is the surface ripples of what must be a torrent. How have you kept me babbling on for these two weeks? I never used to think I was self-centered, but you've got me wondering. I want to know more about Eve Kessler."

I fix on his bright blue eyes. "I'm not sure you'd like what you hear. It might scare you off."

"That hurts, Eve. In three weeks, we've become good friends. I like being with you, just being together. I know you've had a tough life, but I think that's part of what draws me to you. Life has been pretty easy for me, and I think I need a friend with a different perspective, maybe a more real perspective."

"Be thankful for your perspective, Larry. The more you learn about mine, the more you'll know it isn't one you'd want."

"Just trust me, and let me be your friend. Maybe, if you let me in, I could make your life just a little bit better."

"You already have. You're making it better right now."

"Then trust me. I'm not going to run out on you."

"What would you like to know?"

"You moved away from your mom when you were thirteen. You just decided on your own to leave, and she obviously didn't stop you. And you moved in with Vicki, no less. How did that happen?"

"Ett... um, my mom never cared much about me. She doesn't hate me, but she's never really been a mother to me. She's an alcoholic, and she thinks I just add to the problems in her life when I'm around. When she found out I was gone, I'm sure she was glad."

"How did you tell her?"

"Moved out while she was passed out from the night before and left a note."

"Did you tell her where you were going? How to reach you?"

"Nope."

"Unbelievable. Why? Did she hurt you?"

"No, but she always had some man or other around. Some were okay, and some weren't."

"Did... uh... were some of them... bad... to you?"

I look into his worried eyes. I heave a sigh. "No, not really. I was getting afraid that they might be. You know. I was going into junior high. And I was overdeveloped for my age. They all seemed like lechers. I guess I was afraid it was only a matter of time."

"So, that's why you moved out? Because you were afraid one of you mom's boyfriends would force himself on you? Did any of them try? Did you know it was going to happen?"

The memory of all of Gil's assaults hit me with the force of a truck. I exhaled. "I was pretty sure it was going to happen. Yeah. I knew it would happen if I didn't get out."

"God, that's awful, Eve. Man, I wish I could have been there for you back then. I wish I could've helped. Thirteen? And you took off on your own?"

"Val was there. In the crunch, she's always been a good friend for me. She saved me, really. Got me to open up and tell her what I was worried about. Set me up with Vic's mom. Joyce Ann is a good person. I can't think of anyone else in the world who would've taken me in like that. And she did it with no strings. I don't know, maybe I owe her my life."

"But Vicki came with that deal, too. I'm guessin' that opened up a whole new set of problems for you."

"Yeah, maybe. Vic's not a bad person. She's not mean – at least not to people who don't deserve it. She's just Vic – wild, no rules, protective, maybe dangerous. But not mean – spirited."

"She *had* to be a bad influence. She's sex-crazy and drinks like a fish. Drugs, now."

"I can't argue that. You know I've got my own alcohol issues. And I'm no virgin by any stretch. Yeah, she's partly to blame, I guess. Val, too. Maybe even Joyce Ann. But still, the three of them probably saved my life. If they gave me some other problems, at least I'm still here with a chance to beat them. And, see, now I've got *you* to help, since you've vowed to be my friend forever. So, maybe there's hope."

"Tell me about your grandparents. Six years old? That had to be traumatic."

"I don't remember much about them," I lie. "I had lived with Ett – er – my mom when I was little and then for a few years with them. When they had the accident, I went back to live with her. I don't remember much." I stop for a minute and, as inconspicuously as I can manage, swallow the lump in my throat. "I don't know." I force the air out of my lungs along with the words. "I think I liked living with them. It's kinda hard to talk about. I don't know why."

"I'm sorry, Eve. I don't want to make you talk about stuff that hurts."

"It's okay. I'm okay."

"How 'bout old boyfriends? Is that topic okay?"

"That's a little easier." I force a smile. "It's only been Manny. Remember, I'm only fourteen." I open up about Manny, then about some of my experiences with Val and Vic.

By the time we get up to leave, Larry has a partial understanding of the trials and tribulations of the life of Eve Kessler. He'd still be astounded to learn the quantity of partners I've had and alcohol I've consumed in my short life. He has no clue that I was raped fifty-seven times, that I was in the car the night of my sixth birthday when my world came crashing to an end, or that I've ever spoken to one of my classmates named Tom Stanton.

He drives me back to Joyce Ann's and walks me slowly to the door. "We dredged up a lot tonight," he says, touching me lightly on the back of my left arm. "I'm sorry if I made the evening hard for you. I didn't mean to. You okay?"

I turn my head and smile at him. "You have no idea how much it means to me to have a friend to talk to. Thank you."

I reach for the doorknob as he turns to walk back to his car.

I see myself at Val's house three weeks after the biker party. It's Sunday, mid-afternoon. I've avoided going out with Val and her friends since that night.

"I can't do this anymore," I say to Val. "You guys and your friends are all eighteen or older. Some a lot older. I'm barely fourteen. I'm not ready for the stuff you're into."

"C'mon, Eve. You been hangin' with us for two years. You're no kid."

I shake my head. "Vic's too much for me. I mean, she's not tryin' to force me to do stuff, but just bein' around her is trouble for me. That night at the biker farm was too much. I was scared. Those guys were gonna do whatever they wanted to whoever they wanted, and nobody was gonna stop 'em."

"Yeah, that night was one for the books, all right. I'm *still* sore. But Vic held her own, even with *those* crazy bastards. It's probably a good thing you got outta there when you did. So, what're you gonna do? Quit goin' out with us? You're not thinking about moving out, are you?"

"Gil's not at Etta's anymore. I'm gonna talk to her about movin' back in."

"Don't do it. There'll be another guy. Maybe a worse one. He's probably already there."

"Worse than *that* pig? I doubt it. Anyway, I'm not the same girl. If any of 'em come after me now, they better know somethin' about defense."

"Well, I think it'd be a mistake to move back in with your mom. Vic might stand in the way of you coming back. But, whatever you do, I still wanna be friends. You and me. In a way, it'd be kinda cool to have you three doors away again. We could have midnight chats like we used to."

"Sure, Val. I know you guys saved me two years ago, and I really am grateful. You took me under your wing and treated me like one of you. I'll always appreciate that, and I'll always be your friend. But it's time to make another change. I'm gonna give this a try."

"So, your mind's made up? You're gonna go see her? When?"

"Tomorrow afternoon."

"You want me to go with you?"

"Nah. Thanks, but this has gotta be just me."

Even though it's early December, it's almost sixty degrees this afternoon, and the inside door at Etta's house is open. I knock on the screen door. She sits at the table in her robe, a cigarette in one hand and a beer in the other. When she hears the knock, she averts her attention from *Dark Shadows* on TV and stares at me. She looks like she's just gotten out of bed. She hasn't combed her stringy hair or bathed today, or, from the looks of it, yesterday or the day before. The house is a wreck. The odor wafting through the screen door is offensive.

"Can I come in?"

She shrugs. I walk in, sit at the table, and try to ignore the stench. I don't know whether or not I've caught her between men. She gets welfare checks and about sixteen hundred a month from my trust fund, so she's not as dependent on having a man's ready cash as she was before my grandparents died. She spends more than she receives, though, on junk food, cigarettes, and booze, so she never goes without a housemate for long.

"I've been thinking about moving back in," I say.

"Great." Her tone is pure sarcasm.

"Look, you need somebody to clean up the place. You know you'd eat better if somebody'd cook a decent meal once in a while. I'll wash your clothes. I'll earn my keep."

"Who's gonna pay for your food?"

"I can get a part-time job to pay for whatever I need, which isn't much. Are you by yourself?"

She smirks. "I'm workin' on a guy. He'll move in pretty soon. I catch you lookin' cross-eyed at him, and your ass is out."

"Is he coming over tonight?"

"No, I'm meetin' him. We're hittin' the town." She says nothing for a minute. "I was just gettin' ready to get dolled up."

"I'll clean the place up tonight. If it's okay, I'll move back tomorrow."

She shrugs.

I feel her emotions as I absorb the scene. She knows how bad she and the house appear, and she feels a twinge of embarrassment. She's worried that any guy who moves in will want me instead of her. She's jealous of my youth and looks. She feels some relief at the thought that somebody will keep the place presentable – anybody, as long as she doesn't have to do it. She feels nothing for me. No love or bond, but no hate either. I hurt for her.

I'm unimpressed with my actions. I've shown her no love.

I see scenes from the three months after I move back into Etta's house. Etta coerces the new guy, Carver, to move in. He looks old. He has a job and treats Etta and me decently. He buys groceries, and I don't have to get a job. After school, my routine is to go home and cook, clean, and wash. Larry and I spend hours upon hours of platonic time together. As soon as I finish the dinner dishes, Larry picks me up. He drops me off late, and I go straight to bed. About once a week, I see Val on her porch when he drops me off, and I spend an hour with her. I cut back on cigarettes. I quit drinking.

On December 31, at midnight, at his family's New Year's Eve party, Larry kisses me for the first time. After that night, there are many more kisses.

I see us on a Saturday night in early March. We've been to Nickerson Farms again for dinner, and Larry has taken some back roads toward Richmond. He pulls into a drive that leads back to two old barns, cuts the headlights, and drives by moonlight to behind one of the barns. He tunes the radio to a classical station, turns the volume low, and reaches for me across the console. I lean into him, and we kiss, lightly and long.

"Either this gearshift has gotta go, or we should get in the back," he says.

I turn and climb between the seats, showing him no modesty in my short skirt as I wriggle through. I flip over and scoot to the driver's side to give him room to try to navigate the obstacles. He pushes the back of the passenger seat forward to enlarge his path and lurches through. It's cramped back here, even for me. I situate my legs across his lap, unable to change my mindset that, regardless of whether or not I have any desire, I'm supposed to make the guy want more. He does.

For fifteen minutes we make out, wrapped in each other's arms. I'm in no position to resist any advance, and I'm sure he knows he can do anything he wants. His arms stay around me the whole time. His hands don't wander.

"Wow, Eve," he gasps, breaking off an especially long exchange of tongues. "I've gotta take a break before I lose all control."

"Control is overrated."

"No. I'm not taking advantage of you like that. Every boy you've ever gone out with has just taken what he wanted and left you to fend for yourself. That's not gonna happen with me."

I lay my head against his, and we remain wrapped in each other's arms as he tries to cool down. Finally, he gives me a long kiss on the top of my head and says, "Time to take you home, baby."

I have a comfortable feeling that this relationship is developing the right way. Seeing this scene, I approve. I feel Larry's desire overwhelm him but also his compassion, strong enough to win out. I care about him. We help each other feel good about ourselves.

I see myself on the afternoon of Saturday, April 6, at 1:45. I'm washing dishes with one eye on the TV. Carver, much to Etta's chagrin, has enough interest in current affairs to wrest the set away from sitcoms and soap operas from time to time. Carver is watching intently as scenes of rioting in Washington

DC are shown live. Martin Luther King was assassinated two days ago and there is fear that blacks will riot everywhere.

"This is gonna get bad," Carver warns. "Mark my words, it'll happen right here in Richmond."

In the next instant, thunder detonates as if lightning has hit the house. Jerking my head to gape out the window at the bright, sunny day, I'm confused. Then we're hit with another earth-shaking blast.

Carver and I run outside as Etta rolls over on the couch and mumbles something without opening her eyes. Smoke and ash billow from downtown, about a quarter of a mile from us.

"Jesus, they set off a bomb downtown!" Carver shouts. "Git back in the house. We're lockin' 'er down. They'll probably hit the college next."

Sirens begin wailing. We run back inside. Carver locks the doors and windows and pulls shades down. Then he starts flipping TV channels, trying to find out what's happening in Richmond. "Turn on the radio, and see if you can find out what's goin' on," he commands me. "Etta! Git up! We might have to leave fast!"

She rolls and groans. He yanks the blanket off her. "Git up, I said! Now!"

"Leave me alone."

"C'mon, they're rioting! They're blowin' up Richmond. Get dressed."

By 3:00, to Etta's anger and Carver's dismay, radio and TV news reports are emphasizing that the explosion was not the result of bombing or rioting and that civil law is not unraveling in Richmond. The next day, we learn that the initial explosion was caused by a gas leak, which then ignited a gunpowder explosion. It's a horrific disaster for Richmond, with more than forty killed and one hundred fifty injured.

I see myself a week after the explosion with Larry at his parents' house, a three-story plantation-like mansion on Round Barn Road. It's 9:30 on Friday evening, and we've just returned from seeing *The Graduate*. We're alone.

Three days ago, I learned that Gilberto Bartolo, in his office on the afternoon of April 6, was incinerated in the downtown explosion. His absence from the face of the Earth makes me feel more like a person, as if now I have some measure of value.

Tonight, Larry and I are making out on the couch. I'm surprised to feel excitement and desire within myself. I *want* to go further. That's new. That's good. As I urge him on, we inch closer and closer to a point of no return. We reach that point, and all thoughts of anything other than the moment are obliterated – where we are, who might walk in, where we go from here. The world contains nothing except the two of us.

Half an hour later, we're dressed and snuggled together on the couch, watching TV when his parents return home. I'm happy, and the concern in his parents' eyes as they glance at us doesn't dampen my exhilaration. Larry takes me home after midnight. We kiss for a long time before I get out of his car. I'm out of character, joyful, even optimistic.

As I see this night play out, I feel his parents' concern for their son's future. They're friendly to me, but they know enough about where I come from to have decided I'm not the one for their son. They're worried that we're getting too close. I feel Larry's own excitement and happiness, but his emotions are restrained by his parents' concerns and by his own uneasiness that they might be right.

I see myself on a Saturday afternoon in August at Larry's house. His family is throwing him an "off-to-college" party. Larry and I have been dreading the day he'll leave for Purdue. But, he's insisted he'll come home at least once a month. It'll be hard, but our relationship will persevere until I graduate and can join him. Tonight, he seems uneasy and distant.

He drives me home in silence. I sit on a pillow on the hump between the front seats, leaning against him, my left hand on his right thigh. He keeps both hands on the steering wheel. The radio softly plays Herb Alpert's "This Guy's in Love with You." As he turns onto my street, he says nervously, avoiding eye contact, "Eve, we have to talk."

I don't move or utter a sound.

"The way things are working out," he says, "I'm not going to be able to come home before Christmas."

I say nothing. I haven't cried since the morning I started seventh grade, but now I fight tears.

"You know I have to go to college, Eve. It's either that or Vietnam. I don't have a choice. But, Dad says his plastering business took a big hit this summer. He got stiffed for thousands by his main contractor. So, it turns out I have to have a job to help pay my way. My dad lined one up, but I have to work every weekend till Christmas break." He coughs hoarsely. "I'm not positive I'll even get off then." He waits for me to say something. I don't. "It wouldn't be fair for me to ask you not to see other guys, when I don't know if I'll even see you till next summer." There is a long pause. He stops in front of my house. "That wouldn't be fair..." he gulps. "To either of us."

A single tear trickles down my cheek as I open the car door and get out. He drives away as I walk to the house.

Seeing the scene, I feel his pain. He knows he's hurt me. He tries to rationalize that I should have known that a girl with my background could never fit into his future. But he knows how unfair he's been to me, how small and weak he's been. He wants to crawl in a hole and pull it in after him. My judgment of my actions is that I should have talked to him – should have said something to help him feel better. I should have been less absorbed in my own emotions and been more loving. It's a small regret.

## Chapter 8

Scenes flash before me from the first two months of my sophomore year. After Larry dumps me, I revert. Everyone I've hung out with since seventh grade has graduated. I have no friends in my own class. Tom Stanton long ago gave up on me and my decadent ways. He's a top student, involved in lots of extracurricular activities, leading most of them. Despite the turmoil in America in 1968, he has managed to remain patriotic and still be looked up to by both adults and classmates. We never make eye contact.

Val still lives at home, three houses down the street. She works weeknights in a downtown bar. Legally, she's too young, but the owner is on the police force and doesn't concern himself with the fine points of Indiana law. She and I have set aside Sunday nights for porch smoke-and-drink chats. Saturday nights, she and Vic go crazy. Sometimes on Friday nights, I go with her to milder parties. Twice I wake on Saturday morning in a stranger's bed, unable to recall how I got there.

Part of my reversion has been to become more like Val was as a sophomore. She makes enough to buy new clothes and gives me some of her old sexpot wardrobe. I attract almost as many hungry looks as she did.

The senior boys know I hung with the older partiers who've graduated, and they think I should now belong to them. There isn't a girl in the entire school who has any interest in being seen with me.

I see myself in late October. The last class bell has just sounded, and I walk out of my World History class. "Hey, Eve!

Eve Kessler!" a deep voice booms. I glance down the hall to my right and see Eric Kellerman, senior quarterback and team captain, rushing toward me.

He's been trying to get my attention for a month. His family is big in insurance and richer than Larry's. I avoid him. I've had enough of that. He's big, great-looking, athletic, and appears to have it all. He seems thoroughly spoiled. Every girl in school except me would do anything he asked.

As soon as I see him hailing me, I whirl to my left and hasten away. In ten seconds a huge right hand swings around from behind me at chin height and bangs into a locker on my left. I stop in my tracks.

"Hey." His chest is heaving as he grins at me. "Am I poison or what? I've been trying to get you to say hi to me for weeks. Am I too small to see?"

I do a 180-degree spin and take a quick step before his left hand bangs into the locker on that side, and I have a huge arm blocking my path in either direction. I duck under and sprint from him.

"Hey, Eve Kessler!" he bellows. "At least now you know I'm here. Maybe tomorrow you'll say hi to me!" His laugh echoes down the hall.

I see myself walk into school a month later. Eric is waiting for me at the door. He's been relentless, and I've given up rebuffing his hounding. I've grown tired of being treated like a leper by all the girls. If they all want him, and he wants me, then they can all just steam. I'll flaunt.

"Hi, Eric." I smile up at him and slip my arm around his waist as he lays his huge arm down on my shoulder. Although it looks natural, this is the first time we've touched each other.

I see us on our first date the Friday night after football season ends. We go to Frisch's in his hot-rod GTO. After every stoplight, he burns rubber and weaves through traffic to get to the head of the line for the next stop. He looks at me and grins. "See? Invincible!"

At the restaurant, I order a burger and fries, and he orders two. As I pick at my fries, he devours his food, then reaches across the table and takes my burger.

Walking out, he grins and says, "Hey, baby, let's go to Glen Miller Park and park."

"And do what? You barely fit in the front seat. No way you're ever gonna get in the back."

"I got a blanket in the trunk. We could lay in the grass. You know, look at the stars and stuff."

I grin at him. "It's the 'and stuff' that worries me."

"Aw, come on, baby. Man, with that crowd you ran with last year? You gotta know stuff I never *dreamed* of."

"Take me to see *Romeo and Juliet*, Eric." I've decided to experiment with him. He isn't going to hurt me. I learned my lessons the hard way about falling for guys. I'll see how long I can use him while he thinks he's using me. Every girl in school can watch us and turn green.

Eric is a bull and can't be held off for long. By the turn of the year, he's getting what he wants from me. "Man, I was right," he says. "There ain't a girl in the whole school who knows the stuff you know." I want to keep the other girls steaming as long as possible, so I go at him with all I've got just to squeeze every last week out of him.

He's definitely spoiled. This bull insists on getting his way. He's the only guy I've ever been with who refuses to use a condom. "That's like takin' a shower with a raincoat on! If you got pregnant, I'd marry you in a heartbeat. You're the absolute best."

I don't kid myself about his lie, but the thought intrigues me. His family has more money than I can imagine. What if I did get pregnant? I don't want Eric for a husband any more than he wants me for a wife, but a baby might be a good thing for me, especially if his folks provide for their grandchild well. It'd give me something worthwhile to care about. I have nothing else. I decide I don't care either way. If he doesn't want to use a condom, so be it.

I see myself on a warm evening in late April, standing in the northeast section of town in front of the Kellerman home. The grassy, mounded corner lot looks huge, even with the expansive two-story brick and stone manor dominating the landscape. I'm dressed in my nicest and most conservative dress. I drift up the sidewalk to the front door, falter, and then press the doorbell button. In a moment, Ray Kellerman opens the door. He's even bigger than his son.

"Can I help you?"

"Um, I'm Eve Kessler, Mr. Kellerman. Are Mrs. Kellerman and Eric home?"

"We're in the middle of dinner. Is there something I can do for you?"

"I really need to talk to all three of you. It's pretty important. I can wait until you're finished."

He hesitates. "We're almost through. Come in. Have you eaten?"

"Yes, thank you. I'll just wait."

"Come into the living room and have a seat. We'll join you in a minute."

I glance into the dining room as I walk past the archway. Eric's jaw drops. He's never brought me here. I'm sure he's never mentioned my name. I sit on a white couch in the conversational half of the room, facing away from the stone fireplace, the TV, and the furniture set that serves the opposite side, the entertainment area. I hear Mrs. Kellerman say, "We're all done. I'll clear this later." Mr. Kellerman returns, followed by his wife and then Eric. Eric's parents sit in billowy chairs on the other side of a round oak coffee table. Eric stands half in the room and half out, looking dumbfounded.

"Eve," Mr. Kellerman says, "this is my wife, Mary. I'm Ray, and you must already know Eric. What can we do for you?"

I look at Eric, who's staring through me, mouth open. I take a deep breath, let it out, and turn to Mr. Kellerman. "Eric and I have been dating since football season ended. We've gotten pretty... familiar. I... uh... guess, um, I don't really know any way to do this except just come out with it." I turn my eyes to Eric. He looks as if he wants to disappear through the floor. "I'm carrying Eric's baby."

Although I presume they all suspected what I might tell them from the moment I entered the house, each of them is stunned.

After a moment that seems like an hour, Ray looks sternly at his son. "Can this be possible, Eric? Have you two been dating? Have you been intimate?"

Eric looks at me in disbelief. "I… I… never thought it could come out like this." Silence. "Eve. Why? You should've said something."

"Eric!" Ray is loud. "Look at me. Did you use prevention? How could you put yourself – your mother and me – in this situation?"

"I… I never thought *this* could happen."

I'm no longer nervous; I'm the only person in the room who is calm. I see wheels turning in their minds, all of them trying to discern their options and place them into two categories: thinkable and not.

Mary, trying not to shake, asks the question, her eyes locked on mine. "Eve, is it possible that this baby could be someone else's?"

Eric blows it, unable to conceive that any girl he was doing could possibly want anybody else. "No way!" he blurts.

I look at him and back at Mary. "He's right. It can't possibly be anyone else's."

No one speaks. Ray and Mary seem to be trying to communicate telepathically. Eric glares at me. Finally, Ray says, "Eve, we're respectable members of this community, and we're church-going Christians. This family will do right by you. We need a few minutes in private. We're going to go to the basement to talk. Please wait here. We won't be long."

"I'll wait," I say. "Take as long as you need."

They return ten minutes later. Ray says, "Eve, Mary and I know nothing of who you are or your family history. You seem to be an intelligent and courageous young lady. You've obviously conducted yourself in a manner we don't condone, but then, so has our son. Eric tells us you're a sophomore. How old are you?"

"Fifteen."

He shakes his head. "You seem older. Eve, family is more important than anything to us. You are carrying our grandchild. Eric will marry you a few days after graduation. We'll welcome you into our family. We'll also expect you to conduct yourself respectfully and not dishonor this family."

I meet his eyes. "I will do my best, Mr. Kellerman."

I look at Eric. He says nothing. His eyes seem wild and unable to comprehend, like a threatened animal, knowing it has to run fast but unable to decide which direction to bound.

As I absorb the scene, I feel the emotions my actions spawned in the others. Mary is devastated. Her aspirations for her only son's future have been smashed. She's terrified about how Eric will react. He's never given any indication that he could be a responsible, self-sustaining person, and she's afraid he'll vanish. She's never heard of me, which suggests two things that she fears foretell disaster: first, my family has no social status and, second, Eric thinks so little of me that he's made sure nobody in their circle knew he was associating with me. She implodes at the thought of her friends becoming aware.

Ray fights himself. He wants me to go away. Giving me money and sending me away would solve everything. He wants me to disappear from Richmond now, tonight. This impulse battles other emotions. His first grandchild is right here in this room, waiting to be brought into the family. He vowed to himself long ago that irresponsibility on his part would never again endanger one of his own. Sending me away would violate every Christian principle he's grounded in. Sending me away would constitute one more layer of positive reinforcement he would heap upon his only son as reward for thinking of nothing except his own gratification.

Eric feels pure panic. He's incredulous that his father is committing to a marriage. His mind is teeming with schemes for setting himself free of this catastrophe: discrediting me, abortion, driving away forever, getting a friend to claim fatherhood, suicide, getting a more desirable girl pregnant, having me abducted, murder.

My actions created this strife. I allowed myself to get pregnant. It was premeditated. I entered the Kellerman home with purpose. I wrecked their lives. There was nothing loving about my actions. I was destructive. I give myself low marks.

## Chapter 9

I see myself in mid-June on a side street two blocks from Etta's house, opening the passenger door of Ray Kellerman's deep blue Cadillac. The miniscule wedding ceremony is just over a week off. I wonder what he has to tell me that he couldn't say on the phone ten minutes ago when he called and asked to meet in his car. He's shaken.

"I've got tough news, Eve." He looks down at his steering wheel. "Last night, Eric told Mary and me he joined the Army. He's going to Vietnam." Ray waits for me to ask him when. I don't. "He waited to tell us until the day he had to report. He joined back in May." His voice cracks. This big man is about to cry. "He's gone, Eve. He left this morning at five. Wouldn't even let us take him. One of his buddies drove him. His last words when he left were that he'd never come back to Richmond, like he's punishing me for forcing him into this. Mary's beside herself."

He finally looks up at me. His eyes glisten, and his lips tremble. "I lit into him last night. About being immature, thinking of nobody but himself. Not caring about his mother or his own child." He wipes his eyes. "He told me to go to Hell." He shakes his head. "Those were the last words my son spoke to me before going off to war. I guess I've been a much worse father than I ever realized.

"Anyway, he's gotten his way again. There won't be any wedding. So, I'm here to tell you that at least you won't have to worry about how to support yourself and the baby. I'll... we'll provide for our grandchild and you. You need to think about how you'd like to see it work, and we'll talk again." Now he sounds determined. "But the Kellerman family is *not* going to abandon this child."

I know this is Ray Kellerman talking, not Eric or Mary. There's something about Ray – I don't know what, maybe something in his past – that won't let him sever his connection with the life I carry. Mary isn't on the same playing field. It hadn't taken them long to figure out exactly who I was. As far as I can tell, Mary has been unable to find a way to cope with that. I've not seen or spoken with her since the night I sat in their living room and delivered her death blow.

I see myself a month later at Etta's house. It's hot, and I have on a loose top. I've been slow to gain weight, but I'm five months pregnant, and Etta has just figured it out. She looks up from my midriff, gaping.

"Tell me you're not."

"I am."

Etta has just snagged a guy younger than her. He's thirty-three and moved in a week ago.

"That ain't gonna work with Sherm. Can't be no squallin' kid in the house."

I don't have a plan. I've not mentioned the quashed wedding or the Kellermans to Etta. On some level, I never believed any wedding would ever happen. Eric's gone. Ray has called twice since we met in his car, but I've been unable to land on a direction. I think he's scared that I might get an abortion.

"Etta," I say, "I'm not going to mess it up for you. I can move out."

"When?"

"I know you've never wanted me around, but don't you care at all about your grandchild?"

"There ain't nothing good 'bout havin' a kid. You're gonna be payin' for this screw up the rest of your life. I paid my dues already."

"I'll be out of here before school starts."

Val knows everything. She and Vic plan to rent a small house west of town, already dubbed the Volt Jolt, after Vic gets back from some farm field rock concert in New York she's going to with a gang of guys. Val says it'd be fine with her if I live with them, but Vic isn't keen on having a baby interfering with her amorous lifestyle. I can't imagine rearing a child around Vic. I finally decide it's time to talk to Ray. I call his office and tell him I'd like to stop by tonight. I make myself as presentable as I can and walk the two miles across town for our 7:00 meeting.

Ray and Mary sit on the couch, and I face them from the chair Mary sat in the last time I visited. They look at me and wait for me to speak. "I can't sit here and defend my life to you," I say. "I know my past decisions seem terrible. The conditions I live in are a world apart from yours." Mary can't look at me.

"I want to be a good mother to my baby. I care about it and want to raise it right. My life's been so full of problems, I've never been able to think of a future. I've never thought there was any reason for me to do anything except get out of bed in the morning and deal with whatever gets thrown at me that day. Maybe this baby will be a good thing for me."

Mary looks at me as if I'm a lunatic. Ray waits for me to say something he can respond to. "I don't know what you know about my past or my mom. It's bad. She doesn't want me to live in her house anymore, with the baby coming. It's not a good place for a baby, anyway. I'm not sure what to do or how much you might want to help. I know I'm going to have to get a job. I'll have to make enough to pay for a place to stay. It can be really small. I don't see how I can stay in school. I guess I wanted to ask you for a couple things. Mr. Kellerman, I know you have a lot of connections, and people look up to you. I was wondering if you might help me get a job. And, Mrs. Kellerman, the baby is going to be your grandchild. I know everything is awful, with Eric leaving and me not being a person you would pick to be your grandchild's mother, but I was wondering if you might watch the baby while I'm at work."

Mary's head is down. She's crying. I can't tell what she's thinking.

Ray looks at me for a long time before he speaks. He shakes his head sadly. "This is too much, Eve. Our life has been turned upside-down. I know yours has, too. Mary and I haven't been able to bring ourselves to discuss how we need to deal with you... with our grandchild. But, I'm going to tell you what I think." He looks at Mary and says, "Honey, you're going to have to figure out what you think, and if you disagree with what I'm saying, you need to speak up now."

He turns to me. "I think the right thing to do, the best thing – I hope for everybody – would be for you to move in here with us. We've got plenty of room. We could make your own separate area. You're barely sixteen, and you're going to need help with the baby. And as hard as this is for Mary, it will be her grandchild, and she'll never forgive herself later if she shuts it out now. There's no reason for you to get a job. Finish your education. We'll find a way for you to stay in school and graduate. We can easily provide for you and our grandchild. I think that's the right thing to do." He looks at Mary, who is still staring at the floor. "That's what I want to do."

I sit watching them both. Finally, she looks up at him and then turns to me and gives the slightest of nods.

I don't know how to respond. After an awkward silence, I say to Ray, "Are you sure you want to do that?"

"Yes," he says with no hesitation.

As this scene passes before me, I feel Ray's relief. He hopes this gives him the chance to make up for his failings with his son and for some relentless past transgression. Mary feels a collage of emotions. She wants this grandchild to love and care for. She's repulsed by what she knows of me and my life and the thought of bringing me into her home. She's grieving over the loss of her only son. She's mortified about the certain reaction from her social circle.

I judge my actions in this scene to be acceptable. I've laid some groundwork for hope and love.

I see myself near midnight in November.

"*Aaauuugghhhh!*" I scream. Up to this point, I've grimaced and groaned and clamped and cursed under my breath, but I can no longer hold back. My nurse, along with everyone else on the floor, hears my screech and hustles into the labor room. Ray, standing back in a corner gives her a pleading "Save us" look. Mary is white-faced from the pain I'm inflicting on her hand, which is vice-gripped in mind.

I've been in the hospital all day after having been awake the night before in early labor. Three hours ago I thought I was done for, exhausted and unable to withstand any more pain. One hour ago, the nurse told me I was dilated five centimeters, halfway there. *Another whole day? I'm gonna die.*

As the nurse examines me, I bawl, scared to death of the next contraction, willing it away. Mary allows me to continue to crush her hand and harries the nurse with her eyes.

"Seven centimeters. It's going faster now."

"Ow! Ow! *Ow! Aaaaaaaaahhhhh! Stop it! Stop!* Ouch! Oh, ow. Ow." Tears stream down my cheeks, further wetting my ratty hair.

"Can't you give her something?" Mary's voice is fretful.

"Not without an order from Dr. Gershman. And you know how much of a stickler he is on natural childbirth. Keep both the mother and child alert and responsive."

"He ever give birth?" I hiss.

"He'd say women have been doing this since the beginning of time. You'll get through it, honey."

"Oh, *shit!* Here comes another one. Ooooh! *Ow! Aaarrrrrghhhh!*" This one goes on and on and on. I scream through it all. Ray is about to collapse. Even the nurse looks anxious.

Mary whispers, "*Please!*"

"I think we'll go ahead and take her to Delivery," the nurse says, as if moving me will resolve the problem.

Relief floods Ray's face; he knows he won't be going into the delivery room.

After another hour-that-feels-like-ten of screaming, cursing, and being examined, now with the added enhancement of being strapped in stirrups and tied down, the nurse miraculously says, "You're complete. I'm calling the doctor. Don't push yet!"

Mary's breath gushes from her as I feel her thanking God.

"*Oh, no! Ow! Ow! Ohhh!*"

"Don't push!"

"*Aaaaahhhhhhhhhhh. Ow! Ow! Aarrrrgggghhh! Ouch! Oh, Ow!*"

"Don't push. Don't push. The doctor's coming."

The door opens, and in hurries Dr. Gershman. Now the nurse heaves a sigh and thanks God. He smiles. "How are we doing, Eve?"

"Out! Get it out!"

"Easy, Eve. I know labor is hard. It works on its own time. You'll be fine. Women have been doing this for a long time. Okay, let's have a look."

"If you say that again…. Uh-oh. Oh, no. *No!*"

"Looks like you're ready. Push with this one, Eve. Push!"

Six more contractions bring pain worse than anything I've ever imagined. Six humongous efforts at pushing the object within me out through an opening ten times too small, pushing with single-mindedness that knows there is no other existence on earth, only me and pushing… and then it is abruptly over.

"Here he is."

I hear the words but don't comprehend. I steel myself for the next contraction, but I don't feel it coming on. I hear a tiny cry. I hear Mary melt. "Ohhhhh."

I listen to the cry and strain to lift my head, but I'm too spent.

"He's perfect. Ten fingers and ten toes. Would you like to hold your son?"

I see him. My world transforms. I reach for him, unable to respond to the question.

The nurse lays him on my chest. He stops crying and I start. I can't take my eyes off him.

Dr. Gershman beams at me and says, "Am I forgiven?"

I still can't speak, but the answer shines through the wetness in my eyes. Mary stands beside me, looking on in awe. I stroke his hair. "Brent," I say. I silently dedicate him to Grandpa and Gran. "Brent Everett Kellerman." My tears continue to stream.

The nurse smiles at us. "Can I wash and weigh him?" She starts to reach for him.

"Oh, please. Please, let me hold him a little longer."

"Okay, another minute. Don't worry. I'll bring him right back as soon as I've got him ready. He won't be away for long."

As I watch this scene unfold and judge myself, I mark this moment as my best. I have given life. My love is boundless. I have bestowed a priceless gift upon Ray and Mary. It is the greatest of acts.

I see myself on a March evening in the small apartment that has been partitioned off in the Kellerman home for Brent and me. Our apartment has a door into the rest of the house as well as an outdoor entrance. I have a kitchenette, a bedroom with a generously sized closet and an alcove for Brent, a bathroom, and a living room big enough to be comfortable with a couple of guests. The decor is multiple shades of blue. Val visits weekly, and she's holding Brent while *Hawaii Five-O* provides some background noise.

"So, how's school going?"

"I'm gonna be a senior in about three months. A year ago, I never thought that'd happen."

"You thinking about reincarnating your social life yet?"

"My life's full just trying to make passing grades and dealing with this little guy."

"He's the best, but I think I'd still want a life. You wanna go out with us sometime?"

"You and Vic? Man, she'd be so far past me now, my head would spin."

"No, not with wild-woman. Maybe you and me go to a movie. Just get you out for a fun night. Maybe a double date."

"Double date? You know lots of guys itchin' to take out a sixteen-year-old mom? Should I bring Brent?"

"I'm serious! Actually, I do know a guy I think would like you a lot. He's a great guy. I went out with him a half-dozen times when Jack was havin' his little fling with that witch, Rhonda. His name's Doug Pratt. If Jack hadn't come crawlin' back, I'd have latched onto him. Spent a couple nights at his place, and I'll tell you what, it was hard to say goodbye."

"So you dumped poor old Doug, and now you're tryin' to set him up with a teenage consolation prize? How old's this dude?"

"He's a special case. He's twenty-one, but he's different. When he was a junior he collapsed on the basketball floor. Turned out he had a hole in his heart. They fixed it, but it changed the way he looks at things... and kept him out of Vietnam. He works construction, frames houses, so he's got this incredible tan all summer long, at least from the waist up. Pretty white below the belt, but the rest of that tan goes great with his strawberry-blond hair and dark blue eyes. He's six-four. Not as stick-skinny as he was in high school, but he looks great. Kinda long hair, and when he doesn't shave for a couple days he's a god. You'd like him. He's a lot of fun at parties, as long as he doesn't drink too much. Loves kids and says it wouldn't bother him a bit to date somebody who has one."

"You already told him about me?"

"I tell everybody about you. You know that. You're the most amazing person I know."

"I thought Vic was."

"Well, in a different way."

"I hope."

"So, what do you say?"

"About what?"

"A double date Friday night with me and Jack, airhead!"

"Ray and Mary would blow a gasket."

"What, you don't think they want you to have a life? Surely, they don't think their douchebag son's gonna come back and be your knight in shining armor."

"No, they're really pissed at Eric. And they're cautiously impressed watching me with Brent, but they'd flip out if I told 'em I was goin' out on a date."

"So, you've decided to be an old maid, then? C'mon, you gotta break 'em in sometime. I say the sooner the better. You might be surprised. They probably think you deserve a break."

I watch Brent look up at Val. Then I grin and say, "I guess a double date couldn't hurt."

I see myself at 10:30 at night in early August. I'm in Doug Pratt's sparsely furnished half of an aging duplex apartment, in the upper-story bedroom, wrapped in his arms, in his bed. Art Garfunkel croons "Bridge over Troubled Water" on Doug's clock radio. We've been in bed for an hour and a half, and it's past time for him to get me home. He cooked dinner for me tonight: spaghetti – his specialty – complimented with a bottle of wine, all served by candlelight. We topped that off with a second bottle in bed.

"You know I love you," he says.

"Yeah, I know." I tease him.

"I'm serious. You might as well start livin' your life. You've already got Brent, and I love that little guy. I make plenty for us to live on. You got better prospects? You'd better not have. What do you need to go back to school for, anyway? You're *way* more mature than any senior I've ever known. Just get your GED and be done with it. Why waste the whole year going to class with all those teeny-weenies?"

"You worried one of those hot young studs is gonna sweep me off my feet?"

"Dammit, Eve, I'm serious. Let's move on with our lives. You could move in here next weekend."

"I'd have to talk it over with Ray and Mary first. They've been lifesavers for Brent and me."

"You *know* what they're gonna say. They'll do anything to keep Brent at their house. *Forever!* If you let it up to them, they'll *never* let you go. Just tell 'em you got a life to live. It's not like it'd be the end for them. We'd still be in the same town. Ask 'em to watch the little guy a couple days a week. You could get a part-time job like you wanna do anyway, and Mary could watch him while you work."

"I'll think about it."

"Think nothing! Just think about this minute, right here, right now. What's the one thing you'd really like to do right now? Here's the choices I see. We could get out of bed and get dressed and go get in the car and drive across town. Or, we could have another one of those moonshot kisses and see where *that* leads. Wouldn't it be great if you just lived here, and we wouldn't even have to think about it? We'd just go for the moonshot."

"I'll think about it, Doug. I really will. But right now, we're already a half-hour late. You're right, I'd like the moonshot, but it's gonna have to wait till next time. Let's go, lover."

He lays his arm across me, keeping me from sitting up. "All right, I'll skip the moonshot, but I'm tellin' you, I love you, and I really, *really* want you and Brent to move in."

I look into those penetrating blue eyes and say, "Okay."

Chapter 10

My focus is drawn to a weekend in October, two months after I've moved in with Doug. It's just after 5:00 Friday afternoon, and I'm mixing a salad. Eleven-month-old Brent is bouncing in his exerciser, squealing as he grasps and tosses teethers and toys, certain that Mama will retrieve them all for another round of tossing. My cheesy garlic bread is ready to go in the oven, timed to be perfectly toasted when the lasagna is ready to serve. The house is permeated with Italian cooking aromas.

The door opens. "Oh, man it smells good in here," Doug says, beaming. He strides to me, wraps his arms around my waist, and kisses me long and hard, a promise of another weekend of bliss. "Sorry I didn't clean up before that, but I just couldn't resist you for one more second." Then, looking over my shoulder, he gives Brent a monster grin. "Hey, little guy! Are you having a grand time distracting Mommy from her cooking?"

Brent kicks and coos at the sight of his favorite playmate. Doug lifts him, and gives him a half-dozen sky throws, inciting shrieks of laughter. He puts Brent back. "Do I have time to grab a shower before the banquet?"

"If you hurry."

"I can save a little time if I don't put any clothes on."

"I'll make sure you have time to dress."

"Aw, shucks. Back in a jiff."

When he returns, I put the food on the table, and he opens a bottle of red wine. Then he picks up Brent and situates him in his high chair between us. We take turns spoon-feeding Brent between our own bites and sips. The child keeps us hopping. I watch Doug enjoy sharing in the task of keeping Brent satisfied, and I marvel.

After dinner, I clear the table and wash dishes while Doug chases Brent around the apartment on hands and knees. Together, we bathe Brent and get him ready for bed. Doug reads to him, giving me a break so I can relax in my own bath for half an hour. I don my sexiest nightie, Doug's favorite, throw a robe on over it, and take over with Brent. He's gotten tired and fussy, and in ten minutes he's fast asleep. I lay him in his crib in our bedroom, discard the robe, and return to Doug.

"Ooh, what you do to me," he says. "I'd better uncork another bottle."

As he does, I turn off the TV and put a Henry Mancini album on the stereo. He sets the glasses on the coffee table, and we begin to dance. Two hours later, after the wine is gone and we've made love twice in the living room, we go to bed and fall asleep entwined in each other's arms.

Brent wakes up three times during the night. I take the first and last shift, and Doug takes the middle one. He wakes for good at 7:30. I change him and then get back in bed with Doug, placing Brent between us. We play for half an hour until Brent decides breakfast can wait no longer. While I feed him, Doug treks to the bakery and brings back fresh pastries. We cater to Brent most of the morning, except for the hour he naps, when we cater to each other.

It's a beautiful autumn day, seventy-five and sunny with a light breeze. At noon, we head for Glen Miller Park with a picnic lunch. We spread two blankets on the ground and eat while we feed Brent. After lunch, we put him in the stroller and take in the park. He loves the goats, rabbits, and ducks. After rambling for an hour, he falls asleep in the stroller. Doug respreads the blankets, and we lie on our backs, watching the clouds wisp over the rustling gold and red tree leaves. Holding hands, we drift in and out of sleep.

Driving home, Doug says, "You wanna hit the Triangle tonight? Cut loose a little?"

"Sure, if Ray and Mary will watch Brent."

"You think that's a question? Ain't seen 'em say no to that yet."

We arrive at the Kellermans' at 7:00 and make two trips from the car to the house to deliver Brent and all of the paraphernalia required for an overnight.

"So, where are you two off to tonight?" Ray asks. I'm sure we won't need to call you, but it's probably good to know."

"Triangle," Doug replies. "In Greenville."

Mary frowns. "You two be careful driving home. One of you go easy on the drinks. When do you want to pick him up?"

"Do you want to take him to church?" I ask, already well aware of the answer.

"Sure," Ray booms. "You wanna pick him up after lunch?"

"Yeah. How about one or so, before he goes down for his nap."

The exchange made, we speed off in Doug's hot-rod truck, with me sitting so close I'm almost on his lap.

We sit at the bar, chatting with the bartenders and our fellow barstoolers while we each down a beer in a hurry. Doug's second one goes just as fast, but I slow down. He's on his fourth as I finish my second and shake my head at the offer of another. "Maybe later."

He drains two more before slurring, "Let's dance, baby."

He's unsteady as I lead him onto the floor. He leans into me as we slow dance. He locks his fingers at the small of my back, but they soon creep down to my cheeks. As the second dance begins, the hands tug at my short skirt, bringing the hem ever higher.

"Stop it, Doug." I reach behind me, whisk his hands off, and brush the skirt down. "Not here."

He sulks for ten seconds and then is back at it again.

"What are you doing? Trying to show your buddies my panties? Why? Quit!" This time, I reach around and smack his hands.

"Let's get another drink, then," he says, dropping his hands to his side and turning away from me toward the bar.

"You should slow down. I can't carry you back to the truck."

"I can take care o' myself," he says to the air, and then mutters, "bitch," as he slinks away.

I stand and stare at his backside, smarting from the disrespect. Slowly, I make my way back to my barstool. He's already downing another beer and getting loud with the guy beside him, whom I don't know – and I doubt that he does, either.

"Yeah, ma truck's got a three-fifty-one with dual quads. Runs like a scart rabbit! Fire-engine red, man. It'll whoop ass on 'bout any pickup I ever seen. Most Camaros and Firebirds, too, damn GM pieces a crap anyway. Ya wanna see 'er?"

"Maybe later," the guy says without looking at Doug. "Here comes my date back from the powder room. Gotta take 'er out fer a whirl."

"Hey, Doug, I'm sorry." I'm not sure why I'm apologizing, but I try to make amends. Things have been great since I moved in with him. I don't want to mess it up. "I didn't mean to make you mad."

"Yeah, well," he says without looking at me.

After I realize that's all he's going to say, I add, "C'mon, honey, let's go home. You know what they say about makin' up."

"We just got here. I ain't ready yet." He motions to the bartender. "Another beer here."

A girl with a body to advertise and wearing clothes that do it sits down on the empty stool on the other side of Doug. She smiles at him. "Anybody sittin' here?"

"Nope. Been savin' it fer you, sweetheart. Whatcha drinking?"

She grins at him. "Harvey Wallbanger."

"Damn straight. Harvey Wallbanger with that beer," he thunders.

She eyes him. "You by yourself?" She's trying to get under my skin – successfully.

"Nah. I'm here with her." He half-nods his head in my direction without taking his eyes off her. "She's gotta kid. Keeps us up ever' night."

"Yeah, well, what can you say?"

I hiss in his ear. "If we're not what you want, I can end that right here!"

Now, he turns to face me. "Aw, c'mon, babe. You know I didn't mean nothin' by that. You kinda pissed me off out there."

"You're pissin' me off right here. I'm leaving. You comin' or stayin here with this flirt?"

"Jeez. Don't lose your panties. I'm coming. Got one more beer first. Don't know what the hell's wrong with you t'night. You driving?"

"*You're* sure not. Forget the beer. I'm not sure you can even walk."

The beer arrives with the Wallbanger. Doug throws a ten-dollar bill on the bar and slurs, "Keep the change, buddy. Hope you get a real bang outta that Banger, doll."

I vault off my stool and hustle for the door. He grabs his beer and stumbles after me, bumping into a bar stool and the doorjamb on the way. "Hey! Wait up. I'm coming. I got the damn keys, anyway."

I'm standing by the driver's side door when he catches up. He pulls the keys out of his pocket but doesn't hand them to me. He bellows, "Hey, I got an idea. Let's do 'er in the back o' the pickup. Right here under the stars. We ain't never done it there yet."

"Doug, I swear. Give me the keys and get in the truck right now, or I'm *never* going out drinking with you again. *Ever!*"

We don't speak on the way home. He's snoring when we arrive but wakes when the motor shuts off. "We home, baby?"

I get out and go in the house. He stumbles in a minute later. "Okay. Since you wouldn't in the back o' the truck, let's do it now."

"You couldn't do it now for a million dollars. I'm goin' to bed."

"C'mon, Eve!" he shouts. "Brent ain't here. We ain't gonna wake nobody up. Now'd be a great time!"

"Don't touch me! I'm sleepin' on the couch. Go to bed. If you can make it up the stairs." I retrieve a blanket from the closet, kick off my shoes, lie down on the couch, and pull the blanket over me.

"Aw, come on up to bed."

I roll over to face the back of the couch. He clambers up the steps. Within five minutes, I hear him snoring again.

It takes hours for me to go to sleep. When I wake, the room is sunlit. I hear movement in the kitchen and smell coffee. I pull the blanket tighter to my chin.

"You awake, Eve? Man, I'm really sorry about last night. I don't remember exactly what all happened, but I know I was bad. I didn't mean any of it. Sometimes, if I drink too much too fast I get really stupid. I'll make it up to you, sweetheart. I love you. You and Brent. I really do. And I'm not gonna mess this up. Man, everything's been great since you moved in. You and Brent are the best thing that ever happened to me. I'm gonna make this right. Whatever it takes. Are you awake?"

I roll over to face him. "I'm awake. You were awful last night, Doug. *Awful!* Do you have any idea how *bad* you made me feel? You treated me like I was some worthless, dirty tramp. I mean, these last few weeks here with you have been the best of my life – until last night. But, if you ever do that to me again, I don't think I could stay with you. I mean it. I can forgive you this time, but it better never happen again."

"It won't. I swear. I just gotta take it easy when I start drinking. I gotta go slower. I won't get outta control again. I'm gonna make you happy. You and Brent. Watch me. You ready for a cup of coffee? I'll bring it. You want breakfast in bed? I mean, in couch? You name it. Anything you want. Your slightest wish is my command."

I grin at him. "Well, the one thing I really, *really* want you to do for me right now, and I mean it's *urgent*, is go pee for me."

He grins at me in relief. "I'll go do it right now. But I'm not sure it'll help much."

I see us on a Saturday afternoon in February, at Marty and Linda's Griner's house near Centerville. It's this group's annual winter cookout, and even though it's twenty degrees, snowing, and blowing hard, Marty's humongous outdoor stone fire pit is blazing. In addition to Marty and Linda and us, there are three couples. Joe and Jackie are both divorced and have been seeing each other for a month. Joe is the long-term member of the group, and this is Jackie's second appearance. Considering the weather, her getup is too tight and skimpy. After a few drinks, she's too friendly and rowdy. Randy and Bell are married and have two kids, five and three, the same ages as Marty and Linda's two. Crack and Marless have a three-year-old from her first marriage.

At 2:00, a dozen chicken halves hit the fire. The guys pretend to be veteran outdoorsmen, sitting around the fire on lawn chairs held in place by concrete blocks laid on their bottom runners. However, they trek in and out often for bathroom breaks and refills of whiskey-laden coffee, lingering around the women and kids on each trip.

The girls stay in the cozy, aromatic kitchen, tending to the potatoes, macaroni and cheese, rolls, pies, and kids. Inside, beer and wine are the drinks of choice. We've all been here since mid-morning, and I'm the only one going easy on the alcohol. I take on the role of child overseer as the others devote attention to cooking and drinking.

Dinner is served to the adults at 3:00, the kids having maintained their customary eating and napping times. After the feast has been consumed and cleared, two tables of Bid Euchre kick off. One chair at each table is reserved for rotating women in and out to allow for tending to kids and for continuous serving of drinks. Jackie takes my spot in a game versus Joe and Marty, with Doug as her partner.

"Hey, stud," she says to Joe as she scrutinizes the cards in her left hand and rubs Joe's thigh with her right. "You didn't melt away out there in the cold did you."

"If I did, I'm bouncing back now, hot hands."

"Well, let's see. Oh! You are!"

Doug bids three, and Marty passes. Jackie lays a card on the table and says, "I'll take one from my partner, but I need it to be a big one."

Doug slides a card across the table to her. "I got just the big one you need."

The game goes on, and Jackie flirts with all the guys. She's come to this party braless, and her blouse, having been buttoned a notch low all day, now has the next button down unfastened. As I bend to pick Brent up to feed him, I see her foot extend under the table to creep up Doug's leg. For a second, their eyes lock.

By 8:00 it's time for the party to break up, at least for those with kids. Everyone gathers coats, gloves, and hats, except for Joe and Jackie. Joe, who drinks the most freely and has the most trouble holding liquor, is lying on the couch passed out. Jackie says, "Looks like we're gonna need to let him there for the night." She looks at Linda. "If that's okay with you guys, I'll just drive his truck back to my place. I can pick him up in the morning."

Doug says, "I think I can get him home. I'll take Eve and Brent home and come back and load him up."

I drive us home. "You shouldn't drive back to get Joe," I say as I pull a resisting Brent out of his car seat. "You're in pretty tough shape. Marty and Linda won't care if he sleeps there tonight."

"Aw, I'm okay. I'll go get him. But, I might just crash at his place. Don't worry if I'm not back till morning."

I watch out the kitchen window as the truck pulls away. It doesn't turn back toward Marty's house.

Sunday morning, Doug saunters in the door at 10:30 with a box of donuts.

"Did you get Joe home okay?"

He picks up a donut and avoids looking at me. "Naw. Couldn't rouse him. Took him home this morning. You were right. I shouldn't a been driving, so I just stayed."

I let it drop.


I see myself with eighteen-month-old Brent in Doug's apartment on a Friday night in May. Brent has a cold and a low-grade fever, and he's restless. It's after midnight, and I've finally gotten him to stay asleep in his crib at the foot of the bed in our small bedroom. I go downstairs and turn on *Johnny Carson* to try to relax. I'm exhausted. Doug stumbles in, slamming the door behind him.

"Doug!" I hiss. "I just got Brent down." I hear a wail from the bedroom and heave an accusing sigh.

"God, Eve. Just jump all over my case the minute I get home, why don't you? Can't you ever get him to sleep?" Brent is in full swing. "Quiet him down! I'm sleepin' on the couch. At least, I'm gonna try."

I get up off the couch, wishing Doug had stayed out, even if he'd slept with someone else. He relieves himself in the bathroom, not bothering to close the door. Then he staggers to the couch, saying, "You used to be fun, a great lay. What happened to you?"

His words sting, but I know he'll apologize in the morning, and be sincere... if he remembers the conversation. I drag myself upstairs, lift Brent out of the crib, hold him against me, and sit on the edge of the bed and rock. In a few minutes, I hear

Doug snoring. After half an hour, Brent is wide awake and I can't keep my eyes open. I lie down with Brent snuggled beside me and pull the blanket over us.

Doug stirs at 10:00 Saturday morning. I've been up with Brent for three hours.

"Time is it?" he mumbles.

"Ten."

"What day?"

"Saturday."

"Oh, man. When did I get home? Were you up?"

"You came in about twelve-thirty. Woke Brent up."

"Oh. Sorry. I don't remember."

"You were out of it."

"God. We got coffee?"

"Yeah. Stay there. I'll get you a cup."

Brent is fussy, and I struggle with him all morning. Doug stays on the couch watching TV until 3:00. I've just gotten Brent down in his crib.

"I'm startin' ta feel half-decent now. Brent asleep? How 'bout comin' over here and hoppin' under the blanket? Maybe we can feel even better."

"I was awake half the night with Brent. I really need a nap. Maybe after."

"Yeah, right. I'm goin' to the Triangle tonight. You coming?"

"I can't, Doug. I'm so beat. Brent's running a temp. I don't have Ray and Mary set up. I just can't tonight."

"Suit yourself. I'll be outta here, so maybe you can both catch up on your sleep."

"All right. Just try to be a little quieter when you come."

"You won't hear a damn thing."

I know I should try to make this better. I could still salvage the day if I join him on the couch and make it special. I look at him. "I'm goin' up to take a nap."

Brent wakes me an hour later. Doug is already gone. I don't wish that he wasn't.

I hear nothing from Doug until he walks in the door Sunday night at 9:30. Brent went down at 8:00, but I hear him whimper after the door closes. I get up off the couch to go check on him.

Doug's only words are, "I'm gonna watch some TV.  Make sure the alarm's set for six-thirty."

I don't reply as I go upstairs to check on Brent.  I don't return, and Doug doesn't come up.

I see Doug and me at a New Year's Eve party at Marty and Linda's house.  By midnight, I'm exhausted as usual and need to go home and sleep.  And, as is now usual, Doug is drunk.  It's 12:05, and I've been dropping hints about leaving early since 10:30.

"Doug, can you *please* take me home?  You can come back if you want."

"C'mon, Eve!  Man, you're turnin' into a party-pooper.  You just need to cut loose and have some fun.  I'll get you a brewsky."

"I don't want a damn beer!  I'm goin' home.  Are you gonna take me, or do I have to drive myself?"

"Dammit, Eve, I gotta have wheels here.  Get your coat.  Let's go."

He follows me to the passenger door of his truck.  When I open it he says, "Why don't you lay down on the seat?  If I gotta leave, I oughtta be able to go satisfied."

"No!  It's freezing out here, and I'm dead tired.  I think I'm coming down with something."

He slams my door, lurches in behind the wheel, revs the motor up to a thunder, and peels out, fishtailing and missing a parked car by less than a foot.  As I brace for a crash, he says, "I've had it with you.  This ain't working.  It's time for you to live somewhere else.  I'm droppin' you off and goin' back to the party.  Where you wanna go?"

I'm as fed up as he is.  "Val's."  I know she and Vic are at an all-night party, and I know where they hide the key.  He drops me off.  Neither of us speak as I get out and slam the door.  I let myself in and find a blanket.  Before Doug is back at the party I'm asleep on the couch.

Val takes me to pick up Brent the next morning.  Mary is ice-cold.

Two days later at 8:00 in the evening, Val and I sit at the table, talking.  Brent is asleep on a blanket on the floor in Val's bedroom.  She's given us her room for the past two nights, and she's slept on the couch. During the three days I've been here, Vic has spent little time at home. She's not comfortable around Brent. I know she and Val want their lives to get back to normal.

"Maybe it's not all his fault," Val says. "Doug isn't all that hard to keep happy. Heck, if you don't want him, throw him back to me."

It's all I can do to keep from saying, "Take him." But then, where would I go? I say, "It's a lot harder to keep a baby *and* a man happy than I thought it would be. I should never have moved in with him."

"You *think*?" Val has become less intrigued with my life since I moved in with her old boyfriend. "Maybe you should call him and try to work things out."

There's a knock at the door. It's Doug. He looks at me and says, "Hey, Eve, look, I'm really sorry. I know I get outta control sometimes when I'm drunk, but I never mean it. You know I care about you and Brent. A lot. Come on, let's go home."

My heart tells me it's the wrong thing to do. My head tells me I have no choice. "I'll get Brent."

I see myself on a Friday evening in April. I've picked up a cold from Brent and feel lousy. Doug wants me to go out. I decline. Marty picks him up. He doesn't come home Friday night. Saturday afternoon at 1:15, I hear a car pull up on the street, and I look out the kitchen window to see Doug get out of a convertible driven by some long-haired blonde.

Saturday evening at 7:30, Doug says, "Let's go to the Triangle." Sicker than I was on Friday, I say, "Okay." We deliver Brent to the Kellermans.

By midnight, I'm swooning from the combination of drinks and cold medicines, but I'm not pressuring Doug to leave. We finally arrive home at 1:30. I can barely walk.

As soon as we're inside, he says. "Okay, baby, let's see if you can show me as good a time as I had last night." I flounder to the bathroom and throw up. Then I collapse on the bathroom floor and hear him say, "It's over this time, Eve. I'm done." He storms out.

I'm in bed Sunday morning when he comes back half-sober. He wakes me up and says, "Eve, this just isn't working anymore.

Get your stuff together. We're partin' ways. Today. Where ya want me to take you?"

"Doug, please." The last thing I can imagine doing this morning is packing up my stuff, picking up Brent, and moving into someone else's house. *Where?* What if it's permanent this time? It can't work at Val and Vic's. Ray and especially Mary hate me now. There's no place to go. "I'll try to do better. Maybe we should cut down on the booze and parties a little bit, but I think I can make you happy. Let's try to make it work. Let me make it better for you."

"You can't do it, Eve. You got Brent to take care of. You're beat all the time. You *know* what to do in the sack, but you're never interested. All you ever wanna do is sleep. I'm not an old man. I wanna live life. I *need* to! We gotta go our separate ways."

"Doug, there's no place I can go," I utter my real problem aloud.

"What about Val's or Kellermans'?"

"You know neither of those will work. Not permanently. Not even temporary."

"Go back home, then. Your mom's."

"Oh, God."

"C'mon, Eve. I gotta get my life back. I'm goin' crazy. I don't want to hurt somebody."

"You want me to take Brent and go live with Etta." The thought nauseates me.

"You gotta go somewhere. You wouldn't have to live there for long. Get a job. You could get your own apartment in a month or so."

"Doug, I can't."

"My mind's made up! I'm gettin' your stuff." He goes to the dresser and starts pulling my clothes out and piling them on the bed.

"Oh, God." I roll out of bed. "Leave my stuff alone. I'll do it."

At 1:00 on Sunday afternoon, before getting Brent, we pull up in front of Etta's house. I tell Doug to go get lunch somewhere and give me a chance to talk to Etta. "Bring my stuff back in an hour."

As I raise my hand to knock on the door, I hear Etta through the screen. "Where's he going? Ain't he ever heard of a muffler?" She's in her normal pose at the table and hasn't turned to look at me.

"Can I come in?"

She just shakes her head in apparent disbelief, and doesn't respond. I open the door and walk in.

"Now what?" she asks.

"Are you here by yourself?"

"For now. Won't be long, though."

I close my eyes and take a breath. "Do you care if Brent and I crash here for a few nights?"

I'm still looking at her back as she shakes her head again.

"Look, it won't be for long. I'll start lookin' for my own place tomorrow."

"Kick ya out? For good this time? How ya gonna pay for a place? You got a job?"

"I'm gonna get one."

"Tomorrow? You gettin' both a place and a job tomorrow?"

I sigh. "I'm gonna try."

"Where's the kid?"

"At Ray and Mary's."

"You leavin' him there?"

"No, I can't do that."

"Why not? I did. Was way easier than bringin' you here."

*I'm just like her – a replica of my mother.* "No."

"Jeez. You ain't learned *nothing*."

"Etta, can we move in here for a few days?"

No response. I walk past her and start picking up. Doug returns as I'm washing dishes. I go out and start carrying things in as he sits in the truck. Etta has not budged from the table or looked at me. When I have everything moved into the house, I go back out to the truck. "Are you gonna take me to get Brent?"

"Yeah, get in."

I ring the Kellermans' doorbell. Ray opens the door to let me in. The overnight paraphernalia is gathered at the door. "I'll get Brent," he says without looking me in the eye. "You can go ahead and take the stuff out."

I lug it all out in one trip. When I return, Ray is outside holding Brent. The front door remains open as Ray hugs him and says, "I love you, buddy."

Brent hugs him back and says, "Love you, Papaw." Then he turns to me, arms reaching out.

I take him and utter, "Thanks for watching him." Ray goes back inside and closes the door without replying.

I hold Brent on my lap as Doug drives us back to Etta's. He stops in front of her house. I turn to look at him and open my mouth. Doug stares straight ahead. I give up, get out, and carry my son into my mother's filthy home.

Five days later, Friday, I'm at the kitchen table holding Brent and talking to Etta. Life is unbearable. Etta is cleaned up and morphed into her man-ensnaring form.

"I'm gonna bring him back here tonight," she says. "Can you be somewhere else?"

"Where, Etta?"

"I don't care. Anywhere."

"There's no place."

"You gotta keep him quiet, then." She scowls at us. "And make sure you stay in your room in the morning, and don't make a peep till he's gone. Don't screw this up for me."

"I'll do the best I can." *How much longer can I deal with this world?*

"If you mess this up, you're gonna have to get out. I can't keep you floatin' forever."

"Don't worry about it, Etta. Go get your guy. We'll keep quiet."

"You better," she says as she gets up to leave.

As soon as she's gone, I call Doug. "Doug, I'll do anything you want, anytime you want. I'll be better. All you have to do is ask, and I'll do it. I'll go out whenever you want. I won't make you mad at me anymore. Just come get me. Tonight. Please!"

"All right."

The test begins immediately. Friday night, I need no prodding. We pick up carry-out pizza on the way back to Doug's and augment our supper liberally with beer. I have Brent down by 8:00 and come downstairs wearing my skimpiest robe. During the next hour and a half I wear Doug out, making use of every inch of the downstairs. We go to bed at 10:00, exhausted.

At midnight Brent wakes up, and I take him downstairs. An hour later, I lay him down asleep in his crib, strip, slip back under the covers with Doug, and rouse him. Saturday morning I serve him breakfast in bed and leave Brent downstairs in a makeshift pen while I offer up a quickie for good measure.

Saturday afternoon Doug asks, "You wanna go to the Triangle?"

I flash him a smile. "Sure, baby."

I wear my shortest skirt and a low-cut, loose top. I snuggle against him on the drive to Greenville. We order drinks at the bar. I keep one hand on him at all times and keep my thigh against his. After three drinks, we slow dance. I press into him as we make out more than we dance. After an hour and a half-dozen drinks apiece, he says, "You wanna cut outta here?"

"I thought you'd never ask."

He opens the pickup passenger door and lifts me in. Before he can close the door, I slide back across the seat and lie back. He hustles in over me and reaches back to close the door.

When we get home, I take his hand and lead him around behind the house. I lean against the wall, take hold of his hands, and give him my best "take me now" look. Twenty minutes later, entwined in bed, he murmurs, "You're back. Better than ever."

My mind heaves a sigh of relief. *I can make this work. Just keep going.*

I see myself on a Saturday morning in mid-May. I've stretched myself too far, trying to be an attentive mother and satisfy Doug's every whim. We took Brent along last night and went out to eat at a bar, drank too much, and stayed too long. By the time we came home, Brent had cried himself to sleep on the booth bench. At home, between Doug and Brent, I was up most of the night. At 7:00, I take Brent downstairs, stumble through feeding him some breakfast, and set him in his bouncer in front of the TV. I go back upstairs and crawl back in bed with Doug, who's still sleeping off the night.

An hour later, maddeningly I'm awakened by Doug pressing against me. I hear Brent fussing downstairs. I groan and try to muster fortitude. I tune Brent out, force myself to roll over, and put my arms around Doug. Ten minutes later, Doug is spent and rolls over. Brent is screaming. I want nothing more than to grab the closest thing to me – the lamp – hurl it across the room, and smash it to pieces. Instead, I sit on the edge of the bed and with all my might kick my house-slipper into the wall. I drag on my robe, stagger to the bathroom, and sit for five minutes as Brent goes ballistic.

Finally, Doug bellows from bed, "You gonna *get* him?"

I rise and walk out of the bathroom. "Yeah."

Brent has managed to move the bouncer over against the couch, and he has a foot caught under it. I free his foot and hold him until he calms down. Then still holding him, I get a beer out of the refrigerator, sit at the table, and pull out a cigarette. I spend the rest of the day in this mode.

I see myself on a rainy Thursday afternoon in late June in Doug's apartment. I'm on the couch in my robe, with *Truth or Consequences* turned loud to drown out Brent's crying. There's an empty bottle of cheap white wine and a glass on the coffee table. A second bottle is half-empty. I drink from it.

This morning, Doug's crew got rained out before 9:00 and then spent four hours at a bar. He walks in, greeted by a blaring TV, a shrieking kid, and slovenly live-in tramp tipping a half-empty wine bottle to her lips, staring at him through the bottle.

"Eve!" he yells. "Give me that bottle, shut the damn TV off, and *do* somethin' with your kid!"

I snap. I wing the bottle at him, its remaining contents spurting as it pinwheels end over end and crashes through the kitchen window. As soon as it leaves my hand, I charge him, arms flailing, shouting obscenities. He pushes me hard as my first blow lands on his chest. I crash to the floor, gashing my forehead on the counter on my way down. Blood flows from the deep cut and I lie still, stunned.

The man who lives in the other half of the duplex, having been on edge all day from the noise emanating from our apartment, hears the shouting and glass breaking and runs to our front door. He sees me bleeding on the floor and Doug about to lay into me again. He turns, runs back into his apartment, and calls the police.

Two hours and 12 stitches later, Ray Kellerman helps me into his car in the hospital parking lot. He arrived at the hospital an hour earlier, but he waits until we're in his car to speak to me.

"Listen to me, Eve. Look at yourself. You're a *mess*. It's 5:30 in the afternoon. You've been drunk all day. You're still in your bathrobe, haven't even brushed your hair. You're at the hospital 'cause your boyfriend beat you. Your life is completely out of control. You aren't *close* to being capable of raising a child.

"Don't get me wrong. Mary and I do care about you. We did our best to help you turn your life around, but you just chucked it all away. Nothing would please us more than to see you take hold of your life and make something of it. To *not* turn out to be like your mother. But, you've had Brent for two years, and you've shown *nothing* to give us any hope.

"With this stunt today, there's *no way* Mary and I are going to let you continue to destroy our grandson. He's at our house right now. We're taking him. Here's the way it's gonna be. If you're foolish enough to fight us, Eric will file for custody. We had the papers drawn up a month ago, just in case. If you try to fight us, we're going all the way. We'll have you declared as unfit and have Brent permanently taken away from you. Our attorney tells us if we had to, we could even have you committed. If you want to do the smart thing, go along, and let your son be raised in a prominent, caring, God-fearing home. Then we'll let you visit him once a week, *if* you're cleaned up and sober. Do you understand?"

I nod miserably. I can't speak over the lump in my throat. My head is splitting. I'm woozy from the wine. I can't grasp that I'm losing my child, that he's being taken from me because I'm unable to care for him. The thought that consumes my mind is that Ray is right: *I'm exactly like Etta.* I thank God that my grandparents are not alive to see me now.

"All right," Ray says. "I'm taking you back to Doug's. You'll have to find a way to work out your problems, or go to jail, or kill each other. But, you're going to have to deal with your life on your own. Mary and I tried hard, but we can't help you. When you want to see Brent, you call me the day before, and we'll set a time. You come to our house. Alone. I'll be there, and if you're presentable and sober, you can visit him for an hour.  I'll be in the room with you.  Do you have any questions?"

I look at my feet and shake my head, moving it as little as possible. My world has imploded.

## Chapter 11

I see a whir of scenes from the year and a half since that night in June of 1972, when Brent's grandparents took him from me. The first is later that night. Two hours after Ray drops me off, Doug gets home from the police station. We're both shaken from the acts we committed and the consequences that have already slammed into us. We stay up all night and talk about our situation and where we need to go from here. We decide that we're better together than apart and that not having Brent, though tragic for me, will make it easier for us to fix ourselves.

In scenes from the next year, we make progress. I stop drinking during the day, and when we go out we both limit alcohol. I get a part-time job within walking distance at Clara's Pizza Parlor. I try hard to please Doug, and he's less demanding. Our relationship becomes more stable, but passion doesn't rekindle. Without Brent, the biggest chunk of my soul is gone.

I see myself on a Monday evening in January. During the seven months since losing Brent I've been to the Kellermans' every Monday night to see him. Each visit is agony.

Tonight, as on most cold or rainy nights, Doug drives me across town and drops me off two blocks from their home. I walk from there. I ring the doorbell. Ray opens the door.

"Come in, Eve." Neither Mary nor Brent is anywhere to be seen. "Sit on the couch. I'll get Brent." He goes upstairs and returns, carrying my three-year-old son.

Brent's face beams. "Hi, Mommy!"

My eyes moisten as I smile back at him and reach out. "Hi, honey. How's my big boy?"

"Good!" Ray hands him off.

I sit on the couch and hold him on my lap as Ray sits in the nearby chair, his face behind his newspaper.

"What would you like to do tonight?"

"Can you play with me?"

"Sure, what would you like to play?"

He scrambles down off my lap. "C'mon, Mommy, help me get my toys out. We can dump it all out and play with everything!" He takes my hand and pulls me across the room to his toy box. "Dump it!"

In an instant, forty-five minutes is gone. I hear Ray rustle his paper, and I glance to see him look at the clock. My heart plummets. I manage to speak. "Honey, would you like me to read to you before I have to go?"

"Oh, yeah! Let's get some books." He drags me to his bookshelf and dawdles over his choices, finally selecting five books.

He sits on my lap, and I clasp my left arm around him as I read the words through blurry vision and speak them over the grapefruit in my throat.

Precisely one hour after I rang the doorbell, Ray rises from his chair.

"Sweetheart, Mommy has to go now. I'll come back next Monday night. You be a good boy for Grandpa and Grandma, okay?"

"No, you stay and play with me some more."

"I can't, Brent. I have to go. Besides, it's your bedtime."

I hear Mary from upstairs. "Come up now, Brent. It's bath time, and the tub is ready."

"Aw, I have to go upstairs now. I love you, Mommy."

I squeeze him too tightly. "I love you, too, Brent. You have no idea how much."

He wriggles free and slides down off my lap. "I have to go now. See ya next Monday!"

He skips to the stairs and runs up. I look at Ray, tears streaming down my cheeks. He turns away. "Please, Ray, *please*. Think about a little more time. Talk to Mary."

"Ray," Mary calls down, "are you coming up to help?"

"Be right up." He turns to me, expressionless. "Call Sunday if you're coming next Monday."

"I come *every* Monday. I'll be here!"

"Ray!"

"I'm coming, Mary."

"I'll call," I murmur.

I turn and let myself out. My chest is so constricted I can barely breathe as I struggle back to the rendezvous point. I arrive and climb into the pickup. Doug sees my face. "You okay?"

I can't answer. It's the same wretched torture week after week after week. *How much more of this do I have to take? How much more* can *I take?*

I feel like half a person. I want to make life good, but the gash in my soul gets deeper every Monday. I become less and less able to be of value to anyone, including myself.

In September, Doug's inevitable restlessness surfaces. He drinks more. He goes out on some Friday nights without me. In late November, on two Friday nights in a row, he doesn't come home until Saturday afternoon. *I can't even hold my man.* My frustrations overwhelm me.

I see myself at 11:30 on a Saturday night in December sitting at the kitchen table, wearing a nightshirt, stewing. Today, after getting home at noon, Doug slept on the couch until 7:00 and then left. I hear his truck pull up to the curb. He swaggers in. I glare at him. The front of his shirt is soaked and smells like beer.

"So, you decided to come home tonight?"

"I'm just changin' my shirt. I'm headin' back out."

I look out the kitchen window at the truck under the street light as he goes up to the bedroom. I see a full head of blonde hair on the passenger side and whirl to follow him. "Hey! You got somebody waitin' out in the truck? Who is she?"

"Later, Eve," he says, pulling his shirt off. "I ain't got time for this now."

"*Bullshit* you don't! We been workin' hard at making a go of this. What're you *doing*?"

"C'mon. We been tryin' and tryin' but you gotta know it ain't working. Our life's almost as fun as drinkin' castor oil."

"You're drunk. You *know* that's the problem. That's what crashed us last time. You gotta stay sober!"

"Me? *My* drinking crashed us? *You* stay sober. I'm gonna have some fun."

He starts to put on a clean shirt. I rip it out of his hands and throw it across the room.

"Hey! Go pick that up, and give it back! I can't let the truck set out on the street all night."

"I couldn't care less if she sits out there all night. I hope she *freezes* to death!"

He starts to cross the room to get his shirt off the floor. I block his path. He shoves me down on the bed, strides past me, and picks up the shirt. I jump up, jerk it out of his hands, and throw it to the other side of the room.

"That's it, Eve!" He slams me down on the bed and has my underwear off almost before I hit the mattress. I start to bounce back up, and he pushes me down again and unfastens his pants. He's on me before I can move. In less than three minutes he's done with me and rushing out the bedroom door, pulling the shirt over his head.

After he's gone, I get up, go to the refrigerator, and pull out a beer. Then another. Then another. Then another.

I see scenes from the next five months and watch myself sink. The Sunday after Doug forced himself on me, I'm scheduled to work. I'm drunk and don't go. Monday, still drunk, I don't go to work or to see Brent.

I begin to miss more Monday evenings with Brent than I make. Doug doesn't get violent with me, but the remaining fibers of the relationship unravel. He spends every Friday and Saturday night at a bar or party. Sometimes he goes alone, and sometimes he takes me. When I go, by the end of the night I wish I hadn't.

At a bar on a Saturday night in March, when I weave back from the restroom, he pulls me aside. "Hey, Eve, you have to stay someplace else tonight. I'm bringin' somebody home."

"What?"

"Don't make a scene. I called you a cab. It just pulled up. Just go somewhere. Val's or Etta's, it don't matter."

I try to protest as he turns me around and guides me out the door, but I'm too drunk to make sense of anything. I get in the cab and give the driver the Kellerman address.

The cab arrives at 11:00. There are no lights on inside. I tell the driver to wait while I lurch and sway to the door and ring the bell. After a minute, a light turns on, and Ray opens the door. He sees me and is furious. Slurring and stammering, I try to explain that I just need a place to sleep for the night.

He steps outside. "Not only can you not set foot in our house tonight, but if you show up in this shape one more time, you'll *never* see Brent again!"

I stagger back to the cab crying and give the driver Etta's address. She's not home yet, but her door is never locked. I feel my way into my old bedroom, shove the pile of junk on the bed off onto the floor, crawl on top of the blanket, and pass out.

The next morning, Etta and her current man, Woody, are sitting at the table half-clothed at 10:00 when I open my bedroom door and shuffle out, startling them. I see them through slit eyelids.

Etta blurts, "Eve! You scared the shit outta us. How long you been in there? We got stuff goin' on today. Hope you're not plannin' on hangin' around."

Woody has lived at Etta's for a year. We've seen each other before. Etta and I are both well aware of what he'd like to do with me. This morning, having slept in my clothes – shoes and all – I look like I've lived on the street for a week. Regardless, my half-open eyes perceive Etta glaring at Woody as he leers at me. Then her eyes fire daggers at me. I say nothing but continue on past them to the bathroom. I then retrace the path to my bed and for three hours am aware of nothing more.

By the time I get up, Etta and Woody are gone. I drink a glass of water and leave. Then I walk across town to Doug's place and find his truck parked illegally on the street. *So, she's still here.* I sit on the front stoop for an hour. They come out and step past me. No one speaks. They walk to the truck with their arms around each other and their hands slipped into the other's hip pocket, climb in, and drive off.

I go inside and search. They've drunk all the beer and wine. All I can find is a half-bottle of Jack Daniels and one can of Coke. I stretch the Coke thin so it will last out the Jack.

For the next three weeks, I'm never completely sober. My paychecks keep our refrigerator stocked with alcohol. Some nights, Doug and I joke and frolic. Some nights, we yell and fight. I never know which it's going to be or whether it's he who sets the tone or me. It doesn't matter. Half of the Friday and Saturday nights he spends elsewhere. As long as I don't witness the development of the tryst, that doesn't matter to me, either.

I'm scheduled to report to work at 4:00 on a Wednesday in late April. I was scheduled to work the day before but called in sick five minutes after I was supposed to be there. Walking to work today, I've had to stop to lean against trees twice. The second time, I lean over and gag but am able to hold back the vomit. I stagger in the door at Clara's, ghost-white and wind-blown, ten minutes late.

Ken, a high-school senior, is working the cash register when I enter. "Doreen wants to see you."

"Great. What's she want?" The last thing I need is for the heavyset, middle-aged weeknight manager to see me before I can get myself set into work mode.

Ken gives me a blank stare and shrugs.

"I need to use restroom. Then I'll see what she wants."

"Is that Eve?" Doreen blasts from somewhere in the kitchen. "Hey, Eve, I need to talk to you. Come back to my office."

I roll my eyes at Ken and mutter, "Shit."

I walk toward the restrooms and glance down the hall to the left to see Doreen already standing in the doorway to her office. "This'll only take a minute." Instead of wheeling to my right into the ladies' room, I sidle to the left and into her office. She doesn't bother to ask me to sit or to close the door.

"You know what I need to tell you?"

I look blankly at her and shake my head.

"Oh, c'mon, Eve. How many times do you think we can scramble at the last minute to find somebody to work for you? Yesterday was the last time. I already got Janey to cover your shift tonight."

"You want me to go home? I'll be here tomorrow. On time. I promise."

"Forget it, Eve. You're done. I have to fire you. You don't give me any choice."

"But...."

Doreen holds up her left hand to shush me and extends her right toward me with an envelope. "It's too late. Here's your check. Go on. You look awful. Take my advice, and use your last check to get yourself some help."

I turn and saunter out of the restaurant. On the way home, I stop at the cut-rate liquor store that's on my way, cash my check, and buy four bottles of wine.

I see myself at the Triangle on a warm Friday night in May – last night. I'm sitting at the bar beside Doug. Tonight, we're on friendly terms. People are dancing, and there's a TV with a Cincinnati Reds game. We're watching the dancers and the game, making snide comments about both. I'm in mid-sentence yammering about a particularly geeky guy dancing when Doug shouts, "Hey, Tricia! C'mere."

I see a petite, bouncy blonde across the dance floor waving wildly and skipping toward us.

"Doug!"

He jumps up and puts his arms around her. She clings as if she'll swoon if she lets go. I scowl.

"Man, I haven't seen you in ages." He doesn't bother to introduce us. "This seat's open," he points to the barstool on the other side of him. "I been holdin' it, just in case you showed up!"

He doesn't say another word to me for over an hour. I watch the ball game and drink. I glance at them occasionally and see them whispering and grinning at each other as they sit, unable to keep their hands to themselves. By 11:00, I'm pissed and ready to get out of the place. I turn to Doug to make my point, and he's kissing her! It goes on forever.

My instinct is to hit him on the head with my beer bottle. Instead, I get up and go pee. I consider telling him that's where I'm going but give up. When I get back, all three barstools are occupied by people I don't know. I look around and see Doug standing by the door. I can't believe it; he's actually going to take me home. When I reach him, he opens the door and walks out. I follow him.

He pulls his keys out of his pocket and says, "Drive my truck home."

"What? I can't drive like this."

"Drive my truck home!  I'm not comin' home tonight. Here's the thing: next weekend, Tricia's movin' in. You gotta move out this week.  It's been comin' to this forever, and we both know it.  You can stay till Thursday night, if you have to." He drops his keys in my hand and goes back into the building.

*Yet again.*

I try to remember how to take back roads to get from the Triangle to Richmond.

Chapter 12

I've seen my entire life – in sequence, yet all at once, in an
instant. Everyone – everything – God – experiences my life with
me. There is no criticism other than my own. As I judge my
life, I'm bathed in infinite love.

I could have done better. I wish I'd done better. I wish I'd
hurt no one and had given love one thousand fold beyond what I
did. That is my judgment. I regret that I didn't inundate my life
companions with love, but my life was what it was.

Now, everything is ecstasy. The pain and hardship of my
old life are no more. I'm home.

Even though I can't possibly feel any better, my bliss
continues to magnify. Now, the best yet: Gran and Grandpa are
with me! I feel them! We talk without words, and we rejoice in
each other. We catch up on all the missed years in an instant.

I feel Gran say, "Eve, the most crucial thought of your life
was the inspiration that made you abort your suicide attempt."

As this thought penetrates my being, I feel my first negative
emotion since I died. Apprehension. I know the fleeting thought
she wants me to consider, and I'm afraid.

*Don't abandon Brent!*

"It's too late, Gran. I'm dead. I'm *dead*. Please, please,
please, please, *please*, God. *Please*, let me stay here! *Don't
make me go back!*"

"He needs you, Eve. You love him, as Grandpa and I have
always loved you."

"No, Gran! Please, *no*! I *can't* leave you – can't leave this
place!"

"You'll be back, Eve, but Brent needs his mother. And you need your son."

I command the response welling up in my soul to stay trapped within. I'm unable to quash it.

"Yes."


The bliss is gone. Excruciating pain! Everywhere! Stop it!

I hear a voice. "Clear!" Dr. Kenner.

Fire sears my chest, blazes to my core, and spikes to every molecule in my body.

Another voice: Steph. "She's back!"

Everything extinguishes.

## Chapter 13

It requires too much effort to open her eyes, but she hears jumbled sounds. Beeping. Whirring. Murmuring. The sounds intertwine in a collage. She can't move, doesn't want to… not even a finger. Reasoning is impossible.

As Eve's consciousness congeals, she becomes more confused. She doesn't know where she is or who she is. The sounds begin to dissociate into constituents. The murmuring turns into hushed conversation. The voices feel familiar.

"You really think she could've been *tryin'* to drive over it?"

"I dunno, Val. I treated her pretty bad. Man, I was plastered. Saw Trish Weathersby and got carried away."

"What'd you do?"

"I told Eve she had to move out. This week. Told her Tricia was movin' in."

"You gotta be kiddin' me! She's got another year of high school. I know her dad. He'll put you in jail."

"I told you, I was plastered. So was Trish. She said she'd had it at home and was movin' out anyway and needed a place to live."

"You're not goin' through with it."

"C'mon, give me a break. I'm not stupid. I mean, I'm only really stupid when I'm drunk."

"When are you gonna learn, Doug? Some people can handle liquor, and some can't. You gotta start realizing your limits."

"Man, I can't help it. Sometimes Eve drives me crazy. I don't know, too moody or serious or depressed or somethin' when she's sober. She used to be fun and happy. Terrific in the sack... almost as good as you. But, since they took Brent, it's like everything that was exciting in her got sucked out. And there's nothin' I can do. It's like I want two things. I want her back the way she was at first, the girl I loved. At the same time, I just want out of the whole mess, the way she is now. But, she ain't got no place to go. I mean *no* place. Every time I get pushed over the limit and tell her it's over, I end up feelin' like a jackass. Now this."

"It's partly my fault," Val says. "I got you two together. I never should've done it. I felt bad for you both. I was stupid, too, treating you like I did and going back to Jerk Jack. Like *that* was ever gonna work out. I should've stuck with you the whole time. None of this would've happened. And I understand your demons. I could've made things better for you."

Doug's low voice turns to a whisper. "You think she can hear us?"

After a moment, Val whispers back, "Surely not. She hasn't made a peep since we got here. Look at her. Poor thing. They got her doped up somethin' awful. She's out of it." Another silence. "We're not doin' her any good here. Let's go someplace we can talk."

As Doug and Val walk out of the intensive care room, another dose of Demerol pumps into Eve's veins, and the wafts of conversation she's heard disappear from her memory.

A man's voice says, "Has she been cognizant?"

A woman replies, "She comes and goes. Hasn't said anything yet, that I know of. But she's still heavily sedated. Probably a good thing. Those broken ribs are gonna hurt."

"She's lucky to be alive. We lost her for almost three minutes. She came back on the third shock. If she hadn't, that would've been it."

Eve feels a jostle. Something touches her wrist. Fingers?

"She might be waking up," the woman says.

"I hope so. I'd like to talk to her a minute." There's something familiar in the man's voice. "Eve. Eve, can you hear me? Are you awake?"

She doesn't want to move, doesn't want to open her eyes. Maybe just a slit. She sees a vague mix of dark and light. A shadow moves.

"How are you feeling, Eve?"

The voice... it is the last one she can recall, right before being... set on fire? "Clear." A doctor, she thinks.

"Wake up, Eve. You need to wake up for a little while."

"Doc... Kenn... er?" she breathes.

"What was that?" The doctor turns to the nurse. "Did she just call me Dr. Kenner?"

"I couldn't make it out. Does she know you?"

"I don't think so. I don't know her. Eve, can you hear me? Can you talk?"

"Hurts," she whispers.

"You'll get better. You're a fighter. You proved that in the trauma room. We were losing you, but you fought your way back. Do you know what happened to you, why you're here?"

"Where?" The whisper takes all the effort she can muster.

"You're in Reid Hospital, in Richmond. You were in an accident. Do you remember what happened?"

"Time?"

"It's 10:00. Night time."

"Sat... day?"

"No, it's Monday. You've been asleep for a while. We've got you on a lot of medication. For the pain. It makes you groggy."

Eve doesn't want to talk anymore. She hurts and is exhausted and confused. She closes her eyes.

"Hang in there, Eve. I'll stop back and check on you tomorrow."

She hears something, someone entering the room, talking.

"You might be lucky. I think she's waking up. Eve, are you awake? You have a visitor." The nurse glances at the woman following her. "She's awake – her eyelids are moving. She's hurting, and she'll be woozy, but you can have a few minutes with her. Eve, honey, your mother is here. I'll leave you alone for a little bit. I can give you five minutes." The nurse leaves the room.

"Eve, what in the world was you doing? Drivin' drunk as a skunk. Were you *tryin'* to go over the cliff? You almost did. Totaled Doug's truck. Came damn close to killin' yourself. Instead, you're all busted up in the hospital."

Eve doesn't want to hear anymore.  She closes her eyes.

"Hey!  Eve.  Don't go to sleep on me.  We gotta talk.  You awake?  Stay awake.  You could've at least waited till you was twenty-one.  Two more months.  They think I'm gonna *pay* for this.  There ain't no way.  Doug's got insurance, right?  You gotta get his insurance to pay.  My lawyer can get you fixed up with a marriage license.  Woody and me can be witnesses.  We'll sign it.  Say we was there.  A month ago or something.  Listen to me, Eve.  Wake up!  You gotta fix this!"

The nurse taps on the wall and walks back in.  "I think she's gone back to sleep.  She needs rest.  You can sit here with her if you'd like, but she'll need quiet."

"I'll come back later."


Eve opens her eyes.  She sees needles of bright light between closed slats of window blinds.  She's more clear-headed, can put more than two thoughts together.  Tubes and wires droop from all sorts of paraphernalia and snake their way onto and into her body.  Her chest still hurts, but it's easing up or she's getting used to it.  She can turn her head to either side without jump-starting waves of pain.

She sees movement out of the corner of her eye and angles her head to see a nurse walk into the room.  "Hey, you're looking perky!"

Eve starts to talk, gives up, clears her throat, and tries again.  This time she gets some raspy, faltering sounds, "What day... is it?"

"It's Wednesday.  You're in intensive care in Reid Hospital.  You've been here since Saturday.  You had a bad accident Friday night.  Gave us all a scare, but you're going to be all right."  The nurse busies herself for a few minutes while Eve exercises her memory.

"Water?"

"I'll get you a couple of ice chips."

Eve lets three small chips melt in her mouth, swallows, and tries her voice again.  She sounds better, and it's easier.  "Was I... gone... for a while?"

"They almost lost you in emergency.  You stopped breathing, and your heart stopped for a couple minutes."

"Seems longer."

"What?"

"Had to be longer."

"What makes you say that?"

"Saw them. Working on me. Up in the corner. Saw my life. Had to be hours."

The nurse smiles at her. "Those drugs will do funny things to you. I'm glad you're feeling better. Another day or so, and we'll get you out of ICU. Get some of these contraptions disconnected. You'll like that. Get some rest. I'll be back soon."


Thursday morning, Dr. Kenner walks into Eve's room. "Hello, Eve. I'm Dr. Kenner. How are you feeling today?"

"I hurt everywhere, but I can take it if I don't move. I can talk better."

"Good. You're making progress. Has anyone explained your injuries to you?"

"I don't think so."

"Well, you're pretty badly beaten up, but you'll heal. You have five broken ribs. That's causing most of your pain. Three of them had to be set. When they broke, your spleen, diaphragm, and one lung were punctured. We removed the spleen and fixed everything else. You have lots of lacerations and bruises, but the swelling is going down everywhere. You lost a lot of blood. When you arrived in the emergency room, we couldn't get blood pumped into you fast enough. Your heart stopped beating for a couple of minutes. You came within a hair's breadth of leaving us. But, you're going to be all right. Let's have a look at you."

He gently presses here and there and inspects cuts and incisions for a few minutes.

"Can you tell me what happened, Eve?"

"I think I wrecked my boyfriend's truck."

"Do you remember the accident?"

"It's pretty fuzzy."

"Were you by yourself?"

"Yeah."

"Do you know when it happened?"

"Friday night."

"Early Saturday morning, actually. Why were you driving alone so late on those back roads?"

"We had a fight, I guess. Doug told me to drive home."

"By yourself? Were you drunk?"

"Yeah."

"Do you know where you had the accident?"

"Stone quarry. Middleboro. Did I go over?"

"No. Do you remember how you lost control?"

"Not really."

Dr. Kenner touches her forehead lightly and deliberates for a few seconds. "Okay. That's probably enough for now. Do you have any questions?"

She looks at him and wavers. "My heart stopped for two minutes?"

"Yes."

"Could it have been longer?"

"What?"

"Like an hour or more?"

"We tracked the time. It was exactly two minutes and thirty seconds."

"I was awake."

"What?"

"When my heart was stopped. I saw you and the others working on me."

"I don't think so, Eve. Your eyes were closed."

"Not all the time. I saw you. I saw the nurse working on me before you came in. I saw Steph. And Ted, the paramedic. I heard what everyone said."

"You might have been conscious when you arrived and seen and heard them. But, when I came into the room, you'd just flatlined. Your eyes were closed."

"I saw you take over chest compressions. I saw Steph hand you the paddles. I saw you shock me."

Dr. Kenner studies her expression, her eyes. "Sometimes, Eve, patients who are quickly approaching dying are semi-conscious and see or hear some of what is going on around them. I expect that would be very frightening. If you were semi-conscious, we had no idea. Even if we had, there was nothing we could've done about it. We were losing you too fast to anesthetize you. Were you scared?"

"No. It was strange. I was above you, looking down on everything. At first, I didn't know what I was seeing. Thought I was watching you work on someone else. Have you ever lost anyone else and then had them come back while you were working on them?"

He takes her hand. "Eve, the human mind does funny things when the body is dying. We don't exactly understand the whole process, and I'm sure it's different for different people. In your case, you were obviously hallucinating."

"I hallucinated Steph and Ted?"

"You were conscious, or at least awake enough to have heard some of the conversation before I came into the room, maybe even saw their faces. So you knew their names. But you hallucinated when your heart wasn't beating."

They look at each other, he scrutinizing her, she weighing whether or not to tell him more of what she experienced during those two minutes and thirty seconds.

"You need lots of rest. Try to sleep. I'll check in on you tomorrow." He walks out.

## Chapter 14

Friday morning, Eve cracks her eyelids to find the room sunlit, the blinds fully open – a first.  She looks out at a cloudless blue sky and feels eyes on her.  She turns her head and sees a tall, solidly built, middle-aged, bespectacled man in a lab coat studying her.  Neither speaks for a moment.

"Hello, Eve.  I'm Dr. Burgmann.  I'm the chief of the Psychiatric Department here at Reid.  How are you feeling this morning?"

"Okay."

"Are you up to talking?"

"I guess so."

"Is the staff treating you well?"

"Yes."

"Has your doctor explained your injuries and condition to you?"

"Dr. Kenner told me about my ribs and spleen yesterday."

"That's good.  Did he tell you how close they came to losing you the night of your accident?"

"Yes."

"It was very close.  I'm glad you pulled through.  Have you had visitors here in ICU?"

"I think so.  I've been out of it most of the time, but someone might have been here."

"Has your mother stopped in to see you?"

"I think she did, but I'm not sure."

"Anyone else?"

"I don't know.  Maybe."

"Where do you live, Eve?"

The question confuses her. The truthful answer is probably the same as for the last question: *I don't know*. But she can't say that. Not to a psychiatrist. *Why is he here, anyway?* "With my boyfriend."

"What's his name?"

"Doug. Doug Pratt."

"Has he been in to see you?"

"I'm not sure. I've been out of it almost all the time. Because of all the medication. I think so."

"Were you with Doug last Friday night, before the accident?"

She hesitates. "Yes."

"Were you at home?"

"No."

"Where were you?"

"At a dance."

"Here in Richmond?"

"No, in Greenville."

"Ah, the Triangle."

"Yeah."

"Lots of young folks from here go there."

She doesn't respond.

"Were you drinking?"

"That's what everybody does there."

"Do you recall how much you'd had to drink?"

"No."

"Too much to be driving?"

"I probably shouldn't have drove. I guess that's why I crashed."

"Where was Doug when you crashed? Why wasn't he with you?"

She takes a breath, which makes her cough. It hurts. She winces and tries to decide what to say. "I don't know."

"You don't know where he was or why he wasn't with you?"

"I'm really tired. I think I need to sleep."

"I'm sorry, Eve, but we're going to have to have this conversation. The sooner we have it, the less difficult it will be. You just woke up from a good sleep, and your medication levels are not high. We need to continue."

"Why does it matter about Doug? I had an accident. I'm going to be messed up for a few weeks. I was drunk, and I'll probably lose my license, maybe spend a weekend in jail. But nobody else got hurt. Except maybe Doug's truck, and his insurance'll take care of that. Why do you want to talk to me?"

"I have to be sure there wasn't more going on here."

"Like what?"

"Where did you have this accident, Eve?"

"Middleboro. At the stone quarry. Why? You already know that, anyway."

"Do you know anyone else who ever had an accident there?"

Her eyes widen, and her jaw drops. "Leave me alone! Can't you see I've got enough problems?"

"Look, Eve. I'm trying to help you. We're going to help you. That's what we're here for. Tell me a little bit about your life. Let's start with Doug. How did the two of you get together?"

"How 'bout *you* tell *me* about my life. Somethin' tells me you already know it all."

Two minutes of silence pass while Burgmann looks at Eve and Eve looks at the ceiling.

"All right, Eve. Let's try just dealing with the hard question. Was your accident intentional? Were you trying to drive over the cliff?"

"Why would you think that? I didn't go over. It would've been easy enough to do, wouldn't it?"

"Eve, you were in the car with your grandparents on your sixth birthday when they were killed at that very same spot. From that day on, your life has been one disaster after another. Some your doing and some not. On the night of the accident, you felt you had nowhere to go, nowhere to live. You've lost your son. You feel no one in the world cares about you. Yes, I think it's very possible that you decided to drive over that cliff. And maybe it's possible you changed your mind at the last second."

"Who all have you talked to?"

"I can't help you unless I know as much as possible about you."

"Who?"

"Doug. Valerie DeBolt. The police. Dr. Kenner. The Kellermans. I saw your mother, but it would be a stretch to say we talked."

"Why are you doing this?"

"Psychiatrists serve a purpose. Our job is to help troubled people overcome their difficulties and live healthy, productive lives."

"Give me a break."

"All right. Let's have a different conversation. Dr. Kenner told me you were semi-conscious in the trauma room. What was that like?"

Eve looked at the ceiling for a long time before whispering, "Nothing I could have ever imagined."

"Tell me about it."

"I can't." Tears emerge from the corners of her eyes.

"Was the pain excruciating?"

"There was no pain. I felt good... way better than good."

"Dr. Kenner said you explained it to him as if you weren't looking up from your body but were up above it all, looking down."

"Yes," she whispers.

"Did you see the heart monitor go flat?"

"Yes."

"What happened then?"

Eve can't hold it in. She stares at the ceiling and relates the entire experience. When she's done, tears are flowing.

Dr. Burgmann sits silently after she finishes her story. Finally, he speaks. "So, in the end, it wasn't the efforts of Dr. Kenner that brought you back? It was you agreeing that you would not abandon your son? You brought yourself back?"

Eve nods.

"Do you want to go back there, back to that feeling of bliss?"

"More than I've ever wanted anything in my life."

"What about Brent?"

"I came back for him. I need to be his mother."

"Do you have a plan on how you're going to go about that?"

"Not yet."

Dr. Burgmann is quiet, reflecting, and then he says, "Do you think you would have brought yourself back if Dr. Kenner had given up and not shocked you that third time? Or if you had gotten to the hospital several minutes later, after you had already flatlined?"

Eve tries to process the question, the implications. "You're trying to confuse me."

"I'm not. I'm trying to help you think through what happened, to sort out what makes sense from what doesn't. You said knowledge flooded into you, that you knew everything. How the universe works, all the secrets. Do you still know these things? Can you explain some of it to me?"

"That part's gone. I know I knew. But now I don't. I know it all comes down to love. We're all supposed to love each other. Way, way more than we do. Not like between a man and woman − well, that, too − it's no different. We're supposed to love everybody and help each other and be happy for each other."

"But, you can't tell me anything of how the plan works?"

"It doesn't matter. It all just comes down to love."

"Eve, this has been a traumatic experience for you. We don't fully understand how the human mind reacts when the body shuts down, but the mind can take over and wipe out the pain and make the dying process easier. It's nature's way of helping us let go of life and ease out of this world. The story you've told me seems very real to you, but it didn't really happen that way. You didn't really float to the corner of the room and watch yourself die, or talk to your grandmother, or agree to come back to this world. You were dying, and Dr. Kenner shocked you back to life as they pumped blood into your body."

"No! That's wrong. My mind's fuzzy on everything since I felt that shock when I came back to life and on everything that happened before I got to the hospital, but in those two and a half minutes I was dead, I remember everything. It isn't just clear. Every instant of that time, from when I was watching in the corner 'til I got hit with that last shock, is more shining bright than any memory in my life. It's like now all my other memories are dull or colorless or something. You can't say it was all a trick in my head. It's the most real thing that ever happened to me!"

"All right, Eve. If it's all that crystal-clear, tell me more about all that knowledge thrust into you. Just a little bit of it. How do all the pieces fit together in the perfect plan?"

"Stop it!" Eve cries harder. Her convulsions shoot pain through her chest. "You can't say it didn't happen!"

"Okay. Let's approach it like this. Let's both think it over for a day, and we'll talk about it again tomorrow. In the meantime, you're doing well enough that you'll move out of ICU later today. They'll move you onto my floor for a few days. We'll work on sorting through everything together."

"What? I'm going to a psych ward? Why? Just put me in a regular room."

"We can't do that, Eve. You've said you want more than anything to go back to the place you were when you were dead."

"You think I'm gonna kill myself? Right here in the hospital?"

"You also said you want to save your son. And you believe the best place is not here in this world."

"You think I'm gonna take his life! Get away from me, and don't you *ever* come near me again!"

"We're going to help you, Eve."

Eve lies for two hours, trying futilely to make sense of the conversation with Dr. Burgmann and what is happening to her, trying to fit a mandate to love everybody into her situation. She hears the nurse cautioning someone coming in.

"She's had a difficult morning. You can see her for a few minutes, but be careful not to upset her."

Eve turns her head warily and sees the nurse lead Ray Kellerman into the room.

"You have a visitor, honey. Are you up to seeing him for a few minutes?"

At a slight nod of Eve's head, the nurse steps out, leaving the door open.

"How are you, Eve?" Ray asks.

"They say I'm pretty busted up, but I'll heal."

"We're glad you'll be okay. The doctor talked to us."

"Which doctor?"

"Burgmann."

"The shrink. What'd he tell you? I'm crazy?"

"No, Eve. Mainly, he asked us a lot of questions. He was trying to understand what your life was like."

"Well, I'm sure you gave him a stellar report. You know, after talking to all my so-called friends, he thinks I'm a mental case."

"Maybe you do need a little help. Life has never been kind to you. All the things that've happened to you would probably be too much for anybody."

"So, you think I wrecked Doug's truck on purpose, too."

"Look, Eve, I really don't want to make this harder for you. Nobody wants you to get healthy more than I do. For Brent. And for you."

"Mentally healthy, you mean."

"Healthy in every way."

"I need to see Brent. He's the only thing that kept me alive. He's my reason for being here."

"As soon as you get better, we'll try to work something out."

"No! He's my son. I'm his mother. We need each other, and we have a right to be together. Bring him to me!"

"I can't, Eve! You know they don't allow children in ICU or in...."

"Or in where? The nut ward? You're all tryin' to take him away from me! You can't do that! I'm his mother. You go to church all the time. Is that what your church preaches? Steal children from their mothers? If you want them, just take them? To hell with the mothers? You're all trying to ruin me!"

The nurse rushes in. "All right, that's enough. Mr. Kellerman, you have to go."

He meets Eve's eyes. "I really didn't want to upset you. I want to help."

"Get out!"

The nurse takes him by the arm and pulls him out of the room. Eve weeps hard in spite of the agony in her chest.

Half an hour later, she hears voices rising from the nurses' station. "I'm sorry ma'am, but she is not allowed visitors this afternoon. She's had a difficult day. You'll have to come back another time."

"She's my daughter for, God's sake!" Etta. "She's hurtin' and she needs to see her mom. I'm goin' in."

"If you don't leave immediately, I'll call security."

"Look there, who's comin' in now!" Eve hears Etta shriek. "It's the sonofabitch that caused it all!"

"Etta!" Eve hears Doug's booming voice. "What the hell are you doing?"

"Security to ICU! Immediately!"

"You marry her! This whole thing's your fault. Your insurance has to *pay* for this!"

"You're crazy. Get her out of here! She don't care about Eve, never did."

"Yeah – like *you* do. *You* drove her to it! It's *your* fault she tried to kill herself! Just pay the bill and leave her alone, or she'll get it done next time."

"You stupid hag, I'll shut you up once and for all!"

Eve hears doors open and footsteps pounding – a group running in. "Both of you, don't move a muscle! This is over. Come with us. Now!"

The pain in Eve's chest is excruciating. *Gran, how can I love these people? How can I save Brent? Why did you make me come back?*

## Chapter 15

The light causes Eve to stir. She tries to open her eyes, hears something shuffle, and then the light filtering through her eyelids extinguishes. *So groggy. Where am I?* She lies semi-conscious for a several minutes and then manages to crack her eyelids open. The glow of light splaying under a closed door is barely enough for Eve to make out the hands on a wall clock: 3:45. *Night time? Hospital? Whatever drugs they've been pumping in must be wearing off.* She recalls the events of last Friday: Etta and Doug's shouting match; Ray's refusal to bring Brent to her; Dr. Jerk-man, or whoever he was, trapping her. *Seems like so long ago.*

She peeks around in the darkness. The room is stark. She sees the bed she's in, a dresser, a chair, and the door. No window. She attempts to lift her right hand. It moves about three inches, but she can't make it go farther. Her anxiety level rises. She tries to raise her right leg, but it's even more restricted. She strives with what little hand mobility she has to reach for the call button. Neither hand finds a button. She tries to call for help, but all that comes out is a whisper. Panic rises in her chest.

*I want loose! Out of here!* She tries to scream. All that comes out is a soft "Aaaayyyyeee." She keeps trying, even though each effort leaves her increasingly light-headed. Each utterance makes her voice a fraction stronger.

Finally, the door opens and light floods the room. She tries to focus on the figure in the doorway, but the room has become brilliant and she closes her eyes.

A gravelly female voice grumbles, "Easy, now. Have some patience. We've been checking on you every fifteen minutes. You've just started to wake up. It'll be a few hours before your medications wears off." She scrutinizes Eve. "Easy, now. Easy."

Eve strains to hold her head as high as the restraints will allow. Her eyes begin to focus on a tall, tough-skinned, prematurely grey woman with hawkish green eyes. "I'm awake," she pants. "Take these straps off."

"You'll have to talk to the doctor about that."

"Get him."

"He'll be in around eight."

"Call him!"

"No. You'll have to wait. You've been like this for two days. You can take it for a few more hours."

"I have to go to the bathroom."

"You have a catheter. You don't have to get up."

"Take 'em off!" Adrenaline imparting more strength, Eve strains harder against the straps.

"Look, the doctor wants you alert this morning, so we lightened up your meds. But if you won't cooperate, we'll have to dose you back up, and he can evaluate you later. Now, I'm going to turn off the lights and close the door. Relax, and try to go back to sleep. We'll check on you every fifteen minutes."

"Let me loose! Take 'em off, or I'll scream!"

"You try that, and you'll get more Haldol and it'll just be that much longer before you can talk to the doctor. Now, quiet down!"

Eve tries to shoot daggers from her eyes at her antagonist. The light goes off, and the door closes. In instant pitch-blackness, Eve slams her head down on her pillow, creating shock waves in her head and chest. *Owww! Oh, oh. Man. Love everybody? What a crock!*

Eve fumes until 9:45, when the door opens and Dr. Burgmann walks in.

"How are you this morning, Eve?"

"Let me out of here. Get me the release papers. I'm signing myself out."

"It doesn't work like that, Eve. You're here on a seventy-two-hour emergency detention. You can't leave any sooner than that, unless I release you."

"So, release me."

"You have some issues we have to work through first."

"Yeah, I remember. You think I'm a danger to myself and my son. That shows how much you know about me. It's ludicrous. You're the one with issues to work through, and I'm not plannin' to wait around for you to figure it out. I want out of here!"

"Eve, a rational person who understands the rules for getting what they want will play by those rules. I can't release a person who is not rational. Here are the rules. You must be willing to consider and discuss why you tried to commit suicide. Lying to me and to yourself – continuing to insist that your accident was just that and nothing more – simply doesn't admit the facts. So, you're going to have to talk to me about this. You don't get released until you do."

"I don't have to talk to you about anything. When did you lock me up in here? Friday? This is Monday, so my seventy-two hours are up today. I'm outta here."

"I'm sorry, Eve, but weekend days don't count. And, when the seventy-two hours are up, unless I'm satisfied that you are rational and not a danger to yourself or others, the detention can and will be extended until you exhibit stable, safe behavior." He turns to leave. "I'll stop by tomorrow morning, Eve."

"Wait! I need these straps off! Did you tell the nurse to take 'em off?"

"I'll order them off as soon as you are calm and cooperative. You need to think about your accident and why it happened. Tomorrow, if you've decided you're willing to have a meaningful conversation about it, then we'll see what we can do about your restraints." He walks out of the room, closing the door.

"Doctor! Doctor! Get back here! Get back here! *Get back here!*"

After two minutes of Eve screaming this exhortation, a day-shift nurse enters the room. "Hello, Eve. I'm Robin." Robin is younger than the night nurse and offers more compassion. "I'm sorry, honey, but the doctor has instructed that we sedate you if you haven't calmed down in five minutes. Please, relax. Don't make it more unpleasant than it has to be."

"I want a lawyer." Eve glares at her.

"I'm sorry, it doesn't work like that. You aren't under arrest or in any kind of trouble. I know it doesn't seem like it, but we're here to help. Listen, your stay here will be much shorter and more agreeable if you cooperate with the doctor. Don't make us medicate you today. We don't want to. Please, try to stay calm and think clearly about how you want to react while you're with us. Your fastest way out will be to cooperate and talk with the doctor about whatever he asks you to."

Tuesday morning, Dr. Burgmann enters the room. "Good morning, Eve. We'll remove those restraints on two conditions. First, I need you to agree to have a completely honest discussion about the accident. Second, I would like for you to sign yourself into my care here for at least three weeks. Before you make your decision on these requests, keep in mind that if you don't agree to stay, I'll be forced to extend the detention indefinitely, until I'm satisfied that you can function satisfactorily on your own."

"All right. I'll talk. I'll sign myself in for one week."

"Three weeks. And if I'm not comfortable releasing you at that point, you'll have to stay longer."

"What do you want from me? I'm fine."

"You attempted to take your own life, Eve. You are not fine. You need help in understanding and coping with your situation."

She doesn't respond.

"It's up to you. We have plenty of room. You can stay as long as you want."

Eve shakes her head. "What difference does it make? I got nowhere to go anyway. So, all right. You win. I'll sign your stupid piece of paper. Now, please, take these straps off."

They talk for two hours, beginning with the accident and working back through Eve's life. She tears up when talking of Brent. They don't discuss the two and a half minutes that her heart stopped beating. When he leaves, the restraints remain off. Eve is emotionally exhausted and falls asleep.

Thursday morning, Dr. Burgmann tells Eve to spend at least two hours each day in the community area socializing with the other patients. After lunch and a nap, she shuffles her sore body to the open area. It has two tables with four chairs each, a TV with a couch and three chairs grouped around it, a bookcase chock-full of paperbacks, a ping-pong table, and a game cupboard. She sees seven patients scattered about the room.

Two disheveled old men she guesses to be addicts are silently playing Gin at one of the tables. A man who looks younger than she and has a bandage on his left wrist stands motionless in front of the bookcase. A heavy, middle-aged woman and a thirtyish wisp of a woman sit stiffly in two of the chairs facing the TV, watching *The Young and the Restless*. A stocky, fortyish man ambles around the room, stopping behind each of the others to peep over the person's shoulder for a minute or two before ambling on to the next one. The only person making any sound is a girl about Eve's age, who sits alone at the second table, facing away from the others toward the window, eyes fixed on the center of the table. Her hands are folded in her lap, and her lips move nonstop. Eve cannot make out her whispered words. Everyone in the room looks dowdy, *including me.* Two nurses tend to paperwork at their station on one side of the big room. They glance up from time to time but make no sound. *Socialize with these people for two hours a day?*

Eve walks to the couch, eases herself onto it, and slowly pulls one leg up under her. She turns toward Wisp and opens her mouth to speak, then, getting a closer look, thinks better of it. Wisp is rocking back and forth so slightly that Eve didn't notice it from across the room, and she isn't really watching TV. Her head is turned toward it, but her eyes are fixed on the wall above the TV. Eve glances the other way at Big Mama. "Is this any good?"

Mama returns a quick glance but doesn't speak.

"*The Young and the Restless?*"

This time, Mama doesn't even acknowledge her.

Peeper, who had been standing behind Whispering Girl, saunters across the room to stand behind Eve. He stays behind her for two minutes that feel like an hour. Eve can't keep from pulling her robe tighter around her. Finally, he moves on to Mama. He speaks!

"How about we watch *Let's Make a Deal*? I like that Bob Barker."

"I'm watchin' this," Mama grunts.

Peeper stands behind Mama for longer than he was behind Eve. Finally, he moves on to watch the card players. Eve watches the rest of the TV episode. As soon it's over, Mama pushes herself up out of her chair, changes the channel, and plops back down as another soap opera comes on. Eve has never been a fan of daytime soaps. She continues to sit anyway. *Twenty minutes down. Oh man, two hours of this every day?*

Eve knows it's her turn. Peeper's sequence is Shelfman, Card Player A, Wisp, Whisperer, Eve, Mama, Card B. He speaks only to Mama, asking to watch *Let's Make a Deal* each time. "I like that Bob Barker." He gets the exact same response from Mama each time, which is the only time she speaks. Eve keeps Peeper in the corner of her eye. He begins to turn from Whisperer for Eve's fourth turn. She gets up off the couch as quickly as her sore body will allow. *Not this time, Peeper. Maybe a book.*

Shelfman hasn't budged. He's still standing at the center of the bookcase, staring at the books straight in front of him. Eve positions herself to his right and slightly behind him in an attempt to avoid attracting his attention. He doesn't notice her – *or possibly anything else.* Her attempt at leap-frogging her turn with Peeper doesn't work. He ambles up to her and stands behind her and to her right. *Make sure you don't waste my turn on Shelfman, too. You wouldn't want to kill two birds with one stone.* After her two minutes are up and he goes on to ask if he can watch Bob Barker, Eve relaxes enough to peruse the book titles on the quarter of the bookcase she can access without reaching in front of Shelfman. Eventually, she selects *To Kill a Mockingbird.* She's read it before, but it's one of her favorites. *And it's fitting. It has a lunatic in it.*

*Now, where to sit?* There are three choices. Back to the TV area, at the card players' table, or at Whisperer's table. *If I sit across from Whisperer and scoot the chair back to the window wall, Peeper can't get behind me. Anyway, I wonder what she's saying.*

Eve pulls the chair back to the wall and sits, glancing across the table to smile at Whisperer. Whisperer sees only the center of the table. *What is she saying?*

Eve catches bits of it. "Thy will be done"... "our daily bread...."

*The Lord's Prayer?* Over and over and over. Eve tries to read but can't get through the first page. She starts over for the fifth time.

"Forgive us our trespasses...."

Eve sighs and glances at Whisperer. Peeper is turning from Wisp to head for Whisperer. Eve looks back down. As she begins page one for the eleventh time, Peeper leaves Whisperer. Now he's standing beside Eve, looking down at her book. She grits her teeth and clenches the book tightly with both hands. After forever, he moves on to Mama.

"How about we watch *Let's Make a Deal?* I like that Bob Barker."

"I'm watchin' this."

"Lead us not into temptation...."

*Man, I can't take this. I've got to get out of here. Figure out exactly what they want to hear. Tell them anything.*

Trying her utmost to concentrate, Eve finally turns to page two.

"Hey, Mac, that's cheating! You can't do that!" It's Peeper, standing behind Card B and pointing to the player's hand.

"What!" Card A jumps up, yelling and knocking his chair over with a crash. "Are you kiddin' me? Cheatin' again! That's the last straw. Your ass is mine!"

The nurses are in full action now, and buzzers are sounding.

Peeper stands between them, points a finger at B, and shouts, "Cheater! Cheater!"

Card B grabs the table and tips it over toward A. "All right! You been itchin' for this from day one. Come on, you weasel!"

Card A is around the tipped table fast for an old guy. He shoves Card B, and they both fall backward from the force of the push. Card A stumbles into Peeper, taking him down, too. Before any of them can get up, four orderlies are on top of them, pulling them to their feet and keeping them apart.

One of the nurses shouts, "That's it! Everybody, back to your rooms! Now!"

Mama asserts, "I'm watchin' this."

Wisp continues her slow rocking. Whisperer stares at the table and says, "Deliver us from evil...."

Shelfman has turned to watch the commotion – *he's alive –* and now walks away from the open area. Eve closes her book and, heaving a shaky and thankful sigh, rises to go to her room. *Tell them anything they want to hear. Just get out of this place.*

After two weeks in the psychiatric care unit on a Thursday in early June, Eve is permitted a visitor. Val smiles at her as Eve enters the visitation den. "Are they treatin' you okay?" Val asks as she sits.

Eve looks much better than the day Doug and Val were in the ICU room together, which was the last time Val had seen her. "Yeah, I'm all right. Chest still hurts some, but I can move around. No more tubes or needles."

"That's good. It'll be great to get you out of here. We'll have to go out, like we used to – well, maybe a little less rowdy."

"Yeah, that'd be nice."

"Have they talked about a release date?"

"A little. I'm sure everybody knows they think I wrecked on purpose. I guess they're trying to convince themselves I won't do it again before they let me go."

"I don't know why they think that. They've got the blood alcohol reports. I mean, not that that's good, and you shouldn't have been drivin' and all, but you probably just lost control or passed out or something. Don't they even consider that?"

"I told 'em I did it on purpose. Pretty much had to. They made it clear I had to say it before they'd even think about lettin' me outta here."

"Man, Eve. I wish I could get you outta this place, just take you with me this afternoon."

"That sounds good, but where would I go?"

"Doug's waitin' for you to come back. He feels terrible about everything. Have you been talkin' to him?

"They won't let me. You're the first person I've talked to since I got out of ICU."

"Doug saw you there."

"We never talked. I must've only been conscious one time when he came in. Etta was havin' it out with the nurses when Doug came in. They got in a shoutin' match, and the guards took 'em both away."

"Yeah, I heard about that. I hoped you hadn't heard it."

"Everybody on the floor heard. Couldn't possibly have slept through it."

"Man, I wish there was somethin' I could do to help. Is there anything I can do that'd make it easier for you?"

"You're here. I haven't talked to anybody but doctors and nurses for two weeks. They wouldn't let anybody come. I'm glad you're here."

"They said your heart stopped beating for a while."

It's a statement, but Eve hears the question in it. Val knows she told Burgmann what she saw when she was dead; Eve sees it in her face. Val wants to hear Eve tell it. That's Val. "Yeah. They brought me back. I guess I was pretty lucky."

"That must have been awful. Were you conscious at all, I mean when they first brought you in or anything? Or at the accident? Do you remember any of it?"

"I don't know. I mean, not much, really. I don't remember anything from out at the quarry. Barely remember anything from the Triangle."

"So, you were unconscious the whole time, even here at the hospital?"

"I thought I remembered a little bit from here, when they were working on me. I kind of remembered the names of some of the people in the room, and maybe some of what they were doing to me."

"They said they did CPR and shocked you. Were you *awake* through that?"

"Maybe. They said semi-conscious. It was sort of like I was dreaming."

"Was it really painful?"

"No, never felt any pain at all... 'til the last shock. I felt that, and it really hurt. Then I blacked out and don't remember anything 'til like that Wednesday or Thursday."

"Do you remember the dreaming part?"

"The doctors said I was dying, and my brain was shutting down." She looks out the window. "I can't really remember much." They sit silently for a minute. "You said Doug was waiting for me?"

"Yeah. He wants you to come back to his place. If you will. He said he was bad to you that night at the Triangle."

"He say anything else?"

"Yeah, honey, he told me about that thing with Tricia Weathersby. Said he was real drunk and said stuff he shouldn't have."

"What happened with her?"

"She never moved in, if that's what you mean. She's jailbait, and her dad would make sure it happened. Doug knows better, and so does she. He was never gonna do it anyway. She's a kid, and Doug's got you in his system. He loves you, Eve."

"Yeah, well, he's got a bizarre way of showin' it."

"That's just Doug. He's self-destructive when he drinks too much. I never thought I'd say this about any of us, but he'd probably be better off if he'd go to AA."

"Is he planning on coming to see me?"

"He wants to, but they're keeping a heavy hand on who can and can't visit you and when."

"Well, maybe that will keep Etta away for a while."

"They told me I could only stay for half an hour. I probably should go, or they'll be stormin' in here to boot me out. You know, I'm here for you if you need to talk. About anything. If there are things they're making you afraid to say, you can tell me if you want to. I'm always on your side. You know I love you."

"Yeah, I know. Thanks, Val. I'm glad you came by."


The next morning at 8:30, Dr. Burgmann walks in. "Good morning, Eve. I saw Valerie DeBolt's name was on your visitor's list yesterday. How did that go?"

"It was nice to talk to her."

"Were you comfortable with the conversation?"

"Sure. Why wouldn't I have been?"

"Sometimes after going through trauma, people treat you differently, more delicately."

"No. Val was Val. I'm glad she came."

"None of the conversation was difficult for you?"

"No."

"Did you talk about Brent?"

"No."

"Your mother?"

"No."

"Doug?"

"Yeah, we talked about Doug some."

"And that was okay?"

"Shouldn't it have been?"

"You didn't answer the question."

"It wasn't a difficult conversation.  Has he been asking to see me?"

"Yes, he's asked several times to be allowed to visit."

"Why can't he?"

"We've made good progress these past two weeks, Eve. We want to be careful to avoid putting you in a situation that might reverse some of the progress."

"Why would a visit with Doug do that?"

"Well, hopefully it wouldn't, but you and Doug both have deep emotions swirling inside, and we want to be sure you have a handle on yours before we take chances."

"I can handle a conversation with Doug."

"I think you're right.  We'll try to set something up in the next couple of days.  Did you and Val talk about the period of time when your heart had flatlined?"

"Yeah."

"What did you tell her?"

"That I didn't remember much.  I might have had some kind of dream, but it was all fuzzy." *The biggest lie I've ever told.*

"Does it seem less real to you now than it did the day you first told me about it?"

"Yeah.  Probably." *Another lie.*

"Does it confuse you?"

"Yes." *No lie there.*

"Eve, that dreamy state might confuse you for a long time, months, maybe years, and being confused about it is okay.  The thing that will always bring you trouble is telling that story to others and believing it happened.  People will shy away from you if you tell it, especially if you insist on it as reality.  *Nobody* is ever going to believe that truly happened.  They will think you belong back here, permanently.  It's okay for you to think about it and wrestle with it. But, you must realize, or at least allow for the possibility that your brain dreamed it all up and it never happened. Can you deal with it like that?"

Her heart is pounding. "I... I think so." *Never in a million years!*

"All right. We'll step up the visits, starting with Doug."

Sunday afternoon Doug arrives and they walk into the visitation den. Eve is dressed in street clothes for the first time since the crash. Her cuts and bruises have healed, and she looks almost like her old self. She still moves gingerly. They smile at each other and touch hands. She sits slowly and motions for Doug to sit.

"Are you okay?"

"Getting better. How are you doing?"

"I feel really bad about all this. I haven't had a drink since that Friday night. Val tells me I should go to AA, and if I start drinking again, I think I will."

"Work goin' okay?"

"Yeah. We're puttin' in a lot of overtime. Probably a good thing for me."

"What you been doin' when you're not at work?"

"Hangin' out with friends, mostly Marty and Linda. Actually, they're all helpin' me. Nobody's drinkin' much."

"What'd you do about that blonde from the Triangle?"

"Please, Eve. She was nothing. I was drunk. That thing about her movin' in was never gonna happen. I was an idiot. Could we talk about somethin' else?"

"What do you want to talk about?"

"Well, 'bout you gettin' outta here, first of all. Gettin' better."

"What then?"

"We're gonna make it work, Eve. Maybe we should get married. Get Brent back for good. Maybe have a kid of our own."

"That'd be a really big change for you, Doug. We should think it through. Guilt would be the wrong reason for a move like that."

"It's not what you want?"

"I didn't say that. I'm just cautious, maybe paranoid. We've made each other so miserable at times. What if we got married, had a baby, and then it only got worse?"

He frowns and rubs his brow with both hands. "I don't know what to do, Eve. I think I really want it to be like that. You and me settled down, have a family. But how does anybody know how that's gonna work out 'til you just do it?"

"Okay, Doug." She smiles at him. "Let's take it in little steps. If you'll have me back, I'll need a place to go when I get out of here. I mean, I'd like to come back and make it work with us. My life has been such a disaster. I have a lot of work to get it turned around. I have to find a job and keep it. I don't know what I'll do about these hospital bills. I have to find a way to be Brent's mother. I can't be drinking anymore. It's so much. I'm not sure at all I can do it. But I have to try, one step at a time. Marriage? Maybe, but not right away. And, as much as I'd like another baby, I've gotta get the first one figured out before I bring on another."

"So, you wanna try, though. You'll come back?"

Eve isn't sure how much of Doug's sentiments are guilt-driven – probably a good portion. She also knows her own words aren't all heartfelt. She needs a place to live, and she has nothing. "I want to try, Doug. I want to try way harder than we ever tried before."

"Can I hold you?"

"That'd be wonderful."

He helps her rise, gently enfolds her in his arms, and they share a long, light, sweet kiss.

There's a knock on the door, and it opens. "I guess they were serious about my time limit," he whispers in her ear. "I love you, Eve."

"I'm really glad you came, Doug. Come back as soon as you can."


Wednesday at 2:00, she's summoned to Dr. Burgmann's office.

"Eve, I've arranged a meeting with Ray Kellerman. It will be the three of us here in my office. Are you ready for that?"

"When?"

"He'll be here in 5 minutes."

She takes a deep breath, winces, and lets it out. "Yes."

Ray is let in a few minutes later, and they sit around the six-chair conference table in Dr. Burgmann's office. "Thank you for agreeing to visit with us, Mr. Kellerman. Eve has made good progress and will soon be released. Brent is obviously very important to Eve, as well as to you and Mrs. Kellerman. It is crucial to all of you that a set of ground rules be agreed upon – a set of guidelines so that you all know what to expect from each other. I'd like to avoid discussing legal issues, if possible, and just stick to what seems personally acceptable to everyone. Is it all right if I begin with some questions for you, Mr. Kellerman?"

"Call me Ray. I'll be as candid as I can."

"Good. Let's start with visitation. Are you comfortable with Eve spending time with Brent?"

"If Eve is well-kempt, and if the visits are supervised and not inappropriately frequent, at least until a level of responsibility is proven, I'd be open."

"By well-kempt, I assume you mean neatly dressed and groomed and, especially, sober."

"Yes."

"What means of supervision would be agreeable?"

"I'd want all visits to be in my home, at a time when I'm in the house. And with a trustworthy person always in the same room."

"Could that person be a friend of Eve's whom you approve?"

"I don't know of any of her friends that I'd approve. I understand it might be difficult with my wife or me always in the room. I have a niece in town. She's 25 and has two children. I think she'd be willing to devote an hour a week, and I think that she and Eve might get on okay."

"Eve, are these terms agreeable to you?"

Tears stream down her cheeks. "Ray, you have no idea how much I appreciate you giving me another chance. I can *promise* you, I won't mess up again."

"I believe that is a yes. Then, Ray, how soon do you feel the first visit should be?"

"Well, we don't know how long Eve will remain here in the hospital. We certainly think she should be given a clean bill of health first.    And have been on her own long enough to demonstrate both sincerity and ability to function well."

"Do you have a time frame in mind, after her release?"

"I would think not sooner than three months after."

"Eve?"

Her heart sinks, tears still streaming. "I... I want to see him so bad.  Could I do anything to make it sooner?"

"Ray?"

"I don't think so.    Brent is old enough now to be permanently impacted by these visits.  I have to think of him first.  I want to support Eve, too.  Believe me, I want her to work her life out.  But, the patterns we've seen before warrant at least a three-month period.    Enough time to demonstrate solid stability, so we all have a good comfort level that Brent won't get subjected to emotional damage."

"Eve, will you agree to this?"

"What choice do I have?"

"You need to do better than that.  You have to find the strength to approach this positively.  Can you do that?"

"Please, give me a day.  I will, but please give me time to let it sink in.  I can't say I'm happy with waiting three months right now.  I'll be better tomorrow."

"All right, that's an honest answer, and I believe you'll do your best to follow through.  Ray, there's one more concern I need to get in the open.  I know this has been extremely difficult for you, and I believe your approach is honorable and compassionate.    My concern is that Mrs. Kellerman seems unable to find your level of compassion for the situation.  The commitments you are making are for her grandson also.  Will she override your commitments?"

"Honestly, Dr. Burgmann, I need the three months to work through this with my wife as well as to make sure Eve is up to her end of the bargain.  I believe I can bring her to the point of willingness to allow the terms we've set.  If I can't get her to agree, however, she won't override.  If Eve does her part, the Kellerman household will not renege."

*If Eve does her part.*  She knows Ray thinks she'll lose it within a month.  *If I can just hold it together for three months, as soon as I see Brent I'll have the strength to stick with it forever.*  Three months after being released.  *I've got to get out of here.*

## Chapter 16

One week after the meeting with Ray, Eve is again in Dr. Burgmann's office. Since that meeting, she's been a model patient. She knows exactly what they want to see and hear from her, and that's what she's shown them.

"How are you this morning, Eve?"

"I'm fine, Dr. Burgmann. How are you?"

"Good. Your progress has been impressive. Do you feel you're ready to face the day-to-day pressures of your life in the world?"

"Yes. I've been thinking a lot about it, and I'm ready."

"You'll go back to Doug?"

"Yes. We're both committed to give it everything we've got. He's stopped drinking. And I've definitely learned my lesson."

"Do you think you can find a job?"

"I'm sure someone will take me on as a waitress. There are some restaurants within walking distance. And I can always take the bus if I need to."

"Can you deal with your mother?"

"You know she's never really cared much. The only reason she tried to see me is she's afraid the hospital's going to come after her to pay my bill. But the social worker says the hospital will accept whatever payments I can make 'til the bill is paid. She said they'd accept fifty dollars a month. Doug says we can do that, even if I can't find a job. As soon as Etta – my mother – knows that, I won't have to deal with her. She'll never come around."

"Life has been tough for you, Eve. And I'm afraid it might continue to be. But I think you're as ready as you're going to get to deal with it. Keeping you here longer would be counterproductive. I'm planning to release you tomorrow – if I'm sure you have a place to go and if you agree to see me once a week until I determine that is no longer necessary. How does that sound to you?"

Her heart soars. "Wonderful, Dr. Burgmann! I *will* make this work."

It's Sunday morning, three weeks after Eve was released and moved back into Doug's house. He lies beside her, having gone back to sleep half an hour after they made gentle love.

Their new life together has been delicate, but positive. No alcohol. No fights. No tension, at least on the surface. A week after being released, she was hired at Hardees, within walking distance. She works evenings and weekends. She and Doug aren't together a lot, but she thinks that eases their healing.

Lying in bed, Eve's mind, as has become its norm, attempts to fit the puzzle together, to organize thoughts of the past two months, her need to be reunited with Brent, the vivid images from the time when her heart stopped, the mission to love everybody more than humanly possible, and the requisite that she control her life. As always, she's unable to mesh and prioritize these concepts and their corollaries. The intensity of the feelings from those two and a half minutes overpowers everything, making it impossible to formulate order.

Doug stirs and opens his eyes. "Whatcha thinkin' 'bout, baby?"

"I don't know. Everything, I guess."

"About what happened when your heart stopped?"

He's never mentioned it before. She'd begun to think maybe he didn't know anything about what she'd told Dr. Burgmann. But, no – whatever Val knew, Doug probably knew, too. "What makes you ask that? Why would there be anything to think about?"

"I think it's on your mind a lot. You seem like you're somewhere else more than you used to."

"I don't know. I guess I'm troubled more than I used to be. Maybe I should be. Everybody thinks I tried to kill myself. And my life was a god-awful mess. Always has been. I have to fix it. I have to get Brent back. I want to be a good person, to love everybody, you know. I need to change a lot."

"So... when you were in the emergency room, and they were trying to save you... so you don't remember anything from then?"

"I don't know. Why do you want to talk about that?"

"I think *you* want to talk about it. Like maybe you *need* to."

She lies still, staring at the ceiling for a minute. "Dr. Burgmann says whatever I thought happened didn't really happen. It was just my mind playing tricks. He says I shouldn't think about it or talk about it much."

"That's weird for a psychiatry guy. Aren't they s'posed to tell you to deal with all the crap instead of pushin' it back inside? Seems to me like it'd be better to let it out. Get it out of your system."

"I *can't* get it out of my system, Doug. It's like the most real two and a half minutes in my whole life. I can't stop thinkin' about it. I try and try, but I *can't*."

"The pain must've been really bad. Was it awful?"

"No! No, it wasn't like that at all. Just the opposite. I can't begin to explain how great I felt. There's no words for it – way, way beyond ecstasy. There's no way you could understand."

"You're sayin' it felt good to die? Like you wanted to? That doesn't sound right."

"Well, what about you? You know, back when you were in high school and you collapsed playin' basketball. Did your heart stop? Did you see anything?"

"No! Man, when I woke up and they told me what happened, it scared the crap out of me. I mean, I think maybe it changed me, because it showed me I *could* die. Made me think about it. And it terrifies me! All I wanna do is live. Live as much as I can every day! Are you saying you came *this* close to dying, and it don't make you wanna live every second? Instead it makes you wanna die even *more*? *Can't* be right. It *has* to scare you."

"No. Dying doesn't scare me at all. Not anymore. It feels so much better than living – I wish I could explain it better, but I can't. I look forward to it." Tears trickle down her face.

"Jeez, Eve. Maybe your brain *was* haywire when that was happening. It *couldn't* have been like that. A person can't look forward to dying. Burgmann's probably right. Maybe it *is* better to bury that crap... push it outta your head. Man, I'm really sorry I made you talk about it. I won't do that to you again. Wow. I gotta take a shower."

He gets up. She lies in bed and cries.

The party officially starts at 3:00 at the Volt Jolt on Sunday, July 7. It's a combination birthday/hospital release party for Eve, as well as a continuation of the 4th of July four-day blast for Vic, Val, and their dates, Reggie and Jeff. Doug and Eve arrive with Marty and Linda to find the other four partiers in full swing. The music is loud enough for an outdoor concert. Val, Vic, and their guys sway to Marvin Gaye's "Let's Get It On." It's impossible to tell who is dancing with whom.

Val turns the volume down half a notch for the candle and cake ceremony. Val's guy, Jeff, is a law student at Indiana University. Reggie is mulatto and sports an Afro that makes his head look twice the size of even Vic's. Reggie and Vic sit at the counter bar while the other six sit around the table. Val's chair is scooted tight to Jeff's, and her short, low-cut, white summer dress appears to be a continuation of his white tee shirt. The newcomers have soft drinks, and the others wash down their cake with beer.

"So, how long you guys think Nixon's gonna last?" Marty shouts over the music.

"His ass is goin' down like an atomic bomb," Reggie bellows back.

"And it couldn't happen to a more deservin' bastard," says Vic. "That sonofabitch thinks the first rule of communicatin' is to make up the lie before you open your mouth."

"Maybe we should put bets on his last day in office," Doug says. "Everybody throw in five bucks, and whoever's closest without goin' past takes the pot."

"I can't believe you guys let him get reelected." Vic elbows Reggie in the ribs.

"Yeah, well the Panthers was already fallin' apart in seventy-two. We shoulda got more militant instead of meltin' away. Didn't happen. Anyway, chick, watch where you're throwin' elbows," he says as he pulls her neck tighter to him with the crook of his right arm.   Grand Funk's remake of "Locomotion" comes on. "C'mon, baby, let's dance."

"You got a deck of cards?" Marty asks as Val gets up to lead Jeff to the living room dance floor.

Marty, Linda, Doug, and Eve play Euchre, guys versus girls, while the dancing gets more and more risqué. Doug's seat has him looking directly at the dancers. Eve sees him attempting to look as if he doesn't notice Val in her sexy dress, but his eyes are electrified each time Val bends down.

Vic also keeps an eye on Val and Doug. A hint of a sneer shows on her lips. "Hey, Doug, there's plenty of beer in the fridge. You know you want one. Help yourselves."

Halfway through the second card game, the dancers exit the living room. Eve watches the foursome sashay down the hall, all enter the same bedroom, and close the door. *Thank god for cranked-up volume.* She glances at Doug's expression as he watches them go. Smoldering hunger.

They straggle out of the room fifteen minutes later, buttoning, zipping, and hooking various parts of their clothing. Reggie gives the card players a triumphant grin. Jeff is sheepish. Vic, for some reason, looks defiantly at Eve. Eve sees Val's eyes latch onto Doug's.

Vic says, "There's a thing goin' on at Reggie's buddy's," as the pair heads for the front door. "See you guys later. Doug, lighten up and have a beer or two."

The remaining six order in pizza and talk. Eventually, Val says, "Jeff's studyin' Indiana law on child custody for one of his classes." She looks at Eve. "He thinks you'd have a strong case."

"Val told me about your son and your in-laws. They don't have the right to just take him away from you."

Eve's jaw drops. *Why in the world does Val have to bring this up tonight?* "They say their son, Brent's father, will file for custody, and they'll get a restraining order if I fight them."

"The father clearly abandoned the boy. The court isn't likely to grant custody to an absent father and even less likely to grant to the parents of an absent father instead of to a mother who desperately wants the child."

"They have money. Probably millions. I've got nothing. I can't beat their money."

"There are attorneys who would fight for your rights to the end, regardless of the money."

"I don't know any like that."

"I might be able to find you one. Would you want me to do that?"

All eyes are on Eve. Fear wells up in her. She looks down. "They say they could claim I'm not competent." She whispers, "I have a history."

Val speaks up. "I know things are tough for you right now, Eve. But, wouldn't getting Brent back solve everything?" She glances at Doug. "I really think Jeff could help."

"I don't know. Ray says I can start visiting Brent in a couple more months. I think it might be better to go along with his plan. I just have to be good, and then, once I start seeing him, maybe it can gradually get to be more often."

"Yeah," Val replies, "but what guarantee do you have? What if the two months go by, and they change their minds and just say no? Why let them have the upper hand?"

"Let me think about it for a couple days." She's seen what being confined to a psychiatric unit can be like. Panic grips her at the thought of being sent to one permanently. *And Mary would do it in a minute. They've got the money.* "I'll think about it."

On a hot Saturday night in mid-August, seven weeks after her release, Eve is working, looking forward to closing in 15 minutes. Doug walks in, followed by Val and Vic.

"Look what I found," he says. "I was on my way over to pick you up and happened to see the twins out-n-about. We decided to pick you up and take you out for a late-night dinner!"

"Um... okay. We're not very busy. I'll see if Jim'll let me go now."

Doug has a new, shiny, black hot-rod pickup, courtesy of his insurance company. Val and Vic hop into the bed, laughing and pushing. They head for the Lamp Post in New Paris, just across the state line. "No drinks for you and me, babe. Just dinner. The rowdies back there can have whatever they want."

Sitting in a booth, they have a good time talking and laughing about the old days. Doug and Eve drink Coke while Val and Vic down several beers, adding to those they'd obviously had earlier. Val says to Vic, "We haven't seen Rach and Julia for months. They just live four blocks from here. If they're home, I bet they're still up. Probably partyin' way harder than us. Think I'll walk over there and see if they wanna hang out. Domesticated Doug and Eve won't have to take us home."

"I just got this beer," Vic says. "I better finish it first."

"Here." Val slides hers over. "Finish mine, too. There'll be plenty more later. I'll be back in ten minutes." She scoots off the seat.

"Hold on," Doug says. "Even if there ain't any predators out there, I doubt if you could find your way there and back in your condition. I'll take you." He gets up and looks at Eve. "Be right back, baby."

As soon as they're out the door, Vic says, with no concern for being overheard, "So, tell me 'bout when your heart stopped. What was that like, exactly?"

"I was pretty much out of it. Don't remember much."

"Man, that's not what I heard. I heard you were like in heaven or something. I wanna hear 'bout that. Never believed much in it."

*Who's been blabbing to Vic – Doug or Val?* "I don't know where you heard that. I never said that to anybody."

"C'mon, Eve. *Everybody's* sayin' you told 'em at the hospital dyin' was the best thing you ever felt. And you know me. If there's somthin' out there better'n anything *I* ever felt, I wanna know all about that! Fill me in."

"You've had too much to drink, Vic. There's nothing to tell."

"There ain't no such thing as too much to drink. I bet you're feelin' *that* by now. But, I'll tell you what I think. If you thought anything at all when they was poundin' on your chest and puttin' the shocker to you, it was a mirage. There ain't nothing after. Dead's dead. The sooner you figure that out, the sooner you'll see life's for living, and the sooner you'll stop havin' to see that shrink. Do it all, man! Every minute you spend mopin' around 'bout how bad life is and how much better dead might be is a minute of *feelin' the thrill* tossed away."

*How am I supposed to love this person?* "I can't be like you, Vic."

"You never tried!   Always holdin' back.   Afraid a something – I sure as hell don't know what.   But I'm tellin' ya, it works against you.   Live!   You shoulda went to Woodstock. Best damn time I *ever* had!   Do what you wanna do.   Don't let people run over ya.   If it'd been me with Douggy-boy at the Triangle last May, and that prissy Weathersby broad came skippin' over, I'd a let her stick that tongue to Douggy one time, and 'fore she pulls it out I'd a been round behind and yanked her off that barstool so hard she wouldn't a had a clue what hurt worse, her ass or her scalp where the fistful of her hair in my hand used to be.   Then I'd a told Douggy, 'Hey, ain't you gonna help prissy up?' and soon as he gets his ass up off *his* barstool, I'd a kicked his nuts up his esophagus.   Then I'd a latched onto a couple young bucks and told Douggy all balled up on the floor me and my friends was goin' out in the bushes for a while.   What I'd never, *ever* have done is gone home cryin' and try to drive over a damn cliff."

"Stop it, Vic!"

"And I'll tell you somethin' else – and don't get me wrong, I don't want no kid – but if I *did*, there ain't no Kellermans or anybody else that'd be takin' him away from *me*.   Grow a pair, Eve."

"I need to go to the bathroom."

Eve is cherry-red.   As she hurries off, she hears Vic say, "I'll bet you do, sweetheart."

She stays in the stall for fifteen minutes.   When she comes out of the restroom, Doug is waiting at their booth.   Val and Vic are gone.

The following Monday at 5:00, Eve is taking orders at the cash register.   It's dinner rush, and the line has stacked up.   She works as fast as she can, being friendly and courteous, with no time to notice who is backed up in the line.   She hands a high-school boy his change and says, "May I help you?" as she turns to see who she's addressing.

"I heard you was workin' here," Etta says. "I need to talk to you."

Eve's jaw drops. "Uh, can I come by your place tomorrow before work? I can't really talk right now. Um, do you want anything to eat?"

"You buying?"

"Uh, okay. What can I get you?"

"First, let's talk 'bout the hospital bill."

"Please, Etta, I can't right now. There's a big line."

"They can wait. This's important. I haven't heard from the hospital for a while, so they're lawyerin' up. Is your no-count weasel-guy gonna pay up?"

"Look, Etta, I've got it all worked out. You're not gonna hear from any lawyers. I'm taking care of it. Please, what can I get you?"

"Bullshit! How you gonna work it out? You ain't got nothing. If he'd a married you when you was in the hospital like I said, nobody'd have to pay nothing. Just soak the insurance company like everybody's s'posed to. But he ain't buyin' no cow that gushes milk free. Man, you'd think watchin' me all those years you'd a learned something just from bein' my daughter. Too damn stupid."

"Etta, I'm telling you, I've got it worked out! That's why you haven't heard from them! Now, what do you want?"

A voice booms from behind – Joe Eubank, the manager. "What the devil is goin' on? Eve, move that line!"

"Gimme a damn burger and fries," Etta snaps. "And a twenty-ounce beer."

"Burger, fries, and a large Coke. I've gotta keep moving." Crimson-faced, Eve looks at the gaping construction worker next in line and says, "Can I help you?"

She hears Joe mutter, "That's comin' outta your pay."

As soon as the rush is over, he calls her into his office. "What was that all about, Eve? You're a good worker, but I can't have that kind of ruckus here. Was that your mom? Jeez, what a fright growin' up musta been for you. It's a wonder you turned out at all. You tell her she can't come in here and make a scene like that again. I can only give you one chance on stuff like that."

Two days later at, 9:00 on Wednesday morning, she can't wait any longer. She calls Ray Kellerman's office.

"I'm sorry, ma'am, he's not in this morning, but I'll tell you what. We just had this new phone system installed, and I've been dying to give it a whirl. I can push this button, and the call will go straight to his house. He's there. If it doesn't work, call me back, and we'll get you fixed up. Hold on."

Click. Ringing. Another click and then, quickly, one more. "Hello, Kellermans," Ray's voice booms.

Eve is speechless for a moment.

"Hello? Anybody there?"

"Uh... hello, Ray. It's Eve."

Silence.

"Um... I wanted to call you – I guess give you kind of an update. I don't know, maybe Dr. Burgmann's keeping you posted. But, I wanted to make sure you knew I'm doing OK. I've got a job. It's just at Hardees, but it's a job. Full-time. And I haven't even come close to having a drink. Doug hasn't, either. We're doing good, really making it work. I quit smoking, too."

"That's good, Eve."

"It's been two months."

"I know. One more to go."

"Well...." she takes a deep breath. "That's kind of what I wanted to talk to you about." She hears shallow breathing on the phone, but it doesn't seem like Ray's. "I've been really doing good. And I wondered if maybe you might let me see him for just a little bit. Even just 10 minutes. I want to see him so bad. I'm off today, and I was hoping...."

"Don't you dare!" Eve hears Mary hiss.

"Mary!" Eve cries out.

"I'm talking to Ray," Mary snaps. "I won't allow her to ruin Brent's life. She ruined Eric's. That's enough! She'll never set foot in this house again. Ray, don't you dare."

Eve hangs up the phone. She struggles up to the bedroom, collapses face-down on the bed, and sobs. *Gran, I can't do this.*

## Chapter 17

Eve's appointments with Dr. Burgmann are on Monday mornings. She enters his office. He scrutinizes her. "Good morning, Eve."

She falls into the chair, props her elbows on his desk, sinks her face into her hands, and cries. Dr. Burgmann buzzes his secretary and tells her to rearrange his morning appointments.

Until today, Eve has painted a rosy picture. She's maintained that she rarely thinks about those two and a half minutes her heart was stopped. She's not mentioned the conversations she had about that with Val, Doug, or Vic. This morning, after taking ten minutes to gain composure, she admits she can't keep her mind off it. Then she tells of the encounters with Vic and Etta and her conversation with the Kellermans.

"Are you worried that Mr. Kellerman won't be able to live up to his commitment to you?"

"I think she might leave him if he tries to. Or at least she'll threaten."

"They've been married a long time and been through a lot together. They're pillars of the community. Separating would be an extremely difficult decision for both of them. But, for the sake of argument, let's discuss the possibility that Mr. Kellerman can't, or doesn't, do what he agreed. How would you react?"

"How much is a person supposed to take? How much *can* a person take?"

"A person can take a lot. We're not talking about a person. We're talking about Eve Kessler. How would Eve Kessler react?"

"I don't know. I feel like I can't go on another day without seeing my son. I feel like he's the only reason – the *only* reason – I'm alive. My purpose in life is to raise him. Protect him from these damned traps and pitfalls."

"How would Eve Kessler react? One month from today, if you would speak with Mr. Kellerman and he would say, 'I'm sorry, Eve, but I can't let you see Brent,' how would you react?"

"How can I *know* that?"

"Well, then, let's figure it out. Would you sneak in a window at night and kidnap Brent?"

A deep sigh. "No."

"Would you get a gun and shoot Mr. or Mrs. Kellerman?"

"No."

"Would you scream and shout to the world about Mr. Kellerman being a liar and a cheat?"

"I don't think so."

"Would you get drunk?"

"I don't know. Maybe. I don't think so."

"Would you get behind the wheel and drive into a tree? Or over a cliff?"

She closes her eyes. "It seems like a solution. I don't know."

"Let me ask you this. If, one month from today, Mr. Kellerman says, 'No, I will never allow you to see Brent,' do you think that would be the end of it? That nothing could ever change? That future circumstances would never soften the Kellermans' position? Or that you might eventually gain the strength to actually make a change happen?"

"I don't know. I guess maybe it might be giving up too easily to take one 'no' as the final word. Brent's too important for that."

"So, then, do you think Eve Kessler would throw away all the progress she's made so far and have to start all over again, from farther back, by getting drunk or crashing into a tree?"

"It doesn't sound like it would make much sense."

"That's the way it seems to me, but what I would do doesn't matter. The only thing that matters is what Eve Kessler would do."

"God, where would I find the strength?"

"Life isn't always easy. In fact, your life is unjustly difficult. But, it is what it is. You can let circumstances take you under, or you can claw your way above them. You have to make that a conscious choice, and if you're going to take control of your life, you must *never* let your guard down – not for one second."

"Easy for you to say."

"You work on that this week. Find strength to pull yourself up. Next week, we'll work harder on getting those two and a half minutes out of your head."

Three and a half weeks pass, three more appointments with Dr. Burgmann, and she's put on a good front. Yes, everything is getting better. My relationship with Doug improves each day. I like my work. I think of those two and a half minutes less and less. I know they were not real. I'll be strong enough to deal with Ray and Mary. She's almost convinces herself she's making progress.

Her telephone rings on Thursday morning.

"Hello?"

"Hello, Eve. It's Ray Kellerman."

Her heart leaps.

"We need to meet."

"Will you bring Brent?"

"We need to meet... first."

"Why?"

"I want to come to your place."

She glances around, alarmed by what she sees. "When?"

"I can be there in fifteen minutes."

"I need to get dressed," she lies. "Can you give me a half-hour?"

"I'll be there at nine-thirty."

After a whirlwind straightening, cleaning, and dusting, Eve takes a deep breath, looks out the window, and sees Ray's Cadillac pull up to the curb. She clenches her eyes closed, clamps her hands together so hard her knuckles pop, and tells herself to breathe. A knock at the door.

"Come in, Ray." He looks as strained and nervous as she feels. "Do you want to sit?"

They sit at the table. He looks at her. She looks down at the table.

"Eve, I don't know where to begin. When you called a few weeks ago... I think that's when I realized how hard it was going to be to make this happen."

Eve examines the tabletop more earnestly.

"I... I'm going to need more time."

She can no longer see the tabletop and squeezes her eyelids closed, thinking she can lock the tears inside.

"Mary is beside herself. Eric leaving the way he did pushed her over the edge. I'm struggling, really struggling, to save our marriage."

He places a hand over Eve's hand, white from gripping the edge of the table. Her hand jerks out from under his.

"Look, Eve, I'll find a way to make this work. I have to. I just need more time. I need another month. Give me another month."

No matter how tightly she holds her eyes closed, tears plop onto the table.

"Can you look at me, Eve?"

She's rigid.

"I... I don't have any more to say. I'll call you in two or three weeks."

He pushes back from the table and lets himself out. Eve doesn't move for an hour, hardly able to breathe.

Three and a half weeks later, on a Tuesday in early October, Eve retrieves the mail from their box, sits at the table, and opens an envelope from Kellerman Insurance Agency. She unfolds a handwritten letter.

Eve,

I'm unable to bring myself to face you. I know how much Brent means to you. I am not a perfect person. Not even close. I care for, you and I wish you only the best. I find myself too weak to do what I know is right. I cannot fulfill the agreement I made with you. It would destroy Mary, and therefore myself, and probably Brent, and then you along with us. Selfishly, I put Mary and Brent and myself before you. I believe I can help to salvage the three of us, but I can't save all four. May you and God forgive me, and may God be with you. Please, don't contact Mary or me in the future, except that you may contact me only at my office by phone in the following instance. I feel very cheap saying this, but if money would ever help your situation, call me about that, and I will provide it.

    Ray

"Aaahhhggg!" Eve raises her right fist as high as she can and rams it down on the table, breaking the little finger in front of the knuckle. Heedless of the pain, she rips the letter in half, then the remaining pieces in half, and again and again until the fragments are so small she can't stack them. She scoops them up, runs out the door and into the street, and throws them into the wind with all her might.

## Chapter 18

The day after receiving Ray's letter, in the late afternoon of her night off, Eve sits in the living-room chair in her pajamas. There is no sound in the house – no TV, no radio, windows closed, no lights. She stares at the same thing she's stared at all day: nothing. Her mind is a broken record. *What am I supposed to do now? Nothing matters. Maybe I can work double shifts every day. Doug will find somebody else. He should. I'm no future. Or present. Why am I here? What's the point of trying to love anyone? Grandma, why did you make me come back? What am I supposed to do now? Nothing matters....* The refrain replays in her mind over and over and over.

Eve doesn't hear knocking on the door. Again, louder. She doesn't move. The door opens.

"Hey, Eve. You in here?"

She turns toward the door, sees Val, and looks through her.

"C'mon, Eve. Doug will be home in an hour. Time to start your day." She walks to Eve and takes her hand. "C'mon, honey, let's get you dressed."

She coaxes Eve to shower, brush her teeth, and dry and comb her hair. While Eve showers, Val opens the windows, turns on some lights and the radio, and irons a pretty teal and white loose-fitting dress. At 5:00, they're sitting at the table reminiscing about their old late-night porch visits.

Doug walks in. "Hi, sweetheart." He leans over and brushes a kiss on her cheek. "Hey, Val. You two look fresh as daisies, and I'm a dirty tumbleweed. Guess I'd better get cleaned up."

"You want pizza?" Val gets up. "We can pick it up while you shower."

"Sounds great!"

"C'mon, Eve."

When they return with dinner in hand, Doug has the TV tuned to a rerun of *The Sonny and Cher Comedy Hour*. He and Val laugh at it and joke as they eat. Eve smiles and nods occasionally. Val stays until 10:00. The TV stays on: *Hawaii Five-O, The Rockford files*, noise. Doug and Val keep the conversation lively, talk of friends, work, and escapades. When Val gets up to leave, Doug walks her to her car. He comes back inside five minutes later.

"Boy, I'm beat," he says. "You ready for bed, hon?"

"Go ahead. I'll be up soon."

He goes upstairs. She leaves the TV on without changing the channel and lies on the couch. She's there in the morning, still wearing the teal dress, TV still on, as she pretends to sleep while Doug gets ready for work and leaves.

After lying awake all night, she tries to sleep. By 8:30, she gives up and paces around the apartment. Her work shift starts at 3:00, but she leaves the house at 10:30 and walks to Hardees.

"Hi, Joe. I was bored this morning, so thought I might as well see if I can help out here. I won't clock in till three, and I'll work my whole shift. I just need something to do, if that's okay."

"You can work if you want. Diane didn't show up, so we're short-handed anyway."

Eve works nonstop until 11:00. When there are no customers to wait on, she busses tables. When the tables are all clean, she mops floors. When the floors are spic and span, she cleans restrooms. At 11:00, she walks home in the dark, damp, chilly night. Doug is asleep in bed. Dead-tired, she crawls in beside him and conks out.

Friday morning, Eve wakes a few minutes before Doug's alarm rings. She gets up, slips on a worn sweat suit, and fries bacon and eggs for their breakfast. When Doug leaves, she washes the dishes, throws in a load of clothes, and cleans the apartment. It's 9:30. She paces. *I need a routine. Can't go to work five hours early every day.*

She goes out for a walk.  It's a clear, crisp autumn morning.  After walking two blocks, she begins to jog.  When she's exhausted, she turns around and walks back home, arriving at noon.  She showers, dresses, and walks to work.  *Only an hour and a half early today.  Better.*

Saturday and Sunday are sleep-in days with Doug: sleep till 8:00, cuddle and love for an hour, nap, get up, dress, go out for brunch, take a drive and a walk, show up at work on time.

Monday morning: leave at 8:15 to see Dr. Burgmann.

"No, Ray didn't come through.  Says he can't, that I have to stay away from Brent.  Says he's weak.  Offered me money.  The asshole.  Yes, the week has been hard.  Wednesday was awful.  Doug's been very patient with me.  I don't know why – don't see what's in it for him.  Val came over Wednesday night.  To cheer me up... but I think mostly to support Doug.  I worked a lot.  Started jogging.  I have to do something, *anything*, to stay busy, wear myself out, so I can sleep, so I don't drive myself into the ground."

"You're coping, doing as well as could be hoped."

"I'm trying to get through each day."

"Keep doing it.  Have you been able to avoid dwelling on the night of your accident?"

"Not on Tuesday and Wednesday after I got Ray's letter.  Better after that.  I still talk to Gran every day.  Several times.  She never answers.  Maybe I'm beginning to believe you're right.  It was all my mind playing tricks.  Never really happened.  Some days, I try hard to believe that.  Some days, I try hard not to.  I'm starting to think there might be a chance I could actually get past it.  I mean, part of it is maybe a good thing.  The part about trying to love everybody so much.  Maybe that's good, whether it's part of some magic plan or not.  Especially if I can't be with Brent.  If I really care about the other people I'm around, maybe that makes life better.  I'm trying to challenge myself to do that.  I mean, people like Vicki Buholtz?  Now, if I can just feel love for her and no negative feelings along with it, now that would be an accomplishment, wouldn't it?  Or, God, Etta.  Now there's a super-challenge.  Even Val – I mean, she's been a great friend to me – but she's always got her own motives.  Anyway, I think I convince myself a little bit more every day to try harder.  I think that's good."

"When you talk to your grandma, what do you say?"

"Mostly that I don't understand. I want her to help me understand. I mean, it felt so real to talk to her that night. I can't quite get past feeling like she talked me into coming back. Like there was a great purpose in it. That I was coming back to save Brent, and so that he would save me. But, that has only gotten further and further from happening. I want her to explain to me exactly why I had to come back, how my coming back here is supposed to be a good thing for anybody. How I'm supposed to make it work."

"How do you feel about those talks with her?"

"Frustrated. Maybe desperate."

"There *is* another way you could look at it."

Eve eyes him cynically.

"You lived with her for over 4 years, years that were key in developing your character. The best years of your life. She and your grandfather imparted something of themselves into you during those years. Whatever strength you have, and I believe it's considerable, comes in large measure from them. What I'm saying is that part of your grandmother lives inside you. Maybe that's where you should try to look for her answers: inside yourself, to the part inside you that came from her. It's there."

"You think of every angle, don't you?"

"I'm trying to help you. Help you help yourself. Life is out there waiting for you, Eve. You need to find your place in it. For you."

"Now you sound like Vicki. 'Don't let a single experience escape. Try everything,' she says. 'Make sure you get every thrill.'"

"You know that's not what I'm saying."

"Yeah, well, the advice has a familiar ring to it."

"You're arguing with me. You need to get comfortable with the thought that you didn't physically reunite with your grandmother when your heart stopped. You can be mad at me for harping on it, if that helps, but in the end, you need to get past it. You have to find your answers from within."

"I'm workin' on it."

Wednesday is the difficult day. She can't report to work early on her day off. They'd become sure she was off her rocker. The morning is okay: breakfast, clean, run, shower. The afternoon drags. Watch TV without seeing it. Read without comprehending. Pace. Talk to Gran. Spiral.

Val always shows up an hour before Doug gets home. Today is a warm October day and Val walked. They sit on the front stoop like old times, except it's daylight and Eve doesn't smoke.

Val brings her up to date on Vic's exploits. It's the first Eve has heard the details of her antics at that New York field concert, Woodstock. She was rain-soaked three-fourths of the time, naked half the time, and high on booze or drugs the whole time. She was sick for a week when she got back. She claims she has no idea how many guys she laid.

Eve tells Val about her week: Saturday and Sunday morning with Doug, the funny looks she gets from the others when she reports to work early, but nothing of her conversation with Dr. Burgmann. Val asks mostly about Saturday and Sunday morning. "Wistful" is the word that comes to Eve's mind when she sees Val's reaction to hearing about her activities with Doug.

Doug arrives, and Val and Eve continue to sit outside and enjoy the sun while he cleans up. They go to Elizabeth Parker's for dinner and conversation. They return to the apartment and play a game of Monopoly, which Doug ruthlessly wins. At 10:30, Val says she needs to go.

"I'll drive you," says Doug. "Can't be too careful on the back Streets of Richmond."

He's back in fifteen minutes, and he and Eve go to bed.

Eve's routine settles in. Monday mornings: Dr. Burgmann. All other weekday mornings: wash clothes, clean the apartment, run. Saturday and Sunday mornings with Doug. Work the evening shift plus a couple of free afternoon hours every day except Wednesday. Suffer Wednesday afternoon until Val arrives. Spend Wednesday evening as a threesome. She tries with marginal success to avoid thinking of her decision not to die, of a purpose for that, of Brent. She tries, more successfully, to show love to everyone.

The Wednesday before Christmas, Eve decides to fill the afternoon void with an act of reaching out. At noon, she dons her coat, hat, gloves, and boots and walks out into the snow-covered town. Twenty minutes later, she knocks on Etta's door.

After a minute, the inside door opens and Woody appears, sporting his paunch under a sleeveless tee shirt, which hangs down far enough to cover the top half of his briefs. The remainder of his getup consists of a pair of slippers. He leers at her for a moment and then bellows, "Etta. Somebody here ta see ya." No response. "Hey! Eve's here." He opens the screen door and says, "C'mon. Yer lettin' all the cold in." He turns and walks into the bedroom and says, "Hey, get up and see what she wants."

Eve closes the door, takes off her hat and gloves, and unzips her coat. *I should be able to find a way to feel some love for this person.* Standing just beyond the open bedroom door, Woody puts on a pair of pants. Then he walks to the bed, shoves the lump lying under the covers, and says, "Getcher ass outta bed 'fore I throw ya outta it." The lump groans and rolls.

Etta rises to the edge of the bed and sits, keeping covers wrapped around her. Eve hears her mumble, "What the hell time is it?" She slowly rises, drops the covers, and, naked, sticks her feet into a pair of slippers. She shuffles to the hall tree in the corner, pulls a robe from it, and drapes it on. She ambles to the kitchen table, eyeing Eve as she walks, picks up a cigarette pack, bumps one out, and sticks it in her mouth. It bobs up and down as she says, "What you doin' here this time a day?" She picks up a lighter off the table and drags on the cigarette as she lights it.

Woody clicks on the TV, turns the volume up loud, and collapses on the living-room chair.

"Hello, Etta. I haven't seen you for a long time, and it's Christmas. Just thought I'd drop by and say hi. See how you're doing."

"In the middle a the night? Jeez."

"It's after noon. Have you been okay?"

"You still workin' at Hardees? Guess me showin' up there worked. Ain't heard nothing from the hospital since."

"Yeah, I'm still there. I like it. Working's good for me. Keeps me busy, more in a positive frame of mind."

"Positive frame a mind? Good, stiff drink'll do that. Way easier, too. I wouldn't work in a place like that if they paid me."

"You doing anything special for Christmas this year?"

"Gittin' drunk. Same as last year. And the year before. Ya wanna come over?"

"C'mon, Etta. I came to see you because I wanted to try to do something nice, maybe start something. Wouldn't you like it if things were better between you and me? Do you wanna sit and talk over coffee or anything?"

"So, you ran outta coffee at your place? That why you're here? You came over to wake me up so you could drink coffee? Whaddaya mean, better? What's wrong with you and me like we are?"

"Etta, I'm your daughter. You're my mother. It could be better. You might like it."

"Aw, shit. That jerk kick you out again? That why you're here? You wanna move in here again? Steal my man again. I'll tell you what, sugar. That ain't happening. I could give you a run for it, anyway. Ain't as young as you, but I always knowed how ta doll up. Never showed you how. On purpose. Good thing, too, you bein' so man-hungry."

Eve can't stifle a grin. "All right, Etta. I thought it was worth a try. I'm gonna go. I didn't have any ulterior motives. I just wanted to, I don't know, say Merry Christmas or something."

"Yeah, well, Merry Christmas."

Eve zips her coat, puts on her hat and gloves, and opens the door to leave. Before closing it, she looks back and says, "I love you, Etta."

"Jeez, that wreck musta busted somethin' in your head. Go see your shrink."

## Chapter 19

Monday is two days before Christmas.    Eve tells Dr. Burgmann about her visit with Etta. He laughs.

"Eve, this is going to be a short session.    I don't have anything to discuss that we haven't hashed through a dozen times already.    I think you've gotten everything from me I can offer you.    It's time to release you from these weekly consults. You'll have a few rough spots ahead, but you're coping well. I'll always be here if you need me.    Just call and set up an appointment if you want to talk."

This year, Doug's family Christmas gathering is at his aunt's home in Michigan.    He leaves with his parents early Tuesday morning.    They'll return on Sunday.    Eve has to work Thursday, Friday, and Saturday and stays behind.    As soon as Doug leaves, Brent begins to consume her thoughts.    *It's Christmas Eve.    He turned five in November.    The last time I saw him, he wasn't even three.    How can I have missed it all?    Does he remember me?    I'm his mother.    I have to see him.    Somehow.*

She recalls her fifth Christmas, the last time she'd been to Christmas Eve services with Gran and Grandpa.    Now, home alone on the day before Christmas, she feels devastation.    She calls the church.    Services are at 7:30.    Her grief intensifies, and she begins to turn various plans in her mind.    Improbable schemes take on an air of viability.

Eve puts on her knee-length coat at 6:30, buttoning it all the way up to the collar.    It is cold outside.    She wraps a scarf over her head, completely covering her hair, and adds a neck scarf. Her eyes and nose are all of her face that is visible.    She starts up

Doug's truck, drives to a back street four blocks from the church, and parks in the darkest spot she can find.

She arrives at the church on foot forty-five minutes before services begin, stands across the street from the parking lot, and scrutinizes the houses on this side of the street. Two of them look deserted: no porch lights, and all the Christmas lights turned off. The families are probably off to relatives for the holidays. She decides which dark porch has the better view of the parking lot, looks around to see if anyone is watching, and then walks up the steps onto the porch and around a corner where she can watch with little chance of being seen.

Half an hour later, shivering, she sees the car pull into the lot. They park and get out. As they turn their backs to her and head toward the church entrance, she hurries off to follow them. She reaches the door three families behind them and shuffles in, silently extending her gloved hand to the greeters and accepting the bulletin they offer her.

She watches them find a pew, quickly walks to one that is two rows back, and sits directly behind them. The church is warm, but she's so cold that it feels good to remain fully cloaked and covered. They've removed their wraps and taken the little boy's coat and hat off. He's between them, standing on the bench facing the front of the church. Then he turns around and looks at her.

Eve sees Brent clearly for a second before moisture blurs her vision. The piercing in her heart is so intense she can hardly remain upright.

Without turning around, Mary reorients Brent to face forward and pulls him down onto her lap. By the time the service begins, Eve is sweating. After the opening, the children are called to the front and gather on the steps to the altar for their Christmas mini-sermon. Eve cranes to see Brent's face, rising a few inches off her seat. The pastor asks the children what they think they should pray for tonight. Before any of them can blurt out "Baby Jesus" or "presents," she sees Brent look at the preacher and say loud enough that the whole congregation hears, "My mommy."

She gasps and collapses back on her seat.

After a few more responses, a Christmas story, and a short prayer, the children are released to attend their own special

Christmas Eve service. As the children's volunteers lead them out the side door, Eve excuses herself to the side aisle and exits the rear door of the sanctuary just in time to glimpse the group go around the corner toward the Sunday School classrooms. She's aware of no thought process, only *Brent!* She hurries after them and ducks into the dark classroom adjacent to the one they enter. The two classrooms have a communicating door that stands open.

Eve is so warm and sweaty now she's afraid she might swoon, but she doesn't dare remove any of her cover-up. She sways nearer to the open door, trying to get another glimpse of her son. Staying ten feet back from the door, out of the light, she sneaks around in a semicircle. Finally, as one of the teachers begins to read the Christmas birth story, she spies him, sitting on the floor in the midst of the other children. Her eyes cloud again, and she rocks on her heels.

She reaches down to the back of a chair to steady herself. *So hot.* She closes her eyes for a moment. Reopening them, she has a direct view of Brent. He turns his head, sees her, and smiles. A low moan escapes her lips, and other heads turn. Eve backs up a step and stumbles over the chair she'd used to steady herself. She crashes to the floor, overturning the chair.

"What the...?" she hears one of the teachers exclaim.

Then the other cries out, "Somebody's in there! That kidnapper in the news! Count the kids! Get 'em in a tight group. Help!" the teacher shrieks, running to the classroom door. "Help!" she bellows down the hall.

Eve rolls to her feet, falls again, shakes her head, and wills herself to get up and run. She bumps into the doorjamb and bounces off into the hall as she sees the young woman scream a third time for help, then start to come after her. Eve runs hard now. At the fork in the corridor, she goes left, away from the sanctuary. She hears commotion amplifying behind her as she spies an exit sign and runs in the direction. The door she goes out is a rear exit in a poorly lighted area. She runs away from lights into wherever the darkness leads. She trips on a tree root and bangs her head on the frozen ground. She crawls around behind the tree just as she hears the door bang open and a flurry of voices.

"Did he come out this door?"

"I think so. It was a woman."

"Are you sure? Maybe it was a disguise."

"I'm sure. She was small. I saw her nose and eyes and some hair. Had to be a girl."

More voices now.

"What's going on? Is somebody out there?"

"Are the kids all accounted for?"

"I think so."

"That's gotta be first. I don't see anybody out here. Get a head count. Call the police!"

Eve hears the door close. Shaking, she peeks around the tree trunk and sees no one. *I've got to get out of here!* She runs on, staying in the darkest patches, and falls twice more. When she reaches a street sidewalk she sees that her coat and pants are ripped, and her right knee is bloody. She's lost her left glove, and the palm of her hand is scraped, gritty, wet, and freezing. *Where am I?*

She ducks into the nearest alley and hides between two garages while she tries to reconstruct her flight and figure out how to get to Doug's truck. She hears police sirens and trembles from cold and fear.

Carefully choosing her path and the timing of her movements, she makes her way to where she thinks the truck is. After an hour, she finds it and gets in. She shivers, shakes, and cries for half an hour. Finally, she rolls the window down to listen for sounds of nearby activity. When all is quiet, she turns the key and drives southeast out of town. She loops around on dark country roads and drives back into town from the northwest. At 11:00 on Christmas Eve, she finally walks into Doug's apartment and collapses on the couch.

In January, Vic starts coming along on Val's Wednesday evening visits. Eve suspects Vic is protecting her territory. Vic and Val have always had a wild and free relationship, but lately, Vic seems jealous, as if she thinks Doug is the one person who could steal Val away from her.

On a blustery, rainy mid-February evening, the four of them are dining at Connie's restaurant and bar, seated at a table in the bar area. Eve's back is to the bar. Vic says she's buying and everybody's drinking but doesn't seem to care that Eve's drink sits untouched. She's more concerned about Doug's. Eve believes Doug's claim that he hasn't had more than two drinks on any given day since her accident. But Vic keeps trying, applying a bit more pressure each time they're together. *She thinks Val won't want Doug if he falls off the wagon. He's a bad drunk to be with.* Tonight, halfway through the meal he's just finished his second beer and Vic has another on the way.

"Hey, Bill! Long time no see." Eve hears Ray Kellerman's booming voice enter and address the bartender. *That's just great.* Thinking he sounds unusually boisterous, she glances at the small mirror on the wall she's facing, opposite the huge mirror behind the bar. She sees him through the double mirror view. *Oh my God! It's not Ray. Eric!*

Eric is with two of his high-school football buddies, and they noisily claim three barstools. This bar obviously isn't their first stop tonight. Doug's back is to the entrance, and he hasn't caught on. Val and Vic, gaping, obviously have. Eve tries to make herself small and drops out of the table talk. Val and even Vic tone down the volume, although Doug doesn't. Eve, heart in her throat and wanting out of this room, can't keep from stealing apprehensive, veiled peeks into the mirror. As he drains his second beer, Eric's eyes meet Eve's for an instant through the double mirrors. Her eyes dive away.

For a minute, nothing changes in the guffawing at the bar. *Whew. That was close.*

Then there is a moment of silence at the bar.

"Hey! Eve Kessler! Do you remember me?"

*No! Please, no!*

Eric gets up and swaggers to their table. "And lookee here! Damned if it ain't the Volt Twins! You girls look hot as ever. All three a ya. And Doug Pratt! Man, I ain't seen you in years. Heard you and Eve took up, though. That's good, I guess. I tell you what, though, she sure as hell screwed things up for me."

"Eric," Eve whispers. "Please. Don't."

Bill grabs the phone behind the bar and dials.

"Don't what, girl?" he thunders. "Don't wanna talk 'bout old times? Hell, you and me, we had some *great* times. Dang! You did stuff to me I never even dreamed of. I thought I was the luckiest bastard on Earth! I mean, I *know* what attracted *you* to her, Doug. It was damn tough for me to walk away. If it hadn't been for that little bomb you dropped, I'd a kept bangin' you right on till the end a time."

Doug's face is crimson as he kicks his chair back and jumps up.

Eric wears an "I dare you" expression. "How 'bout one for ole time's sake, Eve? Maybe even two or three. What you doin' after dinner?"

Doug barges around the table, but Eric's hands are on his shoulders before he can take a swing, shoving him backward. Doug trips on a chair leg and sprawls on the floor on his back.

Eric doesn't stop talking. "You owe me at least that, Eve. And you better be just as good as you used to be."

Doug is off the floor in a rage, flying at Eric. His diving tackle is intercepted by a smashing right to his jaw. Val lurches at Eric, who tosses her to the floor as if swatting a fly. Vic explodes and is behind Eric like lightning, right arm around his neck strangling him while her teeth sink into his left ear.

He screams, whirling around. Vic doesn't let go, her legs flying out as she whirls with him. He pushes backward, slamming her against the wall. She lets go and uses the wall for leverage to shove his shoulders with both hands and then bring her feet up on his rump to push even harder. He starts to double over backward as he's flung forward, but his feet tangle with Val lying on the floor, and his head plunges forward, crashing into the edge of the bar. Streaming blood, he rolls over in time to see Vic's pointed boot slam into his groin. He's finished, but Vic is livid. She dives onto his doubled-up body, forcing his legs to part. With a hand on each of his knees, she shoves down, lifting her body as his legs slide down to the floor. With his knees pinned down and apart, she moves her left leg aside and crushes his groin again with her right knee. Then she clasps her hands together high above her head and rams them down onto Eric's nose.

Three cops barge in and pull her off.

"You touch her again, you bastard, it'll be the last thing you ever do!" she screams and stomps Eric's rib cage as two of the cops drag her back and cuff her.

Bill is on the phone again. Eve hears him say, "Ray, did you know Eric was in town? Well, he is. He's layin' on the floor in front of my bar right now, bein' handcuffed. He'll be goin' to the station, then probably to the hospital. Maybe to the hospital first. Yeah, I figured you'd wanna know. If you wanna keep it out of the paper, you'll probably need to be at the station when they get there. There'll be a half-dozen or so to greet you. Probably cost a pretty penny to get 'em all outta there and keep it quiet.... Sure. Sorry to be the bearer, though. Hope you can get it worked out."

The police usher Vic and Eric, pressing a towel to his head and face, into the back seats of separate cruisers and keep everyone else inside while a busboy cleans up the mess. Reinforcements arrive, and three policemen tend to each of the two captives in the cruisers while four more question the group remaining in the bar. In less than five minutes, one of the officer's radios crackles.

"Gus, here."

"This one's over, Gus. An ambulance is coming for Kellerman. They're taking him to Indy. As soon as he's gone, turn the others loose."

"You sure? It was pretty rough. Some damage done at the bar. Kellerman's gonna need stitches. I'm not sure the girl wouldn't have killed him if we hadn't pulled her off."

"Everything's already taken care of. Damages are covered. Kellerman flies out of Indy for overseas tomorrow. Let 'em go. And this one doesn't hit the paper, Gus. It never happened. Make sure all respondents know that."

At noon on a Wednesday in late March, Eve sets off for a walk to downtown. She's drawn into Knollenberg's Department Store, to the children's clothing section. *He'll be starting kindergarten this year.* She ambles through, touching everything on the racks for little boys. About a third of the way through, she glances up and sees Mary Kellerman probing through a rack 30 feet away. Beside her, fidgeting and holding onto her skirt, is Brent.

Eve freezes, unable to take her eyes off her son. He doesn't recognize her but fixes on her face, smiles, and waves his free hand. "Hi," he says in a small voice she barely hears. Mary turns to see who has garnered her grandson's attention and looks horrified. She grabs Brent's hand and turns to scurry off.

Eve gasps. "Mary! Wait!" She runs after them. "Wait!"

Mary, dragging Brent along, can't move fast.  She whirls.
"Get away!"

Eve falls to her knees and holds her arms out to Brent.
"Mary, please.  Brent!"

"Ow!"  Brent whines as Mary clamps her hand on his.

"I knew I shouldn't have brought him out."  Confronting
Eve, her eyes are venomous.  "I won't make that mistake again."

"Brent!  It's Mommy."

"We're leaving.  Don't you take one more step.  I'll have
you put away."

"Mary!  Please!"

Mary scoops Brent up and turns away.  Eve doesn't move.

"Is she my mommy?"

"No, honey.  We're leaving."

"She's a nice lady, Grandma."

"She's not.  Forget you saw her."

After a minute, still on her knees, tears streaming, Eve
becomes aware of people staring at her.  She rises and walks
numbly out of the store and back home.  She sits at the first chair
she reaches at the kitchen table, her back to the front entry door.
At 4:30, she's still in the chair with her jacket on, eyes transfixed
on the far wall of the room when the door bangs open.

"Hi, hon!" Doug gushes, carrying two grocery sacks.  "Our
lumber delivery didn't show, so I knocked off an hour early and
picked up Val."

"Hi, Eve!  You have a good day?"  Val enters cheerily on
Doug's heels.  When she sees Eve's face she adds hesitantly,
face reddening, "What's wrong?"

"Saw Brent."

After a moment, Doug replies.  "Where?"

"Knollenberg's."

"Knollenberg's!  What the heck was you doin' there?  You
saw Brent?"

"Went for a walk.  I don't know why I went in there.
Maybe I was thinking about Brent.  Anyway, I was looking at
boys' clothes and saw them.  Him and Mary."

Val's color has returned to normal, and she gets back into
the conversation.  "Did they see you?"

Eve nods her head. "He didn't remember me. I said I was his mommy. She said I wasn't. Said I was bad. Said she'd have me put away."

Doug stares at her. Val drops down to her knees and wraps her arms around Eve. "God, Eve. That's awful." Val gets up. "Let me have your jacket. Did this just happen? Did you just now get here?"

"Got back a couple hours ago," she says, removing her jacket and handing it to Val.

"Um, we picked up stuff to make lasagna. You okay with that for supper? I'll get it started. Doug, why don't you sit and talk to Eve?"

"Uh, okay. Just need to get a shower and cleaned up first."

"You don't look like you need one," Eve says. "Must've been an easy day. When did you get off?"

"Um, around three-thirty or so. Just had enough time to pick up Val and get groceries. We'd have just came straight here if we knew. I'll be right back."

"I'm going to sit out on the porch for a minute," Eve says. "You okay with making dinner?"

"Sure," Val says, not looking at her.

Eve walks out, neglecting to put her jacket back on, sits on the concrete, and leans against the wall. *If I had a cigarette, I'd light up. I have to shake this off. It's been getting better. Can't let this drag me back down.* She takes several deep breaths. *Such a sweet little boy. I have to find a way back in. Have to stay positive. Maybe I'll write Ray a letter. Maybe try to talk to him. Maybe there's a chance.* She mulls over what she might say to Ray... making a plan, discarding it, making another, discarding. Another.

Finally, Doug opens the door. "Salad's on the table, baby." Eve stands up, goose-bump-covered arms folded around herself, teeth chattering. "Jeez, how long you been sittin' out here with no coat?" He pulls her inside.

They eat quietly; the only conversation is between Doug and Val, mostly about work and in needlessly hushed voices. Eve picks at her food. By the time they're done eating, she's stopped shivering. She helps Val clear the table and wash dishes while Doug searches for something cheery on TV. None of them suggests a game of Monopoly or anything else. They watch sitcoms for an hour, and Val says, "Vic told some guy she'd watch his kid tonight, but what she meant is her roommate would watch the kid, since she wouldn't have the first clue what to do. I think he showed up at seven-thirty, so there's already a question of whether or not the kid's survived. I'd better get going."

"I'll take you," Doug says. "If you need me to, I can entertain the kid for a while."

They leave. Doug returns two hours later, saying the kid was a handful. Eve is sitting where she was when they left, TV tuned to the same channel.

It's dinner rush at Hardee's on a Friday night in June, and Eve's immersed in taking orders from the impatient line.

"I was hopin' you still worked here."

Eve turns to her next customer, already chagrined, knowing who it is from the gravelly voice. *Etta.* Deja vu.

"Can I help you, Etta?"

"Yeah, I need five hundred."

"What?"

"I need five hundred bucks."

"I can't talk now. I have to wait on these people. Do you want anything?"

"Can't you hear? I told ya! I want five hundred dollars!"

"I'll stop by your house tomorrow morning." She turns quickly to the next person in line and says, "Can I help you, sir?"

"Hey! Give me the money!"

"I don't have that kind of cash on me. Etta! Move on. You're gonna get me fired."

"I'll move on soon's you hand me the cash. If you ain't got the whole five hundred in that cash register, just gimme everything that's in it."

"Are you crazy? I can't give you cash out of the register!"

"I'm sure you take cash outta it ever' damn day. The only difference today is you're givin' it to your mother. You said you wanted things to be better with us. So, prove it! Gimme the money!"

"Etta! Stop it!"

"Can't you do *anything*? I'll git it myself." Etta puts both hands on the counter and hoists a knee up.

Joe Eubank's voice booms from behind her. *"Hey!* Do I need to call the police?"

"No," Etta says. "Eve's just slow. She's gettin' cash, then I'm outta here."

"Not from that register, she's not. If you're not out that door...." He points emphatically, "In five seconds, I'm callin' the cops, and you're goin' to jail."

"Eve, give me the money!"

"Eve, get to my office! Now! Jason, call the police and tell 'em we got a robbery in progress. Lady, get out of here before I come around there and pin you 'til the cops get here!"

Etta slips down from the counter, glares at Eve, and says, "You're useless." She whirls and darts out the door.

At 6:00, jobless, Eve opens the door to Doug's apartment. Movement catches her eye on the stair. Val is coming down, buttoning her blouse. Eve looks up to the top landing to see Doug saunter out of the bedroom door, shirtless. Three jaws drop.

Val, beet-red manages to mumble, "This isn't what it looks like."

Eve looks up at Doug, standing motionless. "This... uh... never... um... happened before," he stammers. "And we never planned it. It just happened before we knew what we was doing. It looks bad, but it was like... sort of an accident. Um... what're you *doin'* here?"

"I got fired."

"Jesus," Val breathes.

"Fired?" Doug shakes his head. "Today? Like, just now?"

Eve blows the air out of her lungs. "Yeah."

"Why?"

"You wouldn't believe it. It doesn't matter anyway. Etta."

"Etta?" Doug tries to make sense out of it and at the same time make his and Val's transgression disappear. "She got you fired?"

"Tried to rob the place. Tried to get me to give her cash outta the register. Told everybody I take it all the time."

"They *had* to know that was a lie," he says.

"Doesn't matter." She looks at Val. "Button your blouse, and go home."

"I'll run 'er," Doug says and ducks back into the bedroom to put on a shirt.

Chapter 20

*What do I want? If Doug and Val want each other, do I even care? Then what? The only thing I care about is Brent. Try Ray again? Love everybody? How can it be that, after all this, that almost seems easier? I should hate Etta and Mary and Val... and Doug and Vic and Ray and maybe even Joe Eubank. I don't. I hope they all can get past their burdens and be happier. Maybe I do love them. It's almost funny. Everybody pulling me down, trying to rip what's left of me to shreds, and still, I like them and want the best for them. Gran, what have you done to me? What do I want? Brent. Peace. If I can't have both, I'd take either.*

Doug returns at 10:00. Eve sits at the table in the dark.

"I didn't know if you'd come back."

He starts at the words coming at him in the dark. He turns on the light. "Sorry," he slurs.

"Drinking?"

"Vic's fault. She's crazy."

"Tell me about it. But, that isn't somethin' you didn't already know. So, it's Vic's fault your drunk? I mean, far as I know, you've stayed sober for over a year, and now, tonight, you take Val home, and Vic gets you drunk?"

"She's tryin' to take me down. She's scared Val's gonna move out, so she's tryin to take me outta the picture."

"You mean, she thinks you and Val are gonna run off? Like ditch her and me?"

"I don't know. Maybe."

"Is that what you want?"

"I don't know what I want."

"Because, if it is, I won't stand in your way. The past year's been okay, but I know the passion's not there. Since the accident, I haven't been able to care about much. Only Brent. And I can't have him. I think we help each other stay off the booze. But, I know you need passion, and I haven't given you any."

"We've been okay. I like livin' with you."

"How long you been gettin' your passion from Val?"

"C'mon, Eve."

"Two months? Three?"

"I told ya already. Just tonight. It was an accident."

"Oh, come off it, Doug. You never screwed *anybody* by accident. You think I haven't seen the way you always eye her? And the way she leads you on? How long?"

"It don't matter, Eve. Just drop it."

Her voices rises in pitch and volume. "How *long*?"

"All right, all right. Take it easy." He looks at the floor and says nothing for a moment. He mumbles, "Hope I don't need to start duckin' bottles."

"I'm not drunk, and I learned my lesson last time. I'm not gonna attack you. Spit it out!'"

He sighs. "It started when you was in the hospital. I mean, we didn't do anything for a couple weeks, but it started back up between us then."

"So, why didn't you just go for it then? Why are we still doin' this?"

"I don't know. Maybe it bothers me. With Val, I'd be drinkin' all the time. *She* does. You're the only thing that keeps me sober. Besides, she probably wouldn't do it anyway. I mean, Val puts on like she's all about guys and bein' sexy and everything, but she ain't gonna go against Vic. She says she could move out anytime she wants, but it ain't gonna happen."

"So, that's the real gist of it, then. You and Val aren't shackin' up 'cause you're afraid of Vic."

"I'm not afraid of Vic. I just think Val won't go against her, that's all."

"So, what am I supposed to do? Just look the other way while my boyfriend and my best friend get it on?"

"What do you want outta me, Eve?"

"How 'bout some consideration? How about either being with *me* or being man enough to say it's over and go after what you really want?"

"I don't even *know* what I want!" Now Doug is getting louder. "Look, I've had too much to drink. This ain't a good time for this. I'm goin' to bed."

"Whaddayamean, you don't know what you want? *I* know what you want. *Everybody* knows what you want. Any hot chick radiating sex is what you want. And that's about the *only* thing you want."

"I'm goin' to bed."

"Good! I'm staying here on the couch."

"Good!"


The following Monday morning, Eve takes a bus to the mall area on the east side of town to apply for work. She doesn't relish the thought of having to take the bus to and from work, but the east side is closer to Brent. *And farther from Etta.* She's hired as a waitress at Jerry's restaurant to work evenings, with Mondays and Tuesdays off.


On Labor Day morning, Doug's truck rumbles into a secluded picnic area parking lot at Huston Woods State Park. There are a half-dozen cars and twice as many motorcycles in the lot. As Doug and Eve climb out, she sees Vic and Val sitting on a picnic table with a guy sitting between them. Vic wears a skin-tight red tee shirt, jeans, and boots. Val flaunts bright pink hot pants and a white halter top. Vic is scowling at Doug and Eve. *Looks like Val neglected to tell Vic she invited us.*

It's a beautiful late summer day. The sky is crystal-blue without a cloud, and the sun has ousted the early-morning chill. The day will be perfect for partying outdoors until the full moon lights the night.

This is Vic's party, her crowd. There are several couples wearing black leather jackets and smoking who knows what, milling around the picnic table adjacent to Vic and Val's perch. That table has a dozen thermos jugs on it, and everybody carries a 16-ounce cup. Two bearded bikers are setting up a volleyball net. There are blankets and sleeping bags on the ground in a patchwork around the area. Some kind of frenzy is occurring inside one of the zipped double sleeping bags.

"You s'pose that's iced tea and lemonade in those jugs?" Doug asks as Eve looks away from Vic.

"Not a chance."

"I'm not sure why Val invited us. I don't see anybody we know besides her and Vic."

*Yeah, well, I've got a pretty good idea why.* "I'm bettin' Vicious Vic didn't know we were coming. Maybe we can cut out after lunch. This is gonna get wild."

"I don't know. It could be funny. You ever watch falling-down-drunk volleyball? It's a hoot. Speakin' of Vicious, I think she's bringin' those two juice mugs she just filled over to us."

"Great," Eve mutters.

"Hey, Douggie boy," Vic says with a grin that isn't reflected in her eyes, "this'll loosen you up. If you're not wound quite so tight and you get in a brawl today, maybe I won't have to save your ass. Drink up!" She hands Eve the other cup without taking her eyes off Doug.

Val spies the group and bounces off the table, eyes gleaming. "She tryin' to get you drunk already, Doug? Beware! Her goal is to have everybody soused by noon, so nobody'll care that we've got ten times more beer than burgers."

The two bikers who put up the volleyball net slap burgers on three charcoal grills at noon. Vic's goal is achieved. The crowd is raucous. The zipped double sleeping bag is still in continuous action, and two bikers are standing next to it, gulping beer while waiting their turn.

Eve still has her first cup. She's managed to empty it halfway by sloshing a bit here and there out over the rim. Vic hands Doug his fourth. Vic, Val, Doug, and Eve, in that order, sit scrunched together on the picnic table top, hooting at the first volleyball game. By the time the four each down a burger, Doug's beer is gone. The first group of players stagger to the burger platter, and it's time for a fresh batch of players.

"You need a refill," Vic says, taking Doug's cup from his hand and jumping off the table.

Eve murmurs to him, "Doug, don't do this. She's tryin' to get you tanked. C'mon, let's get out of here. I'll drive."

"Aw, you don't have to leave." Val jumps in. "I don't know what Vic's beef is, but we'll stymie her. They need two more for the next game. Eve, you take the beer when Vic gets back. C'mon, Doug. Hurry up! Here she comes."

Val grabs Doug's hand, pulls him from the table, and tows him to the makeshift court. Both are unsteady on their feet. Vic arrives at the table. Her eyes follow Doug and Val as she hands the beer to Eve. "Shit," she mutters, then saunters over to the group of previous players, now chowing down. She joins in the bawdiness as the new game begins, but her eyes never leave Doug and Val. She and Eve have that in common.

Doug and Val play beside each other on the six-person team. Val starts the flirt-bumps. She closes in on every ball that comes near Doug, touching him in one way or another with each effort. Halfway through the first set, he begins to reciprocate. Occasionally, one or both of them goes down from either the force of the bump or lack of balance. They laugh and giggle each time, along with the rest of the out-of-control players and onlookers. Eve sits alone on the picnic table and watches, expressionless and mum. Vic becomes the lewdest of the jeering section. She harasses all the players, as do the other spectators, but her barbs at Doug are venom- tipped.

"Hey, Doug, you forget how to handle beer while you was on the wagon?

"Wow, Doug, that reminds me of the last time I saw you. You know, in that bar, on the floor gettin' pounded!"

"Hey, Doug! Your fly's open. I see somethin' there just the size of yours. Oops, my bad. That *was* a fly!"

Doug and Val's team loses the first game when they're in the back row, and both dive for a dig that's clearly in Doug's area. She collides with him before the ball arrives, and they bounce off each other and fall to the ground as the ball lands between them.

The height of the farce occurs near the end of the second game, when Val is playing in the front row with Doug behind her. A ball is lobbed over top of Val, and she begins to backpedal to take a swing at it. At the last second, she turns around and stumbles into Doug face to face. They go down, and she lands squarely on top of him. She lays on him nose to nose for a few seconds, and then thrusts against him as she lifts herself.

Eve shakes her head. Vic spits in the dirt and goes to retrieve another beer. When the set is over and the players are replaced by the just-fed ones, Vic immediately hands the beer to Doug. He drinks it half-down with one tilt of the cup.

While he's guzzling, she says, "C'mon, Val. Let's go heft Marilyn out of that sleeping bag. She's been in there for three hours, and some of those guys have been back for round three. I know she wants to get in Guinness for redefinin' the meanin' of free love, but I doubt if she can take much more."

Eve watches Doug stumble to the picnic table. By the time he gets there, he's drained his cup.

"Whew! Man, that took it outta me. I can barely walk."

"Yeah, I saw you had a lot of trouble stayin' on your feet out there."

"Dang! Val was all over the place. Was she trippin' everybody else out there as bad as me?"

"Nope. Just you and her."

"Man, I tried to stay outta her way. I don't know *what* she was doing."

"Right."

Val and Vic have unzipped the sleeping bag and spread it open to air out. Marilyn sits on it and giggles while Val tries to help her dress. Vic marches to the drink table.

Eve takes Doug's hand. "She's gonna bring you another one. C'mon, let's go."

"What? Leave? Now? Aw, man, the party's just gettin' started. I ain't leavin' now."

"Can't you see what she's doing? She's jealous. She thinks Val will leave you alone if you start gettin' drunk all the time again. She wants to knock you off the wagon, and she's doin' it. Let's go. Now! Before it's too late. Hurry up! She's coming."

"Don't you order me around! I know what I'm doing. I can handle one bender. I'm already on it, anyway. After today, I'll go another year without drinking. Nothin' to it."

Vic is at the table, beer hand extended. "Here you go, Doug. You look dry."

"Thanks, Vic." Looking at Eve, he takes the cup. "I have a feeling this one ain't gonna last long. You got more?"

"Plenty." She gives him a satisfied grin. "I'll go get you another."

"You're a shweetheart," he slurs.

When she turns, Eve hisses, "If you take one sip of that, I'm leavin' without you."

"You can't. I got the keys."

"Give 'em to me."

He reaches in his pocket, pulls out the keys, and dangles them up high. Then he tips the cup and starts chugging.

Eve jumps off the table, grabs the keys from him, whirls, and strides toward the truck. As she hustles, she hears him mutter loud enough for her and several others to hear, "Bitch. Plenty a better action 'round here anyway."

Five weeks later, Eve is getting ready to go to work. She hears Doug's truck reverberate to a stop in front of the house. Last night was the third Friday night in a row he hasn't slept at home. Neither of them speaks when he enters. He takes a shower, dresses, and comes downstairs ten minutes before she has to leave to catch the bus.

"You wanna call in today?" he asks. "Go out and have some fun for a change, you and me?"

"Can't. I need this job."

"Aw, c'mon, Eve. You been there long enough they know what they got. They ain't gonna fire you for callin' in sick one time. We need some fun time together. It's been a long time. I think you can put the past behind you now. Start livin' again."

"If you mean start partying and drinking again, I can't ever put that behind me. I can't handle that lifestyle."

"It's been a year and a half. You were a kid then, and you've grown up. A lot. I think it might be our only chance, Eve."

"What's our only chance? You mean our relationship is over if I don't start going out and getting drunk with you again? I been there, man, and there wasn't anything about it that made us stronger. More like ripped us apart. Almost killed me."

"It ain't like that anymore, and you know it. I wouldn't do what I did back then. Wouldn't put you through anything like that."

"Like what? Like going out with me and gettin' drunk and ditchin' me for some ditzy, stacked blonde? Or like doin' it again at a Labor Day picnic? Or like again in our own bed while I'm gettin' fired? Like that, Doug?"

"Quit it, Eve. That's not the same. That was just Val."

"Just Val! Just my best friend? Is that supposed to be better? Instead of screwing some piece of jailbait, you're doin' it with my best friend? That's what's wrong with my life. My friends. You and Val. Jeez, no wonder I'm a mess."

"Hey, I come home wantin' to take you out, make things better with us. And all you wanna do is tell me how rotten I am. Pick another fight. I don't even know why I try."

"You come home Saturday afternoon and want to make things better by having me skip work and go out and get drunk and have you humiliate me again? And come home from where? You sure didn't spend the night in my bed. Who were you sleeping with, anyway? And why aren't you gonna be with her again tonight? She get a better offer? I'm going to work. Move."

"We're never gonna make it like this, Eve," he bellows as she walks past him and out the door. "Why do I keep tryin' with you?"

She turns and yells back, "You quit trying when you started drinking again. And you're right, we're never gonna make it like this." Then she slams the door and storms off to the bus stop.

A month later, Eve gets home from work Saturday night. Doug isn't there. He doesn't show up on Sunday. Monday evening, he walks in after work. She doesn't ask for an explanation, and he doesn't offer one. He naps on the couch until after dark while she watches movies on TV. She rises to go to bed, thinking he's still asleep. Then he speaks.

"Me and some of the guys at work are takin' off next week. Don't have much scheduled, so some of us decided to take a cruise. We're leavin' for Florida this Thursday after work and drivin' all night. Cruise leaves Saturday and comes back the next Saturday."

"Just a bunch of guys goin' on a cruise?"

"Yeah, well, there's four of us going. Bill and Girdy think they're gonna find chicks on board and get laid every night, but me and Josh just wanna get away and relax for a while. None of us ever been on a cruise before."

Wednesday night at Jerry's, Eve sees Vic come in and point her out to the hostess. *Great.*

"Hi, Vic. What brings you to a dry place like this, all the way across town?"

"Hey, Eve. Heard you was workin' here and wanted to come see for myself. How long you been here?"

"Around six months. I like it. Get to talk to people more than I did at Hardee's. Like this."

"Yeah, I heard about your mom goin' crazy on you over there. She's still a nutcase, ain't she? It's a good thing we got you outta her house when we did."

"Yeah, it was a bad scene. What can I get you?"

"Just a burger and fries." She opens her coat to reveal the neck of a small bottle protruding up from an inner pocket. "Brought my own beverage."

*I could've guessed that.* "I'll put your order in."

When Eve sets her plate on the table, Vic says, "So, you're on your own next week, huh?"

"Oh, you heard about Doug and his buddies goin' on a cruise?"

"Yeah, but it ain't just him and a couple buddies, you know."

"He told me some guys from work are going. I know some of those cruises are set up for bigger groups from around town."

"Yeah, well this ain't no group. Val told me she was goin' to Iowa to visit her cousins next week with her Mom. I found her cruise ticket yesterday. After all Doug's done to help you stay above water, I'd have sure thought you'd do way more to keep that boy satisfied. You oughta be wearin' him out. Like you actually wanted to keep him home in your own bed. I showed you a lot back in the day. I *know* ya know how. What's the problem?"

Eve stares at her.

"Oh, you didn't know Val was going? Well, I hate to be the one to break the news, but, they been spendin' an inordinate amount a time together. Not sure how you coulda missed that. I haven't. Now, when they get back, I think it'd be a great idea if you'd do a better job of takin' care of business with your man. Keep him home. I'd rather not feel like I have to make sure you get that done. But, then, I've always been willing to do whatever it takes to accomplish the mission. You know what I'm saying? I mean, *somebody's* gotta protect the goods. You'll fare a lot better in the end if *you* do it this time, if you get my drift." Vic scoots her chair back. "Well, Eve, it seems like talkin' about that cruise ruined my appetite. I ain't hungry anymore. Here's five bucks for the burger. You eat it." Vic brushes harder than necessary against Eve as she walks past and Eve stumbles back a step.

That night, Doug is in bed when Eve gets home. She sleeps on the couch and in the morning pretends to stay asleep until he leaves for work. She heads for the restaurant before he returns to pack and pick up Val for their trip.

Friday night, she can't sleep; random fragments flit through her mind at their whim – scenes, real and imagined. Pictures of Doug and Val lying by a pool in the sun, holding hands. *I don't care. Doug and I never had a future, anyway.* Pictures of Vic at night, behind a tree, waiting to pounce as she approaches unsuspectingly. Pictures of Etta climbing the counter to grab money out of the cash register. Pictures of Brent waving to her at Knollenberg's. *I have to change my life.* Pictures of driving a red pickup truck toward a precipice. *Get Brent back.* Pictures of Gil Bartolo pulling off the bed sheet. *It feels so good to die.* Pictures of Tom Stanton sitting beside her on the bench during first-grade recess. *Gran, you made me come back to this. Help me.*

She rises at dawn Saturday morning, feeling drugged. She drinks coffee, goes for a walk, nibbles at breakfast, and tries to make the clock spin faster so she can go to work, all through a haze. She arrives at work a half-hour early, yet is a step behind all night. Orders are taken wrong. Amounts are written and totaled incorrectly. She has to ask customers to repeat their orders. She drags closing out, misses her bus, and has to wait half an hour in the dark for the next one. She's exhausted when she arrives home yet, again, does not sleep.

During the night, Eve formulates a foggy plan to get Brent back and redirect her life. Monday morning, she'll be at Ray's office when it opens. She'll tell him she's going to get her own apartment within walking distance of the Kellermans' home. She's not touched a cigarette or alcohol since the accident. She's done with her old life – Doug and Val and Etta and Vic – leaving the negative influences behind, taking charge. She wants to start seeing Brent regularly, to become part of his life. There will be no stopping her. *I'm doing it. I'll convince Ray. I will be Brent's mother.*

Again at 6:15 on Sunday morning, she gives up on sleep and decides to get up. She rolls over one last time and falls asleep. She dreams the thoughts that skirted through her mind the night before: Doug and Val lost in bliss, Etta jumping on the counter like a monkey, Mary screaming, "She's not your mommy." She lurches, and her eyes spring open just as Vic jumps out from behind a tree, ax raised high. Shaking, she looks at the clock: 6:31. She repeats Saturday morning. The haze is even thicker, and today her hands quiver.

Her first table is a thirtyish couple with two children, a girl around six sitting by her father and a rambunctious boy of three tethered to a booster seat beside his mother. The water ripples in response to her shaking hand as she places their glasses on the table. She reaches too close to the boy as his flailing hand bumps hers, and she tips a glass over, spilling ice water on the girl's Sunday dress.

The girl immediately begins howling. The Dad, already aggravated by his son's unruliness, glares at her. "Jeez! How clumsy can you be? Get us a towel."

An hour and a half into her shift, she's carrying a tray of four meals out of the kitchen, concentrating on not twitching. Her right toe grazes the back of her left heel, setting her just enough off balance that the tray tips off her hand and crashes to the floor, dishes breaking, food and drink splattering. This time, it's the manager glaring. Randy is a good boss and usually understanding. For whatever reason, today he's in his own foul mood. "Get a mop, Eve. Hurry up!"

By 8:00, she's semi-recovered from the mishaps, but she's edgy and trying too hard. A half-dozen people have complained about her throughout the day as they've paid. Four men wearing team bowling jackets enter. They are bawdy. As Eve carries an order to a young couple, she sees the foursome being seated at another of her tables. They've obviously been trounced at their game and aren't in a congenial frame of mind.

Eve quickly wipes a table beside the one she's just delivered meals to and turns to take an order from the table beside the four men. It's a slow order, an elderly man and woman who can't decide what they want. They each finally decide they want meat loaf, green beans, and coffee. Eve turns to rush their order to the kitchen and hears one of the bowlers bawl out, "Hey! Is anybody ever gonna take our order?"

She quickly turns and says, "I'll be right back."

"You better be, you want any tip."

The four of them aren't any faster placing their orders than the couple at the adjacent table, but they're louder. As she leaves to place their order she hears, "She might be slow, but I do enjoy watchin' her walk away." Her face turns red, and her level of self-consciousness rises yet higher, knowing the men's voices carried throughout the restaurant.

The men complain about the food, the service, and the cheaters who beat them at bowling as the old man and woman at the adjacent table quietly pick at their meat loaf. The old man asks for a coffee refill. Eve brings the coffee pot, and with her back to the bowlers hears, "Aw, you're chicken shit. All talk."

Concentrating on controlling her shaking hand, she bends slightly to pour. She senses the bottom of her skirt wisp and feels fingers touch her thigh. She jerks and sloshes coffee past the rim of the cup and onto the table. It floods over the edge and spills onto the old man's lap.

"Ahhg!" He pushes himself up, scooting his chair back with his legs. The chair tips over and crashes to the floor as the bowlers snicker.

Randy runs out of his office and sees the old man bending with his hands on the front of his pants, coffee staining and steaming from below them, and Eve standing agape and flushed, holding the coffee pot.

"Are you all right, sir? Your meals are coming out of her check, and we'll replace those pants. Are you burnt? Eve, go home. Whatever's eatin' you today better be gone by Wednesday. We're short-handed tonight but better off without you. Go! Sir, are you all right?"

"I'm really sorry, sir," she mumbles.

"Go right now!"

She sets the pot down and runs out of the restaurant. She sits on the bench shuddering and waits for the bus, her expression distraught, her eyes wild.

## Chapter 21

Monday morning, after another sleepless night, Eve is in the shower at 6:00. She has difficulty functioning. *I have* got *to fix my life.* Have *to be Brent's mother. Today.* Make *Ray yield.*

At 8:50, she stands at the front door of Kellerman Insurance Agency, waiting for it to be unlocked. At 9:00 she hears the deadbolt click, opens the door, and walks in.

"I need to see Ray Kellerman."

"Do you have an appointment?"

"No."

"May I have your name?"

"Eve Kessler."

The receptionist's eyes widen. "Wait one moment. I'll let him know you're here."

Eve's eyes follow her down the hall. She goes into an office and closes the door. A minute later, the door opens and she hurries back to her desk. Still standing, she says, "Mr. Kellerman has appointments scheduled all morning. He asks that you call him this afternoon."

"No, I have to talk to him in person. I'll wait 'til he can see me."

"That won't be possible, ma'am. Mr. Kellerman has a full schedule today."

"I'm not leaving. Either you go tell him that, or I will."

The receptionist stares at her. "I'll give him your message."

This time, Ray follows her out of his office.

"Please, Eve. I'm very busy today. Can you call me tomorrow?"

"No. Today is it. You can't tell me Brent isn't important enough to rearrange an hour of your day. I'll wait, but I'm not leaving."

"All right. I can give you 15 minutes. June, please put everything on hold for me until I let you know. Come with me."

Eve follows him into his office, and he closes the door. Today, she cannot begin to control the shaking.

"Sit. Are you all right? You don't look well."

"I haven't got much sleep the past few nights. I'm okay."

"I asked you not to do this, not to come here. Why didn't you call?"

"You said I could call if I needed money. That's not why I'm here."

Ray closes his eyes and rubs his forehead with both hands. "Eve, nothing's changed. There's nothing I can do."

"Well, then, I'll have to do what I can do. But I *want* to be together with you on this. I'm taking charge of my life, Ray. I haven't had a drink or a cigarette since the accident. My psychiatrist released me last Christmas. I've been working full-time for over a year. And I'm going to get my own apartment. I don't make a lot, but I can afford a small place. Doug and I are done. I'm done with him. And Val. And Etta. All the people who keep pulling me back. But you're different. I *know* you want to do the right thing. And you *know* what's right. Even Mary. She's pulling me down, too, but not because she's bad. You and Mary are both good. If you and me work together, we can make her see it's worth another chance for Brent to have his mother. All you need to say is you'll try."

"It's not that simple, Eve. You don't understand how deep Mary's resentment runs. There's *no way* I can convince her to let you see Brent. Believe me, I've tried, and it almost broke up our marriage."

"You can't tell me you don't believe Brent and I should be together. Mother and son. I see it in you. You *know* it. And you want it to be that way. Maybe you *should* risk your marriage, if it comes down to that."

"No, Eve! What *I* think is right doesn't matter. There is no right. I won't destroy my wife!"

"But you're happy to destroy me?"

"No! You have to find your own strength. You've got it in you."

"I don't. Back when I had that accident, the only reason I lived was to be Brent's mother. Maybe you think I'm being dramatic. Maybe you can't understand, but I'm tellin' you, *that* thought is the only thing that made me live. And it's been a year and a half, and I've never been with him. I've seen him twice. Seen him for a minute. Couldn't come close. Couldn't hold him. And it ripped me apart both times. No. I don't have the strength. Brent is my *only* strength. If your son was taken from you, maybe you'd understand."

"Don't talk to me about losing sons. I know what it feels like."

"It's not the same. Eric was grown. He left on his own. You had him for eighteen years. You raised him."

"Not very well," Ray says introspectively. "But we lost him just the same. Might have even been harder after having him eighteen years."

"Try losing a baby. Then tell me that's easier."

"I *have*," Ray blurts.

Eve starts. "What?"

"Never mind. It has nothing to do with this."

"It's got *everything* to do with this! You're lying. You could *not* lose a child and still have done what you've done." Eve's voice is shrill.

"Calm down, Eve. This is why I didn't want you to come to the office."

"How the hell can I calm down? I'm tryin' to save myself with the last thread I've got. This is my *life*. Today! Right now! Don't you *lie* to me! You think I'm playin' some kind of game?"

Ray's voice cracks. "Please, don't do this. My thread's as thin as yours."

"Liar!"

"I've never lied to you, Eve. I've made promises I couldn't keep. But I've never lied."

"You're lying right now!"

His chest heaves, and he looks down at his desk. "I lost a baby son.... No, worse... I threw away a baby son."

"What are you talkin' about? Eric never said anything about a brother."

"Eric never knew."

"But, Mary? How could she do this? If *she* lost a baby, how could she shred a mother's heart like this?"

"I didn't say Mary lost a baby. I said *I* did."

"What are you saying?"

"Eve!" He is quaking. "Leave me to my own misery! It doesn't mean anything to you." He looks up, eyes pleading. "Forget I said anything."

"Forget it? You're destroying my life! If you really know what it's like...." She watches him struggle with control as much as she is. "No. I don't know what you're doing, but you never lost a child. You could *not* do this. Lies." She screams, "Liar!"

"I threw him away!" he bellows with a body-racking sob. "Aw shit," he adds in a painful whisper. "Nobody knows, Eve. Only me. And now, you. It was in Korea. I was stationed in Seoul. I had a son there. And I walked away. Ran away. I've never seen him. Never saw his mother after he was born. I just left them. I don't know if either of them lived or died. Don't know if they needed help. Don't know my son's name, only that the baby was a boy. She sent me a note the day he was born. And I've tried – *God* I've tried. Pushed it back, covered it over, told myself it never happened, that he wasn't mine, that she didn't love me anyway, that I didn't love her, that it really wasn't important, that women – unprincipled women – get deservingly left every day, that children get orphaned every day by the hundreds, that it really didn't matter. Liar? Yes. But not to you. I've lied to myself every day for the past twenty-four years. And lived with the guilt that I can't lie away."

"You and Mary were married then."

"Yes."

"Eric?"

"Mary was three months pregnant when I shipped out."

"And she doesn't know? So, you've been lying to her, too, all these years."

"Nobody knows, Eve. I never told anybody. I can't believe I told you."

"So, you're a fake. Pillar of the community. Big Christian. And I put my faith in *you*." She shakes her head. "You took the easy way out then, and you're doin' it again. Doesn't mean a damn how much you hurt anybody else, even if you care about 'em. Just screw 'em and take the easy way out. Now I see where Eric got it. I shoulda been talkin' to Mary all along. At least with her, you get what you see."

"I'm a tormented soul. I'm as lost as you."

"So, fix it. Do the right thing."

"What right thing? What was the right thing in Korea? A man can't have two wives and two families. I had to *choose* which wrong thing to do. Same damn thing now. You tell me I'm destroying you. I don't know. Maybe I am. What I do know is if I take your side, I'll destroy Mary. So, which wrong thing am I supposed to choose this time? I don't have any more control over my choice today than I did back then. I love Mary. I will not destroy her."

"Don't kid yourself. Mary wasn't on the top of your list then, and she isn't now. Ray Kellerman is at the top of your list, just like Eric Kellerman was at the top of his. Who would have been the big loser back then? Ray Kellerman, the big war hero who would come home to his pretty bride and new baby boy and take over the family business. Risk all that money and prestige? For what? Just to take responsibility for the child you created? You didn't have to do that, and you didn't."

"Same deal today. Mary'll survive. Your marriage might not. And what would that do to your precious prestige and your bank account? Ray Kellerman, get divorced? Good Christian Ray? No, that just wouldn't fit into the way things are – the way they *have* to be. Can't risk that. Not for so low a cause as doing the right thing. Not just to reunite a mother and son."

"Look. I tried everything in my power to make this work. You have no idea how hard I tried."

"I know it wasn't hard enough."

"I won't destroy Mary."

"I'll go to court, Ray. I'm his mother. I'm not as naïve as I was four years ago."

"It takes money for lawyers."

"I'm working. I can afford a lawyer. I have some money."

"I have way more. You'll lose. And not just your son. You'll lose everything."

"I'll tell everybody what you just told me. I'm serious. I'm done rolling over. I mean, I'm willing to work out something where we can raise Brent together, but my son and I *will* be part of each other's lives. Don't make me tell Mary about the son and lover you abandoned while she was waiting for you to come home to her and Eric."

"C'mon, Eve. Who do you think would take your word over mine with a story like that? *Nobody* would believe you. You, a desperate, mentally unbalanced girl who'll say or do anything to get back at us for having the audacity to see that our grandson is raised in a good home. You think any judge in the state would take Brent out of a wealthy, respected home and put him with a suicide-risk, alcoholic mother? It just won't happen! Don't make your life any more tragic than it already is. *It won't work!*"

"How can you *live* with yourself? You play God and ruin people's lives. You try to act like you care, maybe try to convince yourself, but you don't! I hope you truly believe in the justice the Bible talks about. And that Heaven's a place you'll *never* see! I hope you believe that deep down in your soul, and I hope it's tearing you apart."

"I gave up on living for myself a long time ago. I live for Mary and Brent. And Eric. Not me. I'm lost. But I'll do everything in my power to save them."

"So, you'll fight every move I make to see my son?"

"And win. I'll get you committed, if that's what it takes. I *know* how bad you wanted out of the psych ward. That place was utopia compared to living in a mental institution. Forever. Live your life, Eve. You can move on, knowing Brent will have everything he needs. Leave Richmond. Why don't you go to California and start over? I'll write you a check for five thousand dollars right now. You go away and *never* come back. Otherwise, you're gonna go under."

Eve feels herself crash. Lack of sleep and food, the events of the past few days, and the confusing conversation and person behind the desk are too much. She slumps. One final shot comes out without her willing it. "I've seen what growing up in your home did to Eric. I can't live with that for Brent. I *have* to change it."

"You can't."

"Gran says I *have* to." Eve is talking to herself more than to Ray. "It's the only reason I came back. She *couldn't* have been wrong."

"See there? That *proves* something isn't right in your head. Mary and I love that little boy. I'm not just doing this for Mary. And not for me. As hard as it is, I have to do this for Brent. You are on the verge of insanity, and you will *never* get Brent. *Take* the five thousand. I'll buy the plane ticket on top of that. Go today. Don't force my hand. Now, you tell me you'll do it."

Whatever is left of her strength collapses. She looks at the floor as Ray stares at her. She has nothing left. "I can't."

"If you don't tell me right now, I'll start proceedings for having you committed as soon as you walk out the door."

Defeat engulfs her. She no longer feels Ray's presence in the room – just her own... and desolation. She murmurs, "Gran, I can't do it. I'm coming home." After a minute, she gets up and stumbles out.

"Eve! Don't make it be like this!"

Ray's words do not register as she makes her way down the hall and out the door.

It's cold for November. Eve wears only a light jacket, but the thought of riding the bus home doesn't enter her mind. She has no conscious thought of anything. She walks in the direction of downtown and home beyond. When she passes a liquor store, she goes in. She comes back out carrying a brown paper bag concealing a fifth of vodka. Across town, she enters a grocery. She places a half-gallon of orange juice on the checkout counter and asks for a carton of cigarettes. Before the cashier begins to ring up the bill, something crosses her mind.

"Wait a minute." She lays the bottle in the bag on the counter and goes to the drug aisle. She returns and adds a bottle of sleeping pills to her purchases.

Back out in the cold, she shuffles home, cradling the grocery bag in one arm and clasping the bottle bag in her free hand. Entering the house shivering, she places her loot on the counter. She opens a cigarette pack, pops one half-out, and lays the pack on the table. She retrieves a glass from the cupboard, fills it – half vodka and half orange juice – and sets it beside the cigarette pack. She sits in front of the banquet and stares. After a while she rises, picks up the sleeping pills, and takes them up to the bedroom. She takes the cap off, digs the cotton ball out, and sets the open bottle on the nightstand. Then she gets a glass of water and places it beside the pill bottle. She goes back downstairs and sits in a different chair, across the table from the screwdriver and cigarettes, so she has to get up to reach them. She takes off her jacket. It's noon.

Eve becomes increasingly lethargic. Lack of sleep, coupled with the events of the past four days, leaves her unable to think coherently. *Just like Etta. No, you can't see Brent. Is she my mommy? Keep Doug in your bed. Over the cliff. I'll have you committed. Feels sooooo good. This never happened before... it's like an accident. All meaningless. Pointless to go on. Gran, I'm coming home.*

She sits motionless for hours. The sun goes down, and she sits on in the dark. As midnight nears, Eve braces herself and stands. The cigarettes and screwdriver are in the same place they were twelve hours ago. She staggers upstairs in the dark and sits on the bed. The moon shines through the window, lighting up the bottle of pills and glass of water on the nightstand beside her. She stares at the bottle for ten minutes, finally reaches down, picks it up with her right hand, closes her eyes, and leans slowly back onto the bed, her head propped on two pillows. She empties the contents of the bottle into her left hand and fingers the glass with her right.

## Chapter 22

Ohhhh, man! Here it is! Ecstasy! All the suffering gone!
Blasting through the tunnel.     Ever closer to the light.
Disintegrating into peace and love and joy.     One with all.
*Exactly* the same. Home!

Gran! This time I *see* her! She's looks exactly as she did
the last day I saw her alive, wearing the same clothes she wore
on the boat, with the late-afternoon sun shining over her
shoulder. I swoon at the sight of her radiant smile; her short,
white hair; the soft, lightly crinkled skin of her face; her radiant,
loving blue eyes. She glows like an angel.

Without touching, we share infinite love. We talk! Not
telepathically, but with words this time.

We reminisce about the scenes I saw from last time, the
scenes that she and Grandpa and I shared – the happiness. Then
we talk of my life after the accident, how each of the difficult
times had value in preparing me to deal with life. My perception
of what is happening vacillates.     One moment it all fits
magically, and I comprehend everything clearly.     Then, the
understanding evaporates. Then it returns. She helps me feel
more love for everyone I interacted with, shows me that the
difficulties they created didn't emanate from evil in their souls.

She already knows every detail of my life. She knows my
innermost feelings during each experience. Still, I sense that
talking about them is enlightening for us both. Each word we
speak intensifies the love and joy we feel in each other. We
relive every experience together as time stands still.

"Few people have the troubles you've had," she says. "Since you were here before, who did you find most challenging to love?"

"Ray. I was the most scared of Vic, the most betrayed by Doug, and the most hated by Mary. But Ray pushed me over the edge. He deceived me. I thought he was my anchor, the one person who, in the end, would care enough about me and Brent to bring us together. But he pulled the rug out from under me. He only cared about himself."

"Do you think your meeting with him yesterday is too fresh to evaluate this relationship clearly?"

"You're saying that in time, I'll overcome my negative feelings toward him and feel only love? It's hard to see that. I can feel love for everybody else. But, Ray?"

"But, you're here. And the *only* thing is love."

I frown. "I'm not supposed to be confused here."

"What will you do now?"

"I'm here."

"If you weren't, what would you do next? What *should* you do next?"

"I would never give up on being Brent's mother."

"What would you do next?"

"Talk to Mary. There has to be a way to get her to talk to me."

"Would you tell her about Ray's other family?"

"I don't know. I'd try get her to understand how committed I am to being a mother to Brent and to convince her that we could all be one family to Brent. But, if she didn't buy it, I don't know."

"Could you feel like part of Mary's family?"

"I think I could, that I'd like to."

"Even with Ray?"

"He said he was going to put me in an insane asylum. That he was starting the process as soon as I walked out the door."

"So, how would you deal with that?"

"Get to Mary first?"

"Would you like to try that?"

"Wait a minute, Gran. You got me to go back last time. It didn't work."

"I'm only asking if you'd like to try approaching Mary."

"It's too late. It's *really* too late this time. There are no doctors. I didn't even see myself. It's over, Gran. I'm dead. I'm dead."

"Do you want to raise Brent?"

"I wanted that more than anything."

"Do you still want that?"

"Yes, but....

"Would you like to try?"

"What? How?"

"Would you like to try?"

"Would you like to try?"

"Would you like to try? Would you like to try? Would you like to try? Would you like to try? Would you like to try? Would you like to try? Would you like to try? Would you like to try? Would you like to try? *Would you like to try? Would you like to try? Would you like to try? Would you like to try? Would you like to try? WOULD YOU LIKE TO TRY? WOULD YOU LIKE TO TRY? WOULD YOU LIKE TO TRY? WOULD YOU LIKE TO TRY? WOULD YOU LIKE TO TRY? WOULD YOU LIKE TO TRY? WOULD YOU LIKE TO TRY? WOULD YOU LIKE TO TRY? WOULD YOU LIKE TO TRY? WOULD YOU LIKE TO TRY?*"

*Light. Not quite so brilliant. Where is the intensity? Gran? Stiff and sore. Where am I? Would you like to try? Would you like to try? Would you like to try? Gran, where are you? Gran! Try? Try? Try? Gran?*

Eve cracks her eyelids and perceives the ceiling of Doug's bedroom. *What happened? How can this be?* She rolls her head toward the sunlit window and sees the full glass of water on the nightstand. Her hand is sticky. She raises it and finds remnants of a few partially melted sleeping pills. She props herself up and sees all of the pills from the bottle scattered on the bedspread beside her.

*A dream? Too real. So much like before. Vivid! Not fading like a dream. Real. Real. Real. Gran, I'll do it. I'll risk* everything!

Chapter 23

Eve glances at the clock. It's after 9:00. She feels well-rested. The shakes are gone, along with yesterday's despair. She gathers the sleeping pills and flushes them down the toilet, drinks a glass of orange juice, tosses the cigarette pack in the trash, and dumps the vodka down the drain. After showering and dressing, she walks to a newsstand and carries a newspaper back to the apartment. She peruses the classified ads, makes a call, and heads for the bus station.

The second-floor efficiency apartment is tiny, but it will be perfect. It's just two rooms and a bath, but it's furnished and has a private, outdoor stair from the sidewalk. There is no couch or any space for one, but there is a corner kitchen table with two chairs, a stove and refrigerator, a reclining chair facing a little TV, a bed, a wardrobe, and a dresser – more than enough to accommodate Eve and her meager belongings. It's cheap enough: a week's pay, $65.00 per month. Best of all, it's only two blocks from Brent.

A retired couple owns the house, and they live downstairs. They're gentle and friendly and remind her of Gran and Grandpa. Eve fills out the paperwork and pays them the required one-month deposit and first month's rent. The $6.37 she has left in her purse will have to last until Friday's paycheck.

To save on bus fare, she walks the two miles back to Doug's apartment stopping at a grocery store to pick up the biggest box she can handle. Jamming the box full, she lugs it to the bus station and rides back to her new home. She repeats the process twice more, carrying the empty box to Doug's and riding the bus with the box stuffed full. Aside from her clothes, her only possessions, she takes a pillow, the bed sheets, one towel and washcloth, milk, orange juice, cereal, crackers, bread, peanut butter, and lunch meat – *my due for the past five years.*

Before leaving Doug's apartment for the last time, she picks up the phone and dials.

"Jolt."

"Hi, Vic. It's Eve."

"Yeah?"

"I thought I should let you know, I'm movin' out. I got a place. I'm finished with Doug."

"So, this is what … the tenth time?"

"This is different. My decision this time. I signed a lease."

"Don't figure ya can compete with Val, huh. Well, you're probably right about that. I woulda thought you'd have been worried about me, though. That why you're calling? Tryin' to decide if you gotta go in hiding?"

"I don't care what you do, Vic. You can't do anything half as bad as what I've already been through."

"Yeah, you're probably right about that, too. Well, it wouldn't have been much of a fair fight, anyway. Better if I go after Douggie boy. He don't stand a chance, either, but it'll be more satisfying.

"So you're actually gonna try to take charge instead o' just reactin' to whatever shit rains on you? Well, hallelujah. I never really had it in for you, you know. Just wanted you to keep your tomcat away from the pussycat. But then, you and Tomcat never was much of a match. Better keep your radar up, though. He ain't never been able to just let any of it go by. He'll come sniffin' around. You wait."

"I'm leaving, Vic. I just wanted to tell you."

"We'll see how that works out. See ya 'round, kid."

After hanging up, Eve exhales, then inhales and picks up the box. She lays her key on the counter and scribbles a note. "I'm gone." She backs out the door and braces the box against the wall to pull the locked door closed. She hears a car door slam and purposeful footsteps approach from behind. Hefting the box, she turns and sees a police cruiser at the curb and a cop marching toward her.

"Eve Kessler?"

She eyes him. "Why?"

"Are you Eve Kessler?"

"Yes."

"Put the box down. I've got papers for you."

She stoops down, pulls her fingers out from under the box, and straightens.

"Here." He extends a hand, presenting an envelope. "You been served."

"What is it?"

"I'm sure you know better'n me. I'm just makin' sure it gets in your slippery little hand." He cocks his head and raises one eyebrow. "Before you bolt."

He turns and struts back to the cruiser, gets in, and starts writing notes without giving Eve another glance. She stares at the envelope from Wayne County Superior Court, and the shakes return.

She wants to take the notice inside and read it, but she's locked herself out. The last thing she wants to do is open it standing out here in the cold, letting the cop relish her reaction – undoubtedly his aim. She folds the envelope in half and sticks it in her coat pocket. Hoisting the box, she cuts across the grass, avoiding the direction of the cruiser.

On the bus she sits and fingers the envelope in her pocket. Halfway across town, she pulls it out, unfolds it, and stares at her name and the return address. After a minute she puts it back in her pocket, hand still trembling.

After lugging the box up the stairs and plopping it on the floor, she lays the envelope on the table and takes off her coat. She stands, looking down at it. The cop's words echo. "Here. You been served." *Commitment papers? A gift from Ray Kellerman. How does this work? You've been ordered to report to the State Hospital? To the police?* She'd thought the "white-coats" would sneak up from behind and bind her in a straightjacket. *Open it.*

Instead of tearing it, she decides to use a kitchen knife. *I brought two of them. They're in this box somewhere.* She begins meticulously sorting through the box, putting things away from the top down. Eventually, there is no avoiding picking up one of the knives.

She sits, holding the knife and staring at the envelope. *What if I don't open it? Lose it? Nobody even knows where I live. Maybe it will all blow over.* She picks up the envelope, carefully slits it, pulls out the three-page document, and unfolds it. Her eyes gravitate to the directive.

> By order of this court Eve Kessler is hereby restrained from intentionally being in the physical presence or general whereabouts of Mary Kellerman, Raymond Kellerman, or Brent Kellerman. Furthermore, said Eve Kessler shall at all times maintain a distance between her person and the forenamed persons and between her person and the Kellerman residence of not less than 500 yards. Violation of this order will result in the arrest of Eve Kessler with potential monetary fine of up to $5,000.00 and incarceration of up to 30 days in the Wayne County Jail. This restraining order shall remain in effect until such time as it may be modified or rescinded by subsequent order of this court. This court order may be appealed, and such appeal may be initiated by filing a request for hearing pursuant to this Order.

*So, this is how it begins. Five hundred yards? How far is that? A quarter of a mile? This apartment is surely closer than that. I'm already in violation. Thirty days' incarceration in the Wayne County Jail. And from there to the asylum.*

## Chapter 24

Wednesday morning, it's raining.  Dr. Burgmann didn't hesitate late Tuesday afternoon when Eve called from a pay phone.  If the rain hadn't stopped, bus fare to and from his office for the early-morning appointment and then later to work would have reduced the contents of her purse to less than $3.00.

Dr. Burgmann studies the document.  "And you just moved into an apartment yesterday that puts you in violation of this court order?"  She nods.  "But, you had no knowledge that the restraining order was about to be issued?  There was no intent on your part to beat or circumvent the order?"

She shakes her head.

"Well, legal action works at a snail's pace.  No matter what, you'll have thirty days before any enforcement action is initiated – *if* you stay away from the Kellerman residence or any place you have foreknowledge they'll be present.  Will you stay away?"

"Yes."

"From what I know about the situation, I believe the court would rescind the order if you pursue a hearing.  You've done nothing to endanger any of the three named, and you have no history of being violent or a threat to anyone."

"Except maybe Doug."

"There is no denying your life has been a struggle.  But, your leasing an apartment and holding a steady job would be in your favor.  It shows you're serious about controlling and improving your life.  And you *are* the boy's mother.  That in itself will carry a lot of weight."

"You think the judge might give Brent back to me?"

"Small steps, Eve. I think the Kellermans' filing of this action might work against them, if you fight it. It's very possible that the court could order that you be allowed regular, supervised visitation. The terms could be better than the Kellermans forced on you before. Small steps."

"How can I fight it? I'm down to my last five bucks. No way I can afford a lawyer."

"You don't need a lawyer. I'll go with you to fill out the paperwork requesting a hearing. The hearing is really nothing more than a fact-finding session for the judge. He'll want to understand the history. From your point of view, my records already document your circumstances fairly well, and if you're willing to let me turn them over to the court, I believe that would be in your favor. Beyond that, there will be testimony.

"You would have to do the best job you can of truthfully explaining some of your past actions. It would be important to stay calm and under control, and to dress well. You will need to identify some witnesses who know you well to help build your case. I'd be willing to be a witness for you. Maybe your boss at work would, too.

"Ray and Mary will also call witnesses. Their efforts – their lawyers' efforts – will be to paint you as unfit and dangerous to Brent. They'll bring up the accident, the fight between you and Doug, your past behavior: alcohol abuse and sexual promiscuity. They'll pull in witnesses who will emphasize the negative."

"Like who?"

"The doctors who saw you after your fight with Doug. The police. Your friends, Vic, Doug, and Val might all be witnesses for their side. Maybe even your mom, if they can find a way to drag her into court. It wouldn't be a pleasant experience for you. It would be very important for you to stay calm and in control of yourself."

"Would Ray and Mary be there?"

He thinks this over. "My guess is they won't be. Let the lawyers do all the dirty work. Actually, I suspect being present might work against them. Your trump card might be to make sure they're on the witness list. Require them to be there."

Eve's eyes grow wide. "I'd have to ask them questions? I wouldn't have a lawyer to do it."

"No. We just need to make sure we've given the judge all the questions we think they should be asked. He'll ask the questions he feels are pertinent for you."

"If I do this, how bad could it turn out? Ray and Mary keep saying they'll have me committed. Could I end up in an insane asylum?"

"Eve, they can't make that happen. I will not let that happen. The worst would be that the restraining order would remain in effect. Even then, the court wouldn't make you break your lease and move. I don't see that you have anything to lose. The Kellermans may have unwittingly helped you by getting this restraining order. You should do this, Eve."

"And you'll stand by me?"

He smiles at her. "How can you even ask that question?"

"I owe you everything, Dr. Burgmann. I suppose it's time I should apologize for the way I was with you back in the beginning. You know, in the hospital, after the crash."

"That's all in the past. Apology accepted, but let's concentrate on the future, shall we?"

She returns the smile. "Yes."

"When would you like to file?"

"Well, after Friday I'll have more bus fare. Could we do it next Monday morning?"

"I could work that in first thing Monday. And forget the bus fare. I'll pick you up. Wear the nicest and most conservative dress you have."


On Friday evening, Eve takes a cutomer's order to the kitchen and reenters the dining room. Two people draw her attention. The first is a man who has just been seated facing away from her. Shaggy, dark blond hair hangs over his collar nearly to his square, solid shoulders. Something is familiar about him. *What is it?*

Before she can pursue that thought, outside the window, a wiry woman slams the passenger door of her jalopy, riveting Eve's attention. *Etta!*

Eve spins around and runs to Randy's office, entering without knocking. She doesn't wait for his surprised face to issue a question.

"Quick! There's gonna be trouble! You gotta stop it before it blows up."

"What the...?"

"There's a woman coming in, and she's gonna make a huge scene. Get her out!"

Randy jumps up and dashes out of his office. Eve picks up the phone. She hears the commotion as she's talking.

"Can I help you?"

"I need ta see Eve."

"She's busy right now. What can I do for you?"

"Bullshit!" Etta yells. "I just saw 'er in the window. She ain't busy. Get 'er."

"Hold on a minute, ma'am. We're not going to have any trouble here. You step outside, and I'll see if I can get Eve."

"You sumbitch. Get outta my way. I saw 'er go that way. Friday's payday, and she owes me money. I'm gittin' it."

Etta steps right to bypass Randy, and he steps left to block her.

"Mother!"

Etta freezes and gapes at Eve, who has just entered the room.

"Don't call me that. You ain't no daughter."

By now, every head in the restaurant is turned toward the fracas.

"Mother, the police are on the way. I don't know what you want, but this is *not* the place."

"You called the cops on *me*? No way. You'd be too scared they'd take *you*. And don't you ever call me that again! You owe me rent. I want it. Now."

"For what? I haven't even *been* to your house since Christmas, and that was only for five minutes."

"You lived in my house a lotta years. And that trust thing of yours ran out when you was eighteen. For all the nights you spent in my house, and cause half of 'em you was sleepin' with my man. That's what for. You owe me at least ten grand. I want half of every paycheck, startin' t'day. Don't care where you git the money. Best bet's git it outta that cash register, like ya always done before."

Eve looks beyond Etta's shoulder. "The police are here."

"Give me the money!" Etta screams.

Randy booms. "That's enough! In ten seconds, you're gonna be arrested for creating a public disturbance. You've got five to get out of here before the police walk in. Go!"

Etta glares at Eve. "I'll git you fer this." She wheels and runs out.

Eve exhales and puts a hand on the checkout counter to steady herself. "I'm sorry, Randy. She's pulled this before. Got me fired from my last job. I didn't know what to do, so I called the cops."

Randy raises an eyebrow at her. "Your mother?" Eve looks back at him hopelessly. "You did the right thing, Eve."

The police walk in as Woody guns his rattletrap out of the parking lot. Jerry looks in the general direction of the dining room and says, "Sorry, folks. It's all over. Nothing that crazy woman said is true. Please, go back to your meals." He looks at Eve and murmurs, "You okay? Can you work after that?"

"I'll be fine."

Two policemen are standing beside them. Randy says, "Would you want to step into my office? I can give you a rundown. We'll call Eve in if we need her."

Eve looks at the floor for a moment and takes a deep breath, trying to compose herself. She looks up to see the familiar-looking man turned toward her in his booth, grinning. His full beard hides his face but the eyes, sad eyes, even with the grin, make her heart leap.

He nods his head in the direction Etta departed and says, "Some things never change, huh."

*Tom!*

## Chapter 25

She doesn't get off until 11:30, but beginning at 10:00 Eve can't keep her eyes off the door and parking lot. Tom didn't order anything. He said she'd already had too much distraction and him being there would only make the rest of her shift harder. He asked if he could pick her up after work, get a cup of coffee, talk.

Even after the scene with Etta, Eve has never been as enthralled at work as she is tonight. She can't remember *ever* feeling so overcome with anticipation. Her past doesn't matter. What his commitments might be don't matter. Just being with him, even for the short minute before he left, was the world. *He felt it, too. I know it!*

Randy is helping the evening crew clean up. He glanced at Eve when he followed the policemen into his office, and he saw the beginnings of the exchange between Tom and her. Watching her work the rest of the evening, he's read between the lines.

Headlights shine into the parking lot at 11:20, and Eve almost leaps. She looks at Randy. "You've had a tough night," he says. "Why don't you knock off?"

In a matter of seconds she retrieves her purse and coat and runs out the door. Tom drives a pickup, a work truck. Eve races to the truck. By the time she reaches it he's jumped out, rounded it, and opened the passenger door for her. She climbs into the spotless cab that smells of fresh furniture polish and waits for him to enter from the driver's side. They lock eyes. They wrap their arms around each other and bury their faces. For ten minutes, they don't speak as tears trickle down their faces.

Finally, they break and look at each other.

"Tom."

"I have no idea where to begin," he says.

She looks into his sad eyes and whispers the thought that's tugged at her all evening. "Are you married? Family?"

He shakes his head. "You? I heard you had a baby back in school. A boy."

"Tom, you wouldn't believe the way my life has gone. Yeah, I have a son. He's the only thing I've lived for... but I haven't been with him for three years. It's a long, terrible story. No, I never got married."

"My life hasn't been anything like I ever could have imagined, either."

"I see it in your eyes. What happened?"

"Also a long, terrible story. Tonight, right now, I only care about one thing. I'm here with you. And it feels like heaven."

"It does."

"Where can we get a cup of coffee?"

"In Richmond? This town rolls up the sidewalks at ten. We don't have to go anywhere. I could talk to you all night, right here." She smiles at him. "I don't think we could find anyplace that's cleaner or smells better, anyway. So, how long did it take you tonight to clean this thing up?"

"Well, it needed it pretty bad. You shoulda seen it when I drove in here for dinner earlier."

"Where did you drive from? I haven't seen you around town since high school?"

"Indy. I'm a surveyor. For a couple years now. I was in the Air Force for a while. Nam. Spent a little time gettin' patched up when I got back. Then tech school on the GI bill for a year. I guess I took surveying to be outdoors. Anyway, there's my life."

"That doesn't touch your life, Tom. Vietnam? Patched up? Tell me about it."

"Another time. If you'll let me have another time. What about you? Tell me about your life."

She looks down. "I'm not sure you'd like me much if you knew it all. You might run. If you're in your right mind, you would."

"You know I told you a long time ago I'd never do that." Silence. "I've always wondered, Eve. Back at the beginning of the seventh grade. For a while, I was sure you fell for some big shot high-schooler. But I watched you some, and it didn't show that way. At least, not for a while. I never could figure out what happened."

There's a light knock on the passenger window. It's Randy. Eve rolls her window down. "Everything okay? I thought you two were going off somewhere, but you're still here. I'm the last one out and I'm leaving. Just wanted to check on you."

"Randy, this is Tom Stanton. He was my best friend in grade school. Best friend I've ever had, really. We haven't seen each other since high school, and I couldn't believe it when I saw him tonight."

"Well, it's good to meet ya, Tom. And, for whatever it's worth to you, giddy is about the last word I would've ever used to describe Eve. Until tonight. And even after that episode with that crazy woman – Mother, I think is what you called her – I'll put it this way, Tom: I hope tonight's not the only night you come around. I kinda like seein' her giddy. Good for business."

"I like seein' her giddy, too, Randy. But, I tell you, I don't think I do half for her what she does for me."

"Okay, then. Well, I'd stay and chat longer, but I have a feeling this chat's gonna last till sunup, and my wife wouldn't take too kindly to me walkin' in tomorrow morning. G'night."

"Giddy, huh?" Tom beams.

"Like you said. Heaven."

"Beyond."

"Would you hold me some more?"

They share another ten-minute embrace. Without letting go or lifting her head from his shoulder she says, "I should have told you. I knew how much I hurt you. But, I couldn't do it. Not sure I can do it now." She stops to avoid talking over the lump rising in her throat.

"It's okay, sweetheart. You don't have to. I learned to live without knowing. I'm okay. Right now, way, way better than okay."

"Tom, it wasn't you. I guess this is where a person's supposed to say, 'it was me.' But, it wasn't me, either. And it wasn't some other boy. I could never, ever have done that. I loved you so much."

Silence.

"You remember Etta's old boyfriend, Gil?"

"Etta? You mean, 'Mother'?" He grins. "Yeah, how could I forget Gilberto? He was a brute. Seemed dangerous. I didn't like you being in the same house. He still around?"

"Nope. Got blown to smithereens in the downtown explosion. I count that as one of the better days of my life."

She sees anger start to build in his eyes..

"What did he do to you?"

"Don't go gettin' all crazy. You can't get him for me. He's already dead."

"Good thing. Probably keep me from goin' to prison."

"I think you're getting the picture."

"That sonofbitch *raped* you? Before school started? Before seventh grade? You were twelve, for God's sake! And when I was gone... I couldn't even help you. You couldn't even tell me."

"You weren't gone. You were back."

"But, we only got back the night before school started. Around midnight.... That night?"

"No. That morning. A half-hour before I had to be at school. Told me I was goin' into junior high. It was time I learned what made the world tick."

Tom crashes his fist on the vinyl dash. It cracks. "No, no, no, no, *NO!*" he shrieks.

"Don't, Tom," she whispers and caresses his neck. "It was a long time ago. A different life. I wish I would've been able to handle it, but I wasn't. I let it rip us apart. I was too weak."

"You were a twelve-year-old girl! Why didn't I see it? Right when you needed me more than ever, I did exactly what I told you I never would. I abandoned you!"

"You couldn't have done anything. It wasn't your fault. Wasn't really my fault, either. I've come to believe that sometimes bad things like that aren't really anybody's fault. They just happen. It wasn't Gil's fault he grew up on his own on the streets of Houston and became what he was. There wasn't much he could do to crawl out of the hole he was born in. It just happened, Tom. And I just wasn't equipped to rise above it. But, it sure ruined everything."

"Eve," he cries. They cleave to each other for a long time as more tears stream.

Finally, Eve speaks. "Well, I've cried my soul out tonight, but the whole time I've felt better than I've felt since the last day we walked down by the river. I'm a complete wreck, but I'm really, really happy. How long you in town?"

"For the weekend. I was gonna surprise Mom tonight, but I found you first. She doesn't know I'm back yet. You wanna go for a walk in the morning? Down along the river, like we used to? It's supposed to be pretty warm for November."

"Yes."

He squeezes her tighter. "You wanna go to church with me Sunday?"

"Yes. You remember that last walk along the river? Remember how we felt?"

"God, do I ever."

They spend the next hour reminiscing. After that, the next thing Eve is aware of is the sun shining through the window. Her face is snuggled in Tom's coat, and her hand is on his chest. His arm is around her shoulder. She inhales, smelling him, and presses her hand to him. He pulls her tighter. She looks up to see him smiling at her.

"You been awake long?"

"I don't sleep much. Way better watching you sleep, anyway."

"Do you need to see your folks this morning?"

"I should go surprise Mom. Make her fix me breakfast. She'll love it."

"You gonna tell them we talked?"

"Don't see how I can help it. I won't be able to think about anything else."

"I don't know what they'll think, Tom. If they know anything about me, they might not be happy."

"It's just Mom. We lost Dad to a heart attack three years ago. But, believe me, she'll be happy. How about if I pick you up around ten? I'll bring a picnic. We can hang out by the river, and then I'll take you to work."

By mid-morning Saturday, it's 60 degrees and sunny. They lay the blanket and food basket in their old favorite talking spot and walk along the river for an hour, holding hands. After returning and eating, Tom lies on his back, and Eve puts her head on his chest and an arm on his shoulder.

"So, what happened after?" Tom asks. "Was it only that one time, or did it go on?"

"It went on." She tells him bits and pieces of her life: how she fell in with Val, how Val and Vic got her away from the abuse, how she got involved with Eric, gave birth to Brent, lived at the Kellermans'... some of her relationship with Doug. She holds back the harder parts.

"Okay, there's mine." She teases him. "Now yours."

"I was born on December twenty-forth nineteen-fifty-one...."

"I have to be at work at three."

"The date is important. My life turned on it. It was a bad day for the seventy-one draft. Number two. You know Dad was career Air Force, and there was no way I was going to run from serving my country. I don't care if everybody else *was* protesting and running. Not me. When my number came up so high, I joined the Air Force.

"The war was winding down, at least for the U.S. But, the fighting wasn't over by a long shot. We didn't have ground troops anymore, but we had advisors and lots of air engagement. I was on a medevac team. A lot happened, but all that really matters is I lost my best friend. Three friends."

"You mean...?"

"Yeah."

"How'd it happen? Were you there? Saw it? Were you hurt?"

"Yeah."

"You wanna talk about it?"

"No," he whispers.

## Chapter 26

Monday morning on the way to the courthouse, Eve tells Dr. Burgmann about her weekend. For a minute, she describes the scene with Etta and then spends the rest of the time talking about Tom. She finishes by telling him about Sunday, how she'd gone to church with Tom and his mother, Janet, and then spent the afternoon with them until she had to go to work. "It was my best three days since I was eleven. And he'll be back Wednesday night for the Thanksgiving weekend!"

They file the paperwork, including service notifications for their only two requested witnesses, Ray and Mary Kellerman. The hearing is set for 9:00 a.m., Tuesday, December 16, 1975, in Courtroom Number 2.

Tom picks Eve up at work Wednesday night. They go to her apartment to pick up clothes, and then on to Tom's mother's house, where Eve will stay until she has to go to work on Friday. On the way she tells Tom about the hearing.

"The hearing is to get a restraining order against your being near Brent lifted? I'm thinking maybe you left out some parts of your life story."

"Some parts you wouldn't want to know."

"I want to know everything about your life. And I'm coming to the hearing."

She envisions the worst. *Doug and Val. And Vic. Etta. The Kellermans. All bashing me and what I've done.* "I'll be fine. Dr. Burgmann will be there. Don't take off work."

"I'm never letting you down again, Eve. Whatever happens, I'll be right beside you. If you've got nothing else, you've got me."

"Please, Tom. Don't come back just for that. Dr. Burgmann is pretty sure everything will turn out good."

"You tell me Brent is your reason for living, that you haven't been with him for three years, and that this hearing might change that... if things all go the way you hope? But, that I shouldn't take off work and drive all the way to Richmond just for that? I'll be there, Eve. Right by your side." They pull in the drive, and he shuts off the motor. "And I've made another decision. I'm moving back in with Mom. She'll be thrilled. There's plenty of survey work in Wayne County. I *will* be by your side."

Eve looks away and is silent. Finally, she whispers, "There's a lot about me you don't know. You shouldn't change your life because of me."

"I gave my two-week notice this morning. I'm coming back."

She takes a deep breath. "All right," she says to herself aloud. "Don't be dishonest with him." She turns wary eyes to him. "Here's what I left out last Saturday. There's a lot."

She begins on the first day of seventh grade, telling the full story of her life. He tries to interrupt at first, but she shushes him. Eventually, he stops trying. After half an hour, the back door to the house opens and Janet walks toward the truck. He rolls down the window. "We're just talking, Mom."

"It's after midnight! And it's freezing out here."

"Leave a light on. We'll be in after while."

She throws her arms up and turns toward the house.

"Hey! I love you, Mom."

"I love you, too. I'm goin' to bed."

"G'night!"

Eve continues for another hour. She tells him everything except that she knows Ray had an illegitimate son, and except that for two and a half minutes she died. And went to heaven.

"So, now you know why I lost Brent. You know I've been a falling-down drunk. I've had sex with half the guys in Richmond. I've been in a mental ward – for tryin' to kill myself. I've been declared an unfit mother who isn't allowed to go near her son." She looks at the floorboard and whispers, "I'm my mother. Worse. Don't give up the life you've struggled to make for yourself for a lost cause."

"You are *not* your mother. I've *seen* her, remember? I'm moving back in two weeks. I'm going to your hearing. I will never leave your side. *Never.* "I can't fathom how you've been able to tough it out through the life you've been dealt. It'll take me a while to sort through everything you've told me tonight. But, I already know two things. First, you're way stronger than me. And second, nothing you can ever do or say will ever shake me loose.

"Now, it's really late and it's really cold, and I'm taking you in the house. And you're stuck here with us until I take you to work on Friday. So buck up."

The Saturday before the hearing, Tom moves into his mother's house. Eve helps in the morning. Janet won't stop expressing adoration of Eve for concocting this miracle. Tom takes Eve to work, then at 11:00 picks her up and drives her to her apartment.

Eve makes coffee for them – decaf for Tom. She doesn't want to do anything to inhibit his sleeping. She knows how tired he is, and she knows he doesn't sleep well – never gets a good night's sleep.

His eyes begin to droop as they sit.

"I'm not sleepy," she says. "I'm going to turn the TV on low. Why don't you go lie down in my room? Sleep for a while. At least rest."

"Okay. I'm really beat. Don't let me sleep longer than a half-hour." He kicks his shoes off, and she leads him into the tiny bedroom. He lies down. She sits on the bed beside him and strokes his hair. In five minutes, he's asleep. She goes back to the main room, leaving the bedroom door open, turns on *The Tonight Show* with the sound barely audible, and sits in the chair. She drifts off.

An hour and a half later, Eve leaps out of the chair to the bursting of shrieks from the bedroom. She races to Tom's side. He bolts upright, eyes bulging, and screams, "Get back! No! No! No!"

"Tom!"

He grabs for something on his shoulder but grasps nothing. He slaps around for it again and again. "Kill you all! Damn you! Rip your insides out!"

"Wake up, Tom! Wake up! It's me, Eve."

He lurches in her direction, catches his toe on the lower bedpost, and sprawls headlong onto the floor.

She drops to his side and touches his shoulder. "Tom, are you all right?"

"Awwhhh. Aw, man. Ouch." He rolls partially onto his side, twists his head so he can see her, and blinks twice. "Aw, man. Nightmare. So real. Like yesterday."

"Are you hurt?"

"Can't tell. Hurts the same as then. Don't know what hurt's real and what's not."

"Can you roll over? Lay your head in my lap?"

Silence. He closes his eyes and then slowly rolls over onto his back. She unfolds onto the floor, lifts his head, and slides under him, leaning her back against the wall. She strokes his forehead.

"You wanna tell me about it?"

He heaves a sigh, closes his eyes, and heaves another. "It was hell, Eve. You should *never* have to hear it."

"If it happened to you, I want to live it with you – at least help you live with it."

"Believe me, you don't want to live it."

"Tell me."

He takes a deep breath, then takes another. "I can't."

Silence.

"It started on April sixth of seventy-two. No, it really started on the fifth, late afternoon. I was at Camp Holloway in Pleiku. In Nam. Got a telegram delivered around four in the afternoon. It was my dad. Heart attack that morning. He was gone.

"The best friend I told you about was with me when I got the note. Barry Wizen. Next to you, he was the closest thing I ever had to a soul mate. Wisp of a guy, 'specially after boot camp, but man, did he have heart."

Tom moves his head back and forth in her lap and blinks. She sits silently, watching his eyes and holding him.

"He was from Texas, and we hit it off from day one. Similar backgrounds. Liked the same things. Had each other's back. After surviving boot camp, we both went to training for support and rescue – helicopter teams. The instructors liked us... you know, hard-working, loyal, energetic, committed guys. They pulled some strings and got us sent the same place. Right after New Year's, we landed together at Pleiku. Got assigned to a Huey support team. The other guys on the team were Dennis Clanton and Darnell Thomas. Great team. Great men.

"We never really saw much action before April. Made a lot of supply deliveries. Transported some wounded Vietnamese soldiers to hospitals. Barry and me were the rookies. Never saw any battlefield action. Denny and Darnell'd been in some scrapes, but nothing where they were ever close to goin' down. In early seventy-two everything was s'posed to be winding down.

"Anyway, I read the telegram, and Barry sees it's bad. I tell him, and he makes me report it and get set up to go home for the funeral. I got scheduled to fly out first thing on the seventh.

"Couldn't sleep much that night. Always slept like a baby before that. Never have since that day. So, I got up around five and was gonna start puttin' stuff together for the trip home. Before I got my teeth brushed, our team got ordered to make a supply delivery and extract wounded Vietnamese soldiers from a hole near the Cambodian border... Loc Ninh. It was a makeshift base beside a little town. They'd had a reconnaissance company ambushed by Viet Cong the day before. We didn't know it yet, but it was the start of the North's Easter Offensive.

"Denny took us in around mid-morning under crazy fire. I couldn't believe what was happening. We couldn't get near the airfield – missiles and bullets flyin' everywhere. Command was tellin' us to get in any way we could. We had a half-dozen advisors in the camp, and we needed to be ready to get 'em out. We had Spectre fighters and Cobra choppers blasting the Viet Cong at the airstrip, and they covered us while we dove into the compound. I don't know how, but Denny got her down without takin' any hits.

"We dumped the supplies and tried to figure out who we were supposed to take out. Shells were explodin' all over the place. We finally figured out our advisers were the ones in charge. The gist of it was the Vietnamese commander, Colonel Vinh, never did want to fight and wanted to surrender right from the start. But, our advisers would have none of that and took over. They weren't leaving. Told us to get ten soldiers that were bein' hauled out of the bunker hospital on stretchers into the Huey and get out. So we hightail it back to the chopper, duckin' and swaying every time we hear a blast, thinkin' we'll probably never reach the Huey. But we did. We get the stretchers secured in about ten seconds, and Denny's takin' 'er up. You wouldn't think a guy could dodge a chopper around, but it was like Denny wasn't dodgin' just missiles, he was skirtin' around machine gun fire. He was good. Did everything humanly possible. More. It just wasn't gonna happen.

"When Barry and me heard glass and steel gettin' ripped to shreds, we dove down among the stretchers. The chopper swung up on its side in a one-eighty back to the compound. I jerked around to see the cockpit and couldn't see Denny, but there was Darnell – already dead. I saw him. Knew it was him. But there was no face."

Tom stops talking and clamps his eyes shut. After a minute, he goes on.

"I puked. I could tell Denny was still trying. We were pitchin' and weavin'; but we weren't out of control. We hit the ground hard, but right-side up, and the engines cut. I looked out the front and saw we were back in the compound. We probably hadn't been off the ground a minute, but it seemed like hours. I still couldn't see Denny, but Barry could. And I could see Barry. And he was turnin' green. I yelled at Denny to see if he was okay. 'Get these guys outta here!' he says. 'Then get under cover. Go!' I yell at him, 'You okay, man?' And he kind of croaks back at me. 'I'm done. Go.'

"Barry and me ram the door open and start runnin' the stretchers back to the hospital bunker. There's nobody to help. Everybody's already got more than they can handle. I can't look at the cockpit while we're haulin' these guys back. After the last one's delivered, I run back to the Huey and look in. Then puke again.

"Barry's standing back, waiting for me to turn around. When I do, he says, 'C'mon. Let's find out what we're supposed to do.' We find one of the American advisors who looks almost crazy himself, and we ask. He wants to know how long we been in Nam. Three months. Wants to know if we ever used the M-16s on our shoulders on human beings. Nope. Tells us to go help in the hospital bunker and do whatever they tell us. And get it in our heads that it's gonna come down to kill or be killed. Says we got about twelve hours to decide which it's gonna be. He was pretty much right.

"The hospital bunker's pathetic. We spend half our time carryin' out the dead. The rest of the time, we're trying to stop blood from running out or holdin' guys down while they're gettin' stuff done they'd rather die than have done. All the while, gunfire and explosions all over the place above us. But there's no time to think about that. No time to even wretch, which seemed like what we needed.

"By ten it's too dark to see, and they tell us to go find someplace to rest – we're gonna need it. I don't know why, but it takes us a while to leave the hospital hole. We try to give a little comfort to some of the guys we worked on. There were around a hundred-fifty left alive in there. We hoped we'd saved some of 'em, maybe comforted them a little. It was hard to leave. I don't know, maybe we were just scared to get up on ground level.

"Anyway, we finally run out and crouch and dodge our way toward where we think the command center must be. We get about halfway there, and...." He stops talking again, shakes his head, and swallows. "And there's a huge explosion behind us – knocks us down. We look back and see there'd been a direct hit on the hospital bunker. Parts flyin' through the air."

He stops for another minute, and then goes on. "Killed everybody there. Everybody we thought maybe we saved that day. The guys we'd just been talkin' to. All the medics. The only thing I wished right then was that I was still back there. I didn't want any more.

"We laid on the ground for a minute. Couldn't believe what we just saw. Then Barry says, 'Let's go,' and he gets up and pulls me up, and we start runnin' again, but no dodging. Just ran straight up as fast as we could. Right before we reach the building, there's what seems like a nuclear explosion. This time, the hit was on the munitions store. From that point on, there was no order. Just chaos.

"Nobody's got time to deal with two green airmen who don't have a clue. We find a barracks that's ninety percent empty and huddle in a corner so if somebody does come back, they won't find us in their bed. We're physically exhausted and emotionally dead. We try to sleep, but there's no way. Before it gets light, Barry says we both know there's only one way. We're probably gonna die today. We're American soldiers. We go down fighting.

"I bury the part of me that says I've got nothing more against these boys that're trained to kill me than they've got against me. I signed up for this. Time to man up.

"So, we ready our weapons and go out and join a group of Vietnamese soldiers. The sun's comin' up. There's a commotion on the flag platform. It's bizarre. Colonel Vinh and most of his Vietnamese officers had just ran out of the compound to surrender. Their executive officer had stayed behind and was bare-chested on the platform. He's trying to pull the flag down, but one of the American advisors is fightin' him over it. He gets it lowered and replaces the flag with his white undershirt, and tries to raise the white shirt to signal surrender. And the soldiers we're standing with all start takin' their shirts off so the North won't be able to tell officers from grunt soldiers, 'cause they just shoot captured grunts on the spot. The American and the officer are still shouting and fighting as the white shirt's goin' up. And then the American pulls out his pistol, points it at the South Vietnamese officer, and kills him.

"The shirt comes down, and the flag goes back up. The American advisor shouts an order, and the soldiers put their shirts back on. The next thing we know, the Viet Cong are storming into the compound from the south. Air power and the group of soldiers Barry and me are with force them back out. We're in the middle of the pack and don't really see or do much.

"At around five the Viet Cong are stormin' the compound from everywhere. Barry and me charge near the front of a group this time. Out of nowhere, a young woman – looked more like a girl, really – runs around a corner straight at us, and she's holding onto a little baby for dear life. For a split second, all I can see is you. You and your little baby boy. Then, around the corner come the Viet Cong, machine guns pointed at her.

"Barry yells out, 'No!' and takes off and dives around her and takes the bullets."

Tom stops again. His eyes are wide open. He's frozen.

"That's enough," Eve murmurs. "Don't go on."

"He dives around to take the bullets," Tom says again. "Takes a lot of 'em. So does the girl. And the baby. The three of 'em are just a pile of ripped-apart flesh and blood and gore.

"Now, I'm nothin' but hate. I'm not a human being. Not any kind of creature. I'm just this all-consuming mass of hate. I open up on the soldiers comin' at us and kill as many as I can. One thought – no, not even a thought. Just kill, kill, kill.

"Then my legs go out from under me, and I go down as two hordes of rage on feet smash into each other. The last thing I feel is something pounding on my head, trying to crush it."

He takes a deep breath as he stares at the ceiling and then goes on with less difficulty.

"It was two days till I came to. I guess somebody saw I was American and figured I was worth more as a live negotiating piece than a dead one. I'd taken two bullets to my left thigh, another above the left ankle that shattered bone, and one just above my right knee. Two'd gone through, but one of the thigh shots and the ankle shot were lodged. My face was a mess from being beat with a gun butt or stomped – broken jaw and concussion.

"I was in a locked log cage in a prison camp in Cambodia. Kratie. Chained. Like I was gonna do anybody any damage. Before I came to, somebody had set my jaw. In a few days I could eat a little – enough to stay alive, but that's about it. They let the bullet wounds fester until I got delirious with fever. Then they tried to interrogate me. Hadn't tried before that. Waited till I didn't know up from down. It took them two days to figure out I didn't know anything and wasn't going to give them propaganda fodder, no matter how bad off I was.

"So then, they let a doc start treatin' my wounds. They took out the bullets and gave me penicillin. In a couple weeks, I was startin' to think I might survive. Then I guess they had second thoughts about me not knowin' anything and tossed me in an underground cell about five feet square and shut me in. They left me in solitary for two weeks and then tried interrogating again.

"After three days, they gave up, and then things got better. I think all they were really tryin' to do was use American prisoners to gain advantage at the peace talks. They wanted us to live. They wanted us to say how America was evil and how good they were treatin' us prisoners. Wanted propaganda. But mainly, they didn't want any more Americans to die in their camps, 'cause it would make negotiatin' the terms of America's withdrawal tougher. If it'd been two years before, they'd have tortured us, but now they thought that'd do 'em more harm than forcing information or lies from us would gain 'em.

"By then, it was June. Living conditions were awful, but I didn't hurt so much, and I could at least talk to some of the other caged guys. It seemed to go on like that forever. My head became my biggest problem. That's when the nightmares started. I was haunted by dreams, both asleep and awake. Over and over, the same scenes, as vivid as when they happened – sometimes worse. Darnell's face. Body parts blasting out of the hospital bunker. Barry and the girl and the baby. Me mowing down teenage boys, boys I didn't know and had nothin' against. Me feelin' nothin' but blind hate, wantin' nothin' so bad as to kill every human being in sight."

"The same dream tonight?" Eve whispers.

"It's the only dream I ever have. If I just nap a little and don't sleep deep, I don't have it. Maybe I get a little better every day, but it's so slow. I don't know. I've always been a Christian. Used to think a pretty solid one. It's taken a long time, but I'm starting to come to terms with the possibility that God might forgive me. I've fought Him hard on that. It don't seem right that what I did could be forgiven. We're supposed to love each other, not hate with such ferocity that the *only* thought that can crowd into my head is to destroy as many of God's people as I possibly can as fast as I possibly can.

"Anyway, after about eight months of torturing myself in that hellhole in Kratie, we were all released – at least, the Americans were. Then I spent a couple months undergoing surgeries and psychological therapy. The therapy and my faith are the only things that kept me from goin' crazy. When I got discharged, the GI bill got me a year of training in surveying. I got a job at it in seventy-four, and here I am. So, if it seems like I'm not quite the same kid you used to know, that's 'cause I'm not. Not even close. I'm tryin' to recapture something of him. Tryin' to remember who that boy was. But the dreams keep comin' at me, hurling me down. And I keep dragging myself back up and tryin' to plod one more step forward."

## Chapter 27

Eve strokes Tom's hair as he lies with his head on her lap. Neither speaks for half an hour. Eventually, he says, "Are you ready for Tuesday?"

"I'm anxious. Half of me can't wait. The other half is scared to death."

"Tell me more about Brent."

She has no trouble recounting story after story about her time with her little boy. Just before 3:00 a.m., Tom's eyelids drift closed. Eve lays a hand on his chest, and soon she nods off. She awakens four hours later from him stirring. He looks up at her and smiles. "I haven't slept like that in over three years. Your reward is getting taken to breakfast."

Getting ready, at the restaurant, and driving to pick up Janet for church, Eve monopolizes the conversation with talk of Brent and the hearing. She isn't sure whether it's because that's consuming her thoughts or because she's afraid to allow Tom's revelations from last night resurface.

In church, Tom sits with Janet on one side and Eve on the other, holding her hand. The sermon is about salvation through grace. The ride back to Janet's house is quiet. Snowflakes meander down. When they arrive, Tom looks at Eve and says, "Let's walk in the snow while Mom does her kitchen magic."

They walk silently arm in arm, enjoying the cold, white world and the feel of each other. After a few minutes, Eve says, "When I confessed my life story, I left something more out."

Tom looks at her and waits.

"When I had the accident, in the hospital they, uh, lost me for a while."

"You were...."

She puts a finger to his lips. "Just listen, Tom. For two and a half minutes my heart stopped. I died for a while. Dr. Burgmann says I should not talk to people about those two and a half minutes – says people will think I'm crazy, start avoiding me, talk behind my back. And he was pretty much right about that with the handful of people I've told. But, here's the thing. That was almost four years ago, and if I had to tell the absolute truth on my life – on Brent's life – if his life depended on me telling the god-honest truth, I'd have to say the most real experience I've ever had in my life was during those two and a half minutes.

"I guess I'm telling you because I want you to know everything about me, to be fair to you. And maybe also 'cause I think there's a chance it might help you.

"When I died, it wasn't just a black world. The farthest thing from it. I could never in a million years have dreamed it up." She told him everything. Then she told him about the dream a month ago, the night she was going to take the pills.

"Here's the thing, Tom. And I know you're a Christian, and I'm not arguing about that. But, I've been there. And I look forward to going back someday. I don't have an ounce of fear of dying. It's like going home and being embraced by the entire universe. Oh, I desperately want to be Brent's mother, and now to be with you. But, I also want to die, when the time is right. To go back there.

"And I really don't think it matters what a person believes about religion. I don't think it matters how a person lives their life. In the end, the terrible things we do – at least some of them – are things we can't stop ourselves from doing. Like me deciding to blow over that cliff in Doug's truck. That thought came out of nowhere. And I started to do it, and another thought, Brent, popped in my head, and I tried to stop it. But with my past and my circumstances, I don't think I could have changed what I did that night. None of it was good or evil. It just happened.

"That day in Nam... there's no way you could have done anything different. It doesn't make you unforgivable, or even bad. The Viet Cong army that killed Barry and the girl and her baby? They were doing what armies have done for centuries, probably what they'd been ordered to do. Does that make those boys evil? Not from what I saw when I was on the other side. Will they go to Hell for what they did? Will Gil Bartolo go to Hell for what *he* did? I think we all just go home, Tom. And there's no doubt in my mind that's where Barry and the girl and that baby are. Their Hell was here. They were mercifully released from it and went home. The boys you shot – they went home. I know how hard it is for you, but, in the end, I'm sure they were and *are* ecstatic about it. It's all okay, Tom."

Tom squares to face her and takes both of her hands in his. "We're a pair, everything we've been through. There's a lot to you, Eve Kessler. The world was stacked against you from the day you were born, but you refuse to let it beat you. You amaze me.

"I don't know what to think about your two and a half minutes, but you won't hear me say you're crazy. I'm closer to going over the brink than you are. And I'll *never* avoid you. Your experience doesn't exactly fit with Christian theology, but then, my faith was never based on a lot of theology. I've always struggled with there being only one way – too many good people out there who happen to have been born in different faiths. Maybe different religions have more in common than we let ourselves see. Maybe people just make too much out of the details. Sometimes I think the only people who are certain of the one and only way are people who won't give honest consideration to any evidence that points in another direction.

"Maybe you're right. Maybe we just all go home. It would be a comforting thought. There's an awful lot about this world I don't have figured out. It scares me some to think my faith could be one of those things, and right now would be a really bad time for me to start questioning that. But, there are a few things I do know. I know I love you, Eve Kessler, and more than ever, I know how much I need you. And now that I've got you back in my life, I'm never letting you go."

Tuesday morning at 8:30, Tom escorts Eve into Courtroom Number 2. The room is empty. They sit on the front bench on the left side, just behind the railing. Tom sits away from the aisle, leaving a place beside Eve for Dr. Burgmann. They sit silently holding hands.

Tom's beard is gone. When he picked Eve up from work Sunday night, he'd shaved it off and gotten his hair cut. He looked more like the Tom Stanton from high school.

At 8:50 Dr. Bergmann walks in, chatting with a man in a suit. When they reach Eve and Tom, he introduces the man as Mr. Bowersley, the attorney for the Kellermans. Eve gapes, but Dr. Burgmann smiles and pats her arm, reassuring her. They pass through the gate in the railing and stand in front of the small table on the right side of the courtroom, smiling and talking like old friends.

Two minutes later, as Eve eyes them, someone sits down beside her in Dr. Bergmann's spot.

"Hey, you doin' okay?" Doug says.

She fidgets. "I didn't know you'd be here."

"Subpoena. Had to be." He lowers his voice, but it still carries. "Hey. This thing with Val ain't workin' out exactly like I thought it would. It's turnin' into kind of an open thing. Like me and her and Vic sort of just sharing. Here's the thing. I think you'd fit right in. Sort of like the four of us all bein' together, but all still free to do our own thing. Whaddaya think?"

"What do you mean, what do I think? I'm done, Doug. Leave me alone."

Tom is on the edge of his seat, glaring at Doug.

"All right. All right." Doug puts both palms up in front of him in a defensive maneuver. "I just thought you oughta know how it's workin' out. Think about it."

"No! Go away."

Tom starts to get up. Eve puts a hand on his thigh, signaling him to hold back.

"Okay, okay." Doug gets up and walks back up the aisle.

Eve glances behind her and sees that the Kellermans have just sat down in the rear bench on the right side. They seem aghast to see their lawyer befriending the opposition. Mary's eyes look haunted. Doug sits two rows in front of Mary, leaving a seat open at the aisle. *Probably hoping Val will sit there and have no room for Vic.* She turns and looks down at her hand in Tom's.

A minute later, she hears the rear doors open and feels an aura of seduction overshadow the room. Everyone looks back to see Val and Vic enter. Val looks sexier than ever in a low-cut, short, black dress. *What is she doing? Is that for Doug or Vic? Or the judge? Or me?* Vic's hair is wilder than ever. She's wearing a camouflage army jacket with tight jeans and black boots. The pair sit on the bench between Doug and the Kellermans, Vic in front of Mary and behind Doug. *Too much is off-kilter in this room. This is going to be bad.*

The court recorder is seated. Mr. Burgmann is still talking with Bowersley. Eve stares at the clock. *The judge must enter at exactly at 9:00.* At the instant the minute hand clicks on 8:59, she hears a thud at the back of the room, like a fist pounding a hard wall. It's followed immediately by an "Uhhhg." *Doug?*

As she turns her head again toward the back of the room, there's a loud crash – something hitting one of the benches. When she takes in the scene, she sees that it's Doug's nose that's hit the bench in front of him. Blood spurts. Vic smirks.

"Awwww. Ow! Ohhhhh." Doug has one hand on the back of his head, where blood is trickling, and his other hand over his nose, where blood is streaming. "Son of a *bitch!* It's broke!"

"Dammit, Vic," Val mutters as she jumps up to help Doug. She's no help, though, keeping distant enough to avoid getting her sex-dress bloodied.

The judge opens the door from his chambers and stares. "What is going *on* here?" he bellows.

"Fell." Doug mumbles the words as loudly as he can. "Tripped." He starts to get up to leave.

"Wait!" the judge orders. "Get that man some help." The recorder runs out of the room. Vic's shoulders quiver as she struggles to contain her snickering.

Within seconds, the recorder rushes back into the room, followed by a man with a first-aid kit.

"Who saw what happened?" the judge demands.

The room is silent. Finally, Val speaks: "He just fell over into the bench."

"What's his name? Is he a witness?"

"Doug Pratt," Val says.

Bowersley speaks up: "Yes, he's on our witness list."

Doug is sitting on the floor with his head tilted back, the medical attendant holding one towel on the back of his head and another over his nose. Val sits on a bench across the aisle, observing Doug's misery, saying nothing.

The judge shakes his head. "When can we reschedule?"

"Thursday, January eighth, at nine o'clock," replies the recorder.

"This court is in recess until Thursday, January eighth, at nine o'clock." The judge surveys the scene again, shakes his head, turns back to his chamber door, and mumbles, "Fell into the bench and broke his nose. Bull!"

The Kellermans look aghast. Eve watches them rise and step toward the door.

"Mary! Wait!" she shouts.

## Chapter 28

Ray and Mary start, turn their heads, and glare at Eve.

The chaotic room is overcome by silence. Faintly, Eve says, "Mary, could we talk for a minute?"

Ray takes his wife by the arm as Doug is helped to his feet. "Let's go, honey."

Mary doesn't move. Still staring at Eve, she gives the slightest of nods.

Ray's eyes on Eve are furious. "That's a bad idea. Let's go, Mary."

As Mary pulls her arm from Ray's grasp, Eve glances at Tom. "I'll be back." She hurries toward Mary.

Ray's face is apprehensive. "We can talk in the lobby."

Mary's eyes are on Eve as she speaks to Ray. "Wait here for me."

Watching Mary turn toward the door with Eve close behind, Dr. Burgmann calls out, "There's a consultation room two doors to the right."

"I'm coming with you," Ray asserts.

"No," Mary commands, stopping him in his tracks.

Eve follows Mary out of the courtroom and into the consultation room. Mary closes the door. There's an oval oak table in the room with six padded chairs surrounding it. The women remain standing near the closed door. Mary looks at Eve with blank eyes that feel accusing to Eve.

Eve struggles with words. She hadn't planned for this. After a moment, she whispers, "Thank you, Mary."

All that Mary offers in response is more of the blank stare.

"Um, you know, after I got out of the hospital, I talked to Ray a few times... and once in the hospital." Nothing from Mary. "The last time we talked, he told me... uh... well, I guess after that time... I guess then I thought maybe my talks with Ray had all been wasted effort. And so hard – so much hurt. For both of us. And probably for you too. The whole time, my life, the whole time since Brent went to live with you, my life... it's torture being separated from Brent. He's the *only* thing I keep going on for. And I can't be his mother. I'm not even allowed *near* him. It's *torture*, Mary. It's worse than dying. Way worse."

Mary stares.

Eve inhales. "I have only one choice, Mary. I'll do anything, whatever it takes, to be Brent's mother. I can't quit. I really want to work it out with you and Ray. I'd never try to cut you out. I'd *never* take Brent away where you couldn't be his grandma and grandpa. But, I can't quit. Whatever you and Ray do to block me, I can never, *ever* quit trying to be with Brent. You'd have to put me in a straightjacket twenty-four hours a day.

"And you *have* to know how hard I'm working on my life. I've left Doug. *I* left, not him. I'm done with him. And Val and Vic. I didn't call them here today. Your lawyer did. I wish he hadn't. That stuff in there today.... I'm *done* with them, Mary. I've got a good job. I stay away from my mother. I wish I could help her, but I can't. *Nobody* can. I'm done with her, too. I've got my own apartment, just an efficiency, but it's mine, by myself. I got it the day before I got served the restraining order. You probably already know it's a couple blocks from you, so, yeah, I'm probably already in violation of that order just by living there. But, I've stayed away like I am supposed to. I haven't come around your house, haven't even walked that direction.

"Anyway, when I saw you and Ray leaving the courtroom, something made me call out to you. Take one shot to try to work this out ourselves. Instead of both of us living on the edge of sanity, waiting to find out what the judge will say. Am I making any sense?"

Mary doesn't respond. Eve waits. Finally, Mary speaks. "Was that Tom Stanton sitting with you?"

"Yes," Eve breathes.

"I knew Tom and his family a little when he was in school. Heard he joined the Air Force, and then I lost track of him."

Eve murmurs. "He had a very bad time in Vietnam. Unbelievably bad."

"How do you know him?"

"He was my best friend in grade school. My only friend. Then, in junior high my life went to pieces, and I lost him. He showed up at the restaurant a few weeks ago. I couldn't believe it."

"You love him." It was not a question.

A tear trickles from the corner of Eve's eye. Her words are barely audible. "I've always loved him."

Mary remains stiff and emotionless. Neither speaks for a moment. Then Mary says, "I've been to the doctor." Now, it's Eve with the blank look.

"A problem turned up last week. I found out for sure yesterday. I have breast cancer."

Eve's jaw drops.

"Nobody knows yet. Just my doctor. And you. I have to tell Ray. He'll take it hard."

"Will you be…?"

"The breast will be removed. Probably next week. We won't know much until after."

"Mary, can we just call a truce until after? We could talk again then. I don't want to make it harder."

"I'll be in the hospital for a while. Somebody will have to take care of Brent. Ray won't be able to."

Eve freezes.

"It has to be you. You are his mother. No one cares for him more than you. I've always known that."

Eve drops to her knees, clasps her arms around Mary's waist, and squeezes as her tears stream. Mary's hand settles on Eve's head.

Fifteen minutes after entering the consultation room, Eve opens the door to lead Mary out. Tom, Ray, Dr. Burgmann, and Mr. Bowersley are huddled across the lobby, making small-talk and fidgeting. Eve is a mess. The little bit of makeup she'd put on has streaked down both her face and her new dress. Her hair is mussed, and her red eyes are distressed.

She hurries to Tom and falls into his arms. As he envelopes her, she reaches out her left hand and touches Ray's sleeve.

Mary looks at Ray. "Everything is all right. This hearing is over. Eve is Brent's mother."

Epilogue

February 2009

Eve, still petite but with salt-and-pepper hair, sits at the breakfast table by the bay window, cradles her morning cup of coffee, and gazes at the snow-covered trees in the backyard. She smiles, thinking of the early-morning hours she's spent with Tom. Today is a big day for him. He left at 8:00 to go to Indianapolis to attend the closing for the buyout of his surveying company. All of the company's six offices around the state are being bought by their managing partners. Turning over the company will be bittersweet for him, but it's a good financial reward for the effort he put into building his company.

A rabbit scampers across the rolling backyard, redirecting Eve's thoughts, reminding her of how much she enjoys sitting in this nook, looking out on the world from inside the old Kellerman home. She reminisces about how it became the Stanton home.

Ray asked Tom and her to move in shortly after Mary died, a little more than eleven years after Mary learned she had cancer. Most of those years were good ones, but cancer being the beast that it is, it never completely released its grip on Mary. The first few years were rich for them all, as Mary rebounded well and they became close to one another. The last two years got progressively tougher for both Mary and Ray. After the funeral, Ray asked Eve, Tom, Brent, and their then eight-year-old daughter, Tara, to move into the house with him. He took the small living space that he'd originally remodeled for Eve and Brent.

After Eric's fiasco in the bar at Connie's, he'd never been back and had not stayed in touch. The last address Ray and Mary had for him was in Germany. He didn't come home for his mother's funeral.

When Ray died nine years after Mary, he left most of his wealth to Brent and Tara, whom he considered his full-blooded granddaughter, and he left the home to Tom and Eve.

Eve's reminiscences are interrupted by the front door bursting open. Her snow-covered sixteen-year-old granddaughter, Sarah, neglects to close the door and stands in the entry foyer, her face the definition of agony.

"Sarah! Why aren't you in school? What's wrong?"

The girl heaves sobs as Eve rushes to her, engulfs her, and pushes the door closed with a foot. "Oh, Gran, it's awful. You're the only one I can come to."

"What is it, sweetheart?" More than any of her other five grandchildren, this one reminds her of herself: smart, too independent, and too impulsive. Looking at her face from the side, she's the image of Eve. "Are you hurt? Is anybody hurt?"

Sarah shakes her trembling head and buries her face in her grandmother's neck.

"Come. Give me your coat. Your hair is soaked. How long have you been out in the snow? I'll make you a cup of hot chocolate. Here, you sit at the table and get hold of yourself while I make it. Then tell me what happened."

By the time Eve sets the cup in front of her, Sarah has stopped crying.

"Now, tell me, sweetheart."

Sarah, hands folded in her lap, looks at her grandma with pleading eyes and then looks down at the table. "You remember my boyfriend? Jeremy?"

"Look at me, honey. You don't have anything to worry about with me. Yes, I remember Jeremy. He's a senior, right?"

Sarah nods. "Well, I loved him *sooooo* much. And we'd been together for sooooo long. From the prom last year, then all summer. He was so cool and always had these older girls flirting with him all the time. I mean, it made me jealous, but he always said he didn't care about any of them, just me. But then, last fall he got more like, you know, a guy has needs and stuff. And he loved me so much, and he *needed* me so much. Just me. But these other girls – especially Lisa Reece – were always coming on to him. Then, after the Halloween dance he told me that sexy tramp wanted him to go to her house after, that she had just what he needed. And he said he only wanted it from me, but a guy his age couldn't just hold off forever. So I did it."

Sarah glances into her grandma's eyes, but no look of shock, disappointment, or disapproval is there – just softness and love. "We did it a lot, Gran. What I didn't find out 'til later was that he was doin' the same thing all along with that bitch. And then, after Christmas break, he told me she missed her period, and if she was pregnant it was his, and he loved her and was gonna marry her. I hate him now."

Eve reaches down to Sarah's hands, pulls them up onto the table, and envelopes them in hers. "Everything will be okay, Sarah. Go on."

"I missed two of my periods. Friday I skipped school and went to a clinic. I'm pregnant, Gran," she moans and again bursts into tears. "I *can't* tell Mom and Dad," she sobs. "They'll *kill* me. I have to have an abortion and you're the only one I can come to. I'm going to Hell."

Eve rises to her feet. "Come here, Sarah."

Sarah stands, and they embrace while Sarah cries and Eve repeats, "We all love you, Sarah. Everything is going to turn out all right. And you are *not* going to Hell." Finally, she says, "Now, sit and dry your eyes, and let's talk this through."

They sit. "Sarah, have you ever gone to bed at night after a really bad day, and the problems just seemed insurmountable, like the world is just going to crush you? You think you'll never be able to sleep because of all the hurt and trouble. But, somehow, in five minutes you're asleep, and you wake up eight hours later with the sun shining in the window and birds singing, and you just feel good and you smile. And the end of the world last night just feels more like a new beginning today. Ever have a night like that?"

"But, Gran, *this*...."

"Shhhhhh. I know. This is different. This is big. But still, in a way it's like that. It's not an overnight thing, but it can be like that. I've been there, honey. The worst, worst, *worst* thing that could possibly ever happen really *can* somehow turn into the best, best, *best* thing that ever happened."

"But, you *can't* be saying that about *this*. I'm *pregnant*, Gran! I'm *sixteen*! You gotta help me. I need money for an abortion, and Mom and Dad can't *ever* know. And you're wrong about Hell. I committed adultery and now I'm gonna commit...." She can't say the word. "Everybody would be better off if a semi just runs over me in the street when I leave. Nobody would have to know."

"Listen to me, Sarah. I'm not just trying to make you feel better. I *know* what I'm talking about. Believe me. I've lived this."

Sarah looks at her, questions developing in her expression.

"Peaches, you're only sixteen, and I'm not sure your father would approve of what I'm gonna tell you. But, what can he do to me? I'm his mother. And you aren't a little kid anymore. You've got yourself in a mess. You're old enough to figure out how life really works. It's not a fairy tale where nothing bad ever happens. Terrible things happen every day, but that doesn't mean life's not worth living.

"I'm going to tell you about my life. And about your grandpa's life. This is gonna take some time. You're not going to make it to school today. Will they be calling your mom?"

"No. I turned in a note."

Eve raises her eyebrows.

"It said I have a doctor's appointment in Indy. Yeah, I signed it. I can sign Mom's name pretty good."

"All right, then. My story starts with my mother, before I was born."

Hours later, after lunch, when Eve finishes telling her story and Tom's, holding back nothing, Sarah seems more absorbed in their lives than in her own problem.

"Does Grandpa still have those awful nightmares?"

"He hasn't had one for a long, long time."

"When we all sit in church on Sunday, does he feel bad about what he did to those soldiers that day?"

"He did for a long time. But, eventually, he came to believe that what I saw that night I had my accident wasn't just a hallucination, that when we die, we all just go home. Not that it isn't important to be a good person, but even if you can't stop yourself from doing things that hurt other people, that doesn't mean anybody is going to burn in Hell forever. We're here to love each other, but we aren't all born with the same tools to do that. And that isn't our fault – each of us can only do our best. We're Christians, Sarah, but there are lots of variations in how Christians see the details. Your grandpa and me see heaven maybe a little differently than they preach about it on Sundays."

"I never heard you talk about your mother before, my great-grandma. What happened to her?"

"After your grandpa and me got married, she got sick. She wouldn't go to the hospital until she couldn't get out of bed anymore. She had sclerosis of her liver, from all the alcohol. She was so far gone she never got out of the hospital. She died before you were born. This world was never kind to her. She went home."

"And your bad friends? I thought I picked some bad ones, but yours were crazy, Gran. Do you ever see them?"

"I put them behind me. They're still around, and once in a great while I'll see one of them from a distance. But I haven't spoken to any of them since the day your great-grandma Kellerman told me she had cancer. They were negative influences on me, dragging me down. Once I decided nothing was going to stop me from taking control of my life, I knew I had to put the people who were pulling me back out of my life. And with your grandpa's help, I did."

Sarah gets quiet, and Eve senses the weight of the girl's problems settling back over her. "Anyway, Sarah, my point in telling you all this is that what looks bleak and completely unresolvable at his moment can look brighter on another day. It might not be tomorrow, but it *will* get better.

"For me, it started getting better when my own gran, your namesake, convinced me in my sleep that the issue boiled down to me taking charge of my life. And I was way closer to the end of my rope than you are. If I'd caved in – if I'd taken those pills, or if I'd not swerved to avoid going over the cliff, or not said 'yes, I'll go back and be your dad's mother' – then you would not be faced with this problem of yours today. You wouldn't be faced with it, because you'd never have been born. I would never have had the unimaginable treasure of being your grandma, of knowing and loving you the way I do. The same for your brothers and sister and your Aunt Tara and little Natty and Timmy.

"I look forward to the day when I'll see my own Gran again. In some ways, I just can't wait for that. But, honey, if you and my other grandkids and Tara had never been born, if I'd never stepped up and really became your dad's mom... well, even thinking about that for a second brings me to my knees. Not only do I know how glorious everything will be when I'm done in this world, but I've also experienced heaven right here with your grandpa and all of you. I would never, ever, *ever* trade it for anything.

"So, take my word for it. There *will be* a brighter tomorrow. And whatever comes for you, your grandpa and I will *always* be standing right by your side. As will the rest of us, including your mom and dad. Will they be disappointed and angry with you? You bet they will. Will they turn their backs on you? Never in a million years.

"You ask for my help? You've got it. You want money for an abortion? My help will be way stronger than that. If I thought you could actually go through with that, you and I would tussle right here and now. And I would win, and I would hogtie you until you came to your senses. You understand, this is my great-grandchild we're talking about. My first, just like your daddy was my first child and you were my first grandchild. I'll fight just as hard to save this little, unborn baby as I'd fight to save every one of you. I'll fight to my last dying breath."

Sarah buries her face in her arms on the table and moans her words between gentle sobs as Eve strokes her hair. "I can't believe... what you and grandpa... went through. But... what am I... gonna do... Gran. Everything... is such a... a god-awful mess.... Stick with me... Gran.... I love you."